Stone Barrington is left hanging in a financial windfall in the latest novel from *New York Times* bestselling author Stuart Woods.

Stone Barrington is enjoying his usual dinner at Elaine's when his boss at Woodman & Weld, the law firm where Stone is "of counsel," walks in, sits down, and hands Stone a check for one million dollars. It seems Stone's undercover dealings with MI6 have brought in a big new client for the firm, and they're willing to pay Stone a huge bonus and put him on a partnership track. But almost as soon as he's taken the deal, Stone gets wind of an impending scandal that might torpedo his big promotion: It seems the lucrative new client he's introduced to the firm might be a devil in disguise. . . .

Praise for Stuart Woods's Stone Barrington Novels

Lucid Intervals

"Woods's Stone Barrington is a guilty pleasure. . . . He's also an addiction that's harder to kick than heroin."
—*Contra Costa Times*

"Smooth. . . . Woods mixes danger and humor into a racy concoction that will leave readers thirsty for more."
—*Publishers Weekly*

"In *Lucid Intervals*, [Woods's] blend of booze, broads, and bullets remains a winning formula. In an ever-changing world, it's nice to have reliables such as Woods and his characters on which to depend." —*Bangor Daily News*

"Fans of Woods's long-running series will not be disappointed by this romp, which is peppered with plenty of humor." —*Booklist*

"[A] first-class page-turner." —*Albuquerque Journal*

continued . . .

Kisser

"POW! He's back with more twists and trysts."
—The Mystery Reader

"A fun, breezy page-turner." —*Booklist*

Loitering with Intent

"Have a margarita handy when you read this fun page-turner." —*Southern Living* magazine

"[A] solid, action-packed thriller."
—*The Globe and Mail* (Canada)

Hot Mahogany

"[A] fun ride from Stuart Woods." —*Bangor Daily News*

"Series fans will find all their expectations nicely fulfilled."
—*Publishers Weekly*

Shoot Him If He Runs

"Fast-paced . . . with a whole lot of style."
—*Bangor Daily News*

"Woods certainly knows how to keep the pages turning."
—*Booklist*

Fresh Disasters

"Fast-paced, hilarious, and tragic."—*Albuquerque Journal*

"Good fun." —*Publishers Weekly*

Dark Harbor

"A vigilante detective in the manly-man mode . . . [a] rat-a-tat tone." —*The Washington Post Book World*

"Fast pacing and an involving mystery." —*Booklist*

Two Dollar Bill

"A smooth and solid thriller." —*The News-Leader* (Springfield, MO)

Reckless Abandon

"Fast action, catchy plot, and spicy dialogue." —*The Calgary Sun*

"[An] amusing, full-throttle sex-and-crime romp." —*Publishers Weekly*

Dirty Work

"High on the stylish suspense." —*The Sante Fe New Mexican*

"Sleek and engaging." —*Publishers Weekly*

The Short Forever

"A tight mystery right up to the end . . . good-guy charm." —*The Palm Beach Post*

Cold Paradise

"A delightful tale of sex and violence . . . Sopranos-style . . . slick, sophisticated fun." —*The Washington Post*

"Woods delivers his most riveting and glamorous Barrington novel yet." —*Vero Beach Press Journal* (FL)

BOOKS BY STUART WOODS

FICTION

TRAVEL

MEMOIR

*A Holly Barker Novel   †A Stone Barrington Novel
‡A Will Lee Novel   §An Ed Eagle Novel

STRATEGIC MOVES

Stuart Woods

A SIGNET BOOK

SIGNET
Published by New American Library, a division of
Penguin Group (USA) Inc., 375 Hudson Street,
New York, New York 10014, USA
Penguin Group (Canada), 90 Eglinton Avenue East, Suite 700, Toronto,
Ontario M4P 2Y3, Canada (a division of Pearson Penguin Canada Inc.)
Penguin Books Ltd., 80 Strand, London WC2R 0RL, England
Penguin Ireland, 25 St. Stephen's Green, Dublin 2,
Ireland (a division of Penguin Books Ltd.)
Penguin Group (Australia), 250 Camberwell Road, Camberwell, Victoria 3124,
Australia (a division of Pearson Australia Group Pty. Ltd.)
Penguin Books India Pvt. Ltd., 11 Community Centre, Panchsheel Park,
New Delhi - 110 017, India
Penguin Group (NZ), 67 Apollo Drive, Rosedale, Auckland 0632,
New Zealand (a division of Pearson New Zealand Ltd.)
Penguin Books (South Africa) (Pty.) Ltd., 24 Sturdee Avenue,
Rosebank, Johannesburg 2196, South Africa

Penguin Books Ltd., Registered Offices:
80 Strand, London WC2R 0RL, England

Published by Signet, an imprint of New American Library, a division of Penguin
Group (USA) Inc. Previously published in a Putnam edition.

First Signet Printing, September 2011
10 9 8 7 6 5 4 3 2 1

 REGISTERED TRADEMARK—MARCA REGISTRADA

Printed in the United States of America

This book is for Sandi Butchkiss

STRATEGIC MOVES

I

Elaine's, late.

Stone Barrington was uncharacteristically late in meeting his former partner at the NYPD, Lieutenant Dino Bacchetti, for dinner, and Dino was not alone at the table. Dino ran the detective bureau at the 19th Precinct. Stone's other dinner partner, Bill Eggers, managing partner at the prestigious law firm of Woodman & Weld, pretty much ran Stone, who, working from his home office in Turtle Bay, handled cases and clients of Woodman & Weld that they did not wish to be seen to handle.

"You're late," Eggers said.

"I'm late for dinner with Dino," Stone said, "but since I didn't have a date with you, I prefer to think of myself as right on time for our meeting."

Eggers managed a chuckle. "Fair enough," he said. "I'm buying tonight."

"For me, too?" Dino asked.

"For you, too, Dino," Eggers replied.

A waiter set a Knob Creek on the rocks before Stone; the other two men already had glasses of brown whiskey before them. Stone raised his glass, but Eggers put a hand on his arm.

"No, I'll do the toasting tonight," he said, raising his own glass. "To Stone Barrington, who has earned more than a night out on my expense account."

"Hear, hear," Dino said.

"I'll drink to that," Stone offered, raising his glass and taking a pull from it. "Is there an occasion, Bill, or are you just feeling magnanimous?"

"A little of both," Eggers said, taking an envelope from his pocket and handing it to Stone.

Stone saw, through a window in the envelope, his name, which indicated to him that it might be printed on a check. "Bill, have you taken to personally delivering payment of my bills to the firm?"

"Open it," Eggers said.

Stone lifted the flap and pulled open the envelope far enough to see the amount of the check, which was one million dollars. His mouth worked, but no sound came out.

"Don't bother to thank me," Eggers said. "After all, you earned it, and may I say that this is the first annual bonus the firm has ever paid to an attorney who is 'of counsel'?"

Stone recovered his voice. "Why, thank you, Bill,

and please thank anyone else at the firm who had anything whatever to do with this."

"This event is occurring because you were substantially responsible for bringing in Strategic Services as a new client, and they have turned out to be a very good client indeed. The death of Jim Hackett has increased their need for your counsel and ours."

Jim Hackett had been the founder and sole owner of the firm, which served many corporations around the world in security matters of all sorts. He had been shot to death while in Stone's company, on an island in Maine, by a sniper employed by two senior members of the British cabinet who believed Hackett to be someone else.

"Thank you again," Stone said.

"I want you to know—and I realize I'm saying this in front of a witness—that if the growth of the Strategic Services account continues as I believe it will, then by this time next year I may very well be recommending you for a partnership at Woodman & Weld," Eggers said.

Stone was once more dumbstruck. That this might happen had never, in his years of service to the firm, entered Stone's mind. Furthermore, he knew that a partnership in Woodman & Weld would bring an annual income that would be a considerable multiple of the check in the envelope he held. Stone had always been an outsider at the firm, only occasionally visiting its offices and listed as "Of Counsel" only at the bottom of its letterhead.

"I will take your silence as evidence of shock," Eggers said.

Stone nodded vigorously and downed half his drink while signaling for another.

"Make it three," Eggers said to the waiter, "and let me see the list of special wines."

Stone had seen the list of special wines, but he had never once ordered from it, because the wines started at $500 a bottle.

"Well," Dino said, raising his glass again, "I'm happy I could be here on this special occasion."

"Dino," Eggers said, "you've done Stone many favors on our behalf over the years, so I'm happy you could be here, too."

"Feel free to add me to the bonus list," Dino said wryly.

"Only should you die in our service," Eggers said pleasantly.

"I figured," Dino replied.

Eggers opened the wine list, glanced at it, then closed it. "Order something that will go well with a Château Pétrus 1975," he said, opening his menu.

Stone turned to the waiter, who was braced beside the table, holding his pad and pencil ready. "I want one of Barry's secret steaks, medium rare," Stone said, "and I'll start with the French green bean salad, hold the peppers, use truffle oil."

"Same here, rare," Dino said.

"Make it three," Eggers echoed, "and mine medium."

The waiter dematerialized.

"Tell me," Eggers said to Stone, "have you figured out why Jim Hackett was murdered?"

"I've never said this to anyone before," Stone replied, "but I am under the constraint of the British Official Secrets Act and am, therefore, unable to respond to your question."

"You're shitting me," Eggers said.

"I shit you not," Stone replied. "You will recall that my client, at that time, was an arm of Her Majesty's Government. They made me sign the Act."

More specifically, Stone's client had been a lovely redhead, who also happened to be the head of MI6, the foreign arm of British Intelligence.

"And," Eggers said, "I perceive that your work for them resulted in the resignation and arrest of the British foreign secretary and the home secretary."

"I cannot either confirm or deny your perception," Stone said, "but just between the three of us, I would be very much surprised if those two gentlemen ever came to trial."

"I suppose, if that happened, too much embarrassing information would come to light," Eggers said.

"That is what I suppose, too," Stone replied, "though no one has said as much to me. The government managed to keep it out of the British newspapers by employing the Official Secrets Act."

"It made the *New York Times*," Eggers said.

"All copies of which were banned for sale that day

in the UK," Stone said. "I don't think that sort of thing has happened since the abdication of Edward the Eighth."

"I'm glad your name was kept out of it," Eggers said. "The firm would not have liked that sort of publicity. Our London office has too many clients who might have been embarrassed by your participation."

"I'm glad, too," Stone said. "Believe me."

Dinner arrived, and the bottle of Pétrus, which Eggers tasted with some ceremony. "We'll drink it," he said to the waiter, and they did.

2

Stone took the elevator down from the third-floor bedroom of his Turtle Bay town house and walked into his ground-floor offices. He had inherited the house from a great-aunt and had done much of the restoration work himself. He walked down to the office of his secretary, Joan Robertson, and handed her his bonus check. "Get this into the account, please, and send the IRS the taxes."

Joan nodded, then looked at the check. "WOW! What is this for?"

"It's my year-end bonus," Stone said.

"They've never given you a year-end bonus before," Joan pointed out.

"I brought them the Strategic Services account," he said. "Eggers liked that. By the way, write yourself a check for ten thousand; I think you're entitled to a year-end bonus, too."

"Yes, sir!" Joan said, turning to her computer.

"I'm going to a memorial service for Jim Hackett in a little while, so I may not be here when you get back. I'll call you later."

"Got it," Joan said.

Stone walked back to his office and began reading correspondence.

Jim Hackett's memorial service was held at a small Episcopal church on Park Avenue. As he entered, Mike Freeman, Hackett's successor at Strategic Services, beckoned him to a front pew.

The priest made some rambling remarks about Hackett, then turned the pulpit over to Mike Freeman, who spoke movingly of his long relationship with Hackett, who had mentored him and had made him number two at the firm.

The service ended, and Freeman said to Stone, "I'm giving a lunch at the Four Seasons for our branch managers, and I'd like you to be there. Come ride with me."

Stone got into a Mercedes with Freeman and two other men, who were introduced to him as the heads of the London and Tel Aviv offices. They lunched in a private dining room, and much drink was taken. Stone held back on the wine, wanting to keep a clear head and to remember as many of the names as he could.

When the dishes had been taken away, Mike Freeman stood and addressed the group.

"Gentlemen, Strategic Services is not a publicly

traded company; it was owned in its entirety by Jim Hackett, who in his will has left me twenty-five percent of the stock and each of you two percent of the stock."

There were murmurs of surprise in the group, and they burst into applause. Stone looked around the table and counted twelve noses, not including himself. If the gift of stock applied to him, then the branch managers now owned twenty-six percent of the stock.

"The remaining stock of the company will be owned by the Hackett Foundation, and the board of directors will control how it is voted. The new directors are Derek Barnes, head of our London office, Jake Green, head of Tel Aviv, and Bill Chu, head of Hong Kong. Stone Barrington is our corporate counsel, and I am chairman and CEO. I will also perform the duties of my previous position as COO. Each of the directors will have one vote; I will have two, and I will vote the foundation's stock.

"That is the new structure, and each of you will run his local office as in the past, subject to budget constraints and the will of the board. I am grateful to all of you for attending Jim's memorial; none of you had to come. I know that many of you have airplanes to catch this afternoon and evening, so we will end this meeting now and go our separate ways."

The men got up from their seats, spent a few minutes saying good-bye to each other and Freeman, and then everyone departed.

"Ride with me," Freeman said to Stone, and they got back into the Mercedes.

"I was very surprised to be included in the gift of stock," Stone said.

"Jim thought highly of you, Stone, from our first tennis match. He admired the way you played against him, the fact that you were not intimidated. As you will recall, Jim was a very intimidating tennis player."

"I was hanging on by my fingernails," Stone said.

"He also admired how quickly you mastered the Citation Mustang." Hackett had suggested during their acquaintance that Stone learn to fly the airplane.

"I was glad of the opportunity to learn a new airplane," Stone said.

"I'm delighted to hear that, because Jim left you the Mustang in his will. It was his personal property."

"You're kidding!" Stone said.

"I am not, and I have a proposition to offer you. Strategic Services has bought a hangar at Teterboro and we have on order a CitationJet 4, which will be delivered shortly. We would like to continue to use the Mustang for business flights of less than a thousand miles, and if you will consent to that, we will offer you space for your airplane in our new hangar, and we will continue to make the payments on the maintenance programs covering the airplane. Also, we'll have an in-house mechanic at the hangar for smaller maintenance jobs, and one of the company pilots will fly the Mustang up to the Cessna Service Center at Newburgh, New York, for periodic inspections. The firm would also like to buy your old Jetprop," he said. "We'll pay whatever you paid for it."

"I am delighted to accept," Stone said.

"You'll always have first call on the Mustang," Freeman said. "If you'd like your old tail number on the Mustang, we'll have the change made for you."

"Yes, thank you."

"I'm also happy to tell you that I am assigning the remainder of all our legal work to Woodman & Weld, where we would like you to join Bill Eggers in supervising it."

"Thank you very much, Mike. Have you told Bill yet?"

"We spoke on the phone this morning; he was very pleased."

The car drew up in front of Strategic Services' building on East Fifty-seventh Street.

"The car will take you back to your office," Freeman said. "By the way, would you like an office in our building?"

"I don't think that will be necessary," Stone said.

"We'll reserve my old office for you, on the occasions when you're in the building," Freeman said.

The two men shook hands, and the car took Stone home.

Stone went into his office and sank into his chair. He had just had the best twenty-four hours of his life, and he was still stunned. He was now a stockholder of

Strategic Services, he had a new airplane, and he had not only his bonus of the night before but he would have cash for the sale of his old airplane to the company. What more could he ask for in this lifetime?

The phone rang, and Joan buzzed him. "Bill Eggers," she said.

Stone picked up the phone. "Hello, Bill."

"I had a call from Mike Freeman this morning," Eggers said.

"I heard."

"Then you know we're getting all their business?"

"I heard."

"You and I will work closely to supervise it," Eggers said.

"I heard."

"And I hear you have a new airplane."

"I heard."

"Is that all you can say?"

Stone sighed. "Bill, I can hardly speak. I'm just letting it all sink in."

"You do that," Eggers said, and hung up.

Stone buzzed Joan.

"Yes?"

"Please book me a table at Elaine's at nine."

"I'm afraid you have plans for this evening."

"What?"

"It's Herbie Fisher's wedding reception at the Hotel Pierre, at seven, dinner to follow."

"Oh, no."

"Oh, yes, and remember, Herbie is your second-biggest client."

Stone groaned. Herbie Fisher was a royal pain in the ass, one of those unfortunate people who never did anything right. Herbie had won a big number in the lottery a while back and had offered Stone a million-dollar retainer to handle all his legal affairs. Stone had been in a financial bind at the time, and in a weak moment he had accepted the money. "How much would it cost me to buy my way out of representing him?" he asked Joan.

"You couldn't afford it," Joan said, and hung up.

3

Stone arrived at the Pierre late and, consulting the list of private rooms, was surprised to see that Herbie's wedding reception was in the Grand Ballroom. Stone made his way there and found an acquaintance, Peter Duchin, at the piano, leading a full orchestra. He stopped by the bandstand.

"Hey, Stone," Duchin said.

"Evening, Peter. Who the hell is paying for all of this?"

"The father of the bride, of course." Duchin nodded toward a couple dancing past the bandstand. "Jack Gunn, the financier." Gunn was a handsome man in his sixties, who was dancing with a much younger woman.

Stone thanked the bandleader and made his way to the bar. Suddenly, Herbie Fisher was at his elbow, dressed in white tie and tails and towing his new wife.

"Hi, Stone," Herbie shouted over the din. "This is my wife, Stephanie."

"How do you do, Stephanie," Stone said. "I wish you both every happiness." Privately, Stone felt that little happiness was in store for the couple. Herbie's last fiancée had taken a dive off the terrace of the Park Avenue penthouse Herbie had bought with his lottery winnings.

"I've heard a great deal about you from Herbie, Stone," the young woman said. "I hope we'll be good friends."

Stone thought she sounded quite normal for someone who had just married Herbie Fisher. "May I have this dance, Mrs. Fisher?" he asked.

"I'd be delighted," Stephanie replied.

Stone led her to the dance floor and they danced. Stephanie was brunette and small, around five-two, Stone thought, without the heels. "How did you and Herbie meet?" he asked her.

"At P.J. Clarke's, at the bar," she replied. "I had just come back from a year abroad after graduating from Smith."

"Are you going to have a career?" he asked.

"I'm joining my father's firm after the honeymoon," Stephanie replied. "I'll be working as a trader, to start."

"Are you his heir apparent?"

"I am."

"I hope you'll take charge of Herbie's money," Stone said. "He can be rather impulsive in the way he spends it."

"Oh, I already have," she replied, laughing, "and just in time, too."

"I'm glad to hear it."

"Herbie has such a good heart," she said, "but no head for figures, unless they're female. I'm going to make him a rich man."

"I thought he was already rich," Stone said.

"He's down to his last ten million after the lottery win," she said. "In my family, that's not rich—that's slightly well-off. I've put him on an allowance, and I'm redecorating the apartment with my own money and some family things."

"I'm glad to hear that, too," Stone said, remembering what the apartment had looked like on his only visit there.

"Oddly enough, Herbie has very good taste in art. We've already bought some pictures he chose. He's not so good on furnishings and fabrics, though."

"Herbie has very good taste in wives, too," Stone said.

She laughed again. "Thank you, Stone. By the way, I've paired you with my aunt at dinner, my mother's recently widowed sister, Adele. You're at table number one, with us."

"How delightful," Stone said, trying not to clench his teeth.

Stone returned the bride to her new husband and got himself a glass of very good champagne. He sneaked a look at the bottle: Veuve Clicquot Grande Dame. If they were giving this to what looked like about seven hundred people in the ballroom, Jack Gunn had done very well indeed in business.

Stone wandered through the crowd, and they were a very presentable lot. Herbie had fallen into a pot of jam, he figured, and he wondered how long it would take before the boy screwed up.

The orchestra stopped, and a headwaiter took the microphone. "Ladies and gentlemen," he said, "dinner is served."

Stone found his way to table number one, where he located his place card, between Stephanie and her widowed aunt Adele. The bride arrived with Herbie and introduced her father, Jack, and her mother, Christine, who turned out to be the much younger woman he had seen Gunn dancing with.

"Good to meet you, Stone," Gunn said in a velvety bass-baritone voice.

"And you, Jack," Stone replied. He held Stephanie's chair for her. And turned to find a very beautiful blonde, wearing a gold lamé sheath, standing behind him. She appeared to be in her mid-thirties.

"Good evening," she said. "I'm Adele Lansdown." She offered her hand.

Stone took it. "How do you do? I'm Stone Barrington." He held her chair for her, then sat down, unable to believe his good luck.

"You," she said, "are apparently the most eligible man at this shindig; otherwise, Stephanie would not have seated you next to me. She's been trying to fix me up ever since my husband died."

"I'm very sorry for your loss," Stone said.

"Well," Adele replied, "you're about the only one who is."

"Was he ill?"

"Only for about three seconds," Adele replied. "He died of a gunshot wound."

"Who shot him?" Stone asked.

"I did," Adele replied.

Stone was taken aback for only a moment. "And yet you are a free woman. Or are you out on bail?"

She laughed. "I was not charged in his death," she said.

"You must have had a good lawyer."

"No, I had a black eye and a broken arm—the detectives in charge of the investigation deemed that sufficient evidence that I was defending myself."

"I used to be a police detective," Stone said, "and I would never have dreamed of arresting you."

"Are you still?"

"No, I retired some years ago. I'm an attorney."

"You went to law school after being a police officer?"

"Before," Stone said. "I took the bar afterward."

"At what firm are you?"

"I'm of counsel to Woodman & Weld."

"A very fine firm," she said. "I considered hiring them to deal with my husband's estate."

"I trust you found competent counsel."

"I found them; whether they were competent is another matter. I wish I'd gone with your firm. What does 'of counsel' mean?"

"It means I'm not a partner, and I work from my own offices."

"Hmmm," she said. "Are you what they call a fixer?"

"I've been called worse," Stone said, "but all attorneys are fixers, or at least they'd better be, if they want to hold on to their clients."

"And what clients do you represent?" she asked.

"I range across the client list," Stone replied, "but my principal responsibility is a company called Strategic Services."

"Oh, I read an article in *Vanity Fair* about them last year," she said. "Very interesting outfit."

"They are, indeed."

"I'm impressed, Mr. Barrington."

"Stone."

"And I'm Adele," she said. "Perhaps we could talk later about Woodman & Weld handling my affairs."

"I'd be happy to introduce you to the managing partner, Bill Eggers," Stone said, "but I'm not sure I want a business relationship with you."

"And why not?" she asked.

"I'd rather take you to dinner and discuss that," Stone said.

She smiled for the first time. "What a good idea," she replied.

4

The party eventually waned, and Stone escorted Adele Lansdown down to street level to look for a cab.

"I've got my car," Adele said. "I'll give you a ride."

They got into a white Mercedes sedan and were driven away. Stone gave the driver his address.

"Is that Turtle Bay?" Adele asked.

"Yes; I have a house there."

"I'd like to see it," she said. "I've always thought that an interesting neighborhood."

The car parked out front, and they went inside, where Stone began turning on lights.

"This is very handsome," Adele said, looking around the living room and dining room. "Beautiful woodwork."

"My father did all the woodwork in the house,"

Stone said. "In fact, this was his first big job, for my mother's aunt. She left me the house some years ago, and I renovated it."

"You did a lovely job. You did everything yourself?"

"I hired an electrician and a plumber and some casual labor, but the rest I did myself. Come, I'll show you the kitchen and garden." He led her downstairs, walked her through the kitchen, then opened the doors to the garden.

"Oh, a common garden," Adele enthused. "How pleasant."

"In warmer weather, yes," Stone said, taking her back indoors. "Would you like to see the bedrooms?"

"Perhaps another time," she said, smiling.

"My offices are on this level, too. My aunt's tenant was a dentist, and when he retired I took over the space. It works very well."

"I must be going," she said, "but I'll take you up on the offer of dinner."

"When are you free?"

"The day after tomorrow?"

"Good, I'll pick you up."

"Seven-forty Park," she said.

"Eight o'clock?"

"That's fine."

He put her into her car and watched her drive away. Some widowed aunt!

*   *   *

When Stone wandered into his office the following morning he found Herbie Fisher sitting on his sofa, waiting for him.

"Good morning, Herbie," Stone said. "I thought you were honeymooning."

"I'm afraid that's off," Herbie said.

Oh, God, Stone thought, he's screwed up already. Stone took a chair. "What's the problem?"

"We've just heard that Jack Gunn was arrested early this morning."

"Arrested? For what?"

"I'm not sure; some sort of financial irregularities in his firm. It should be in the papers tomorrow."

"This is not another Madoff thing, is it?"

"I hope not," Herbie said.

"Herbie, have you invested with your new father-in-law?"

"I'm not sure; Stephanie is handling that."

"Where is she?"

"With her mother."

"Herbie, you should get over there immediately and find out where your money is, and if it's with Gunn, you'd better move it fast."

"Okay, I'll go talk to Stephanie."

"Have you canceled your travel plans yet?"

"No. I guess I'd better call the travel agent. We were supposed to fly to Saint Barts this afternoon."

"That's exactly what you should do," Stone said. "If

this is a financial scandal, you and Stephanie are better off not being in New York."

"I'll see what Stephanie thinks," Herbie said, then left.

Joan came into his office with a copy of the *New York Post*. "Is this Herbie's new father-in-law?" she asked, handing the paper to Stone.

"I'm afraid it is," Stone replied. "I met him last night."

"There's no mention of the wedding in the story," she said.

"They'll get around to it, don't worry." His phone rang and Joan picked it up. "Mr. Barrington's office . . . One moment."

She covered the phone with her hand. "Somebody called Adele Lansdown."

Stone took the phone from her. "Good morning, Adele."

"Have you heard?" she asked.

"Yes, Herbie was just here. He's on his way to the Gunns' place to see Stephanie."

"Stop him, if you can," she said. "There's a mob scene over there."

"Hold on, please. Joan, see if you can get Herbie on his cell. Tell him to go straight home, not to the Gunns', and to try Stephanie on her cell and tell her the same thing." He went back to Adele. "My secretary is trying to reach Herbie. Do you know anything about what's led up to this?"

"Not a thing. Jack is the most upright man I have ever met."

"Do you have money invested with him?"

"Yes, most of my liquid assets."

"Can you get it out?"

"I can't do that; it would look awful if Jack's sister-in-law appeared to have no faith in him."

"Have you talked to Christine?"

"Just for a moment. She has no idea what's happening, except some people showed up at their house at breakfast time and took Jack away."

"Is there anything I can do for you?"

"Do I need a lawyer, Stone?"

"Are you in business with Jack, except as an investor?"

"No, I'm not."

"Then just sit tight and get somebody to screen your phone calls. Don't talk to anybody from the press."

"Not even to support Jack?"

"Not even for that, until you know more. Call me if you need any help."

"All right. Thanks, Stone." She hung up.

"Do you know anybody who invests with Gunn?" Joan asked.

"That was his sister-in-law; she does, but nobody else that I know of. Did you reach Herbie?"

"Yes, I caught him in a cab. He's going home, and he's trying to reach Stephanie."

The phone rang again and Joan answered. "It's Mike Freeman at Strategic Services," she said.

"Hello, Mike."

"Morning, Stone. Have you heard about this Jack Gunn thing?"

"Yes, just a few minutes ago."

"We're having a board meeting in half an hour. I'd like for you to be here."

"I'm on my way. What's the agenda?"

"Strategic Services has got more than ten million dollars invested with Gunn. That's the agenda."

Stone was in a cab when his cell phone vibrated. "Hello?"

"It's Bill Eggers."

"Good morning, Bill."

"I assume you've seen the papers, about Jack Gunn."

"Yes. I met him last night at his daughter's wedding reception."

"I just had a call from his corporate counsel, Leighton Craft. He wants us to represent Gunn, and I'd like you to help me handle it."

"We've got a conflict, Bill. Strategic Services has a big investment with him; I'm on the way to a board meeting there right now."

"It may not be a conflict. Leighton says that Gunn has done nothing wrong and is cooperating with the U.S. Attorney. I'm meeting with them this afternoon, and I'd like you to be there."

"All right, but I'll have to tell Mike Freeman about it."

"Go ahead and do that. I'll see you at three o'clock here."

Stone hung up. Yesterday he had never heard of Jack Gunn, and now he was up to his ass in the man's problems.

5

Stone arrived at Strategic Services, and the receptionist sent him in to Mike Freeman straightaway. Mike had moved into Jim Hackett's old office.

"Sit down, Stone," Freeman said. "I'm going to place a conference call to London, Tel Aviv, and Hong Kong in just a minute, but I wanted to talk to you first. What do you know about the Jack Gunn arrest?"

"Just what I've read in the papers," Stone said. "I attended his daughter's wedding last night—his new son-in-law is a client of mine. I'd never met Gunn before."

"Jim Hackett was a good friend of Gunn's; it was Jim who invested the firm's money with him."

"You said ten million. What part of your cash reserves does that represent?"

"Only a small part; we're sitting on over half a billion in cash."

"Well, that's good. Have you checked your insurance policies?"

"What insurance policies?"

"In your corporate portfolio you may have something that protects corporate funds from theft."

Freeman pressed a button on his phone. "Get me the legal department, an insurance specialist."

"I'll get right back to you," his secretary said.

"It would certainly make things simpler if we're covered for that," Freeman said.

"Mike, I have to tell you that I had a call from Bill Eggers on the way over. He's meeting with Gunn's corporate counsel, a man named Leighton Craft, this afternoon to discuss the firm's representing Gunn, and he wants me to help handle that."

"Wouldn't that be a conflict of interest, since you represent us?"

"If it looks that way, we can seal me off from any contact with the representation of Gunn," Stone explained, "but I understand that Gunn's position is that he's innocent of any wrongdoing and is cooperating with the U.S. Attorney."

"Not like the Madoff thing, huh?"

"I hope not. Bill wants me at the first meeting this afternoon. I'll need to look into this some more, to be sure there's no conflict, but in any case, my first loyalty is to Strategic Services."

Stone's cell phone buzzed, and he looked at it. "It's

Eggers. I'd better take this." He got up and walked across the room. "Yes, Bill?"

"Stone, I'm going to seal you off from the Gunn representation. I don't want it to interfere with your representation of Strategic Services, and you should tell Mike Freeman that I can't work on his account until the Gunn thing is cleared up, which could be some time."

"I understand, Bill."

"This means you're going to have to handle the Strategic Services account without consulting me. Most of the rest of the firm will be available to you, if you need help."

"Thanks, I'll let Mike know." Stone hung up and returned to his seat. "I'm all yours," Stone said.

"Good."

"But Bill is going to have to be absent from your account while he's dealing with the Gunn thing."

"I understand."

"Have you made any attempt to move your investments from Gunn to another firm?"

"Not yet."

"I think it would be good if you moved those assets to another entity, say, your bank, for the time being. You should talk to your banker before you call the Gunn firm. Who is your account manager there?"

"Jack Gunn."

"You'll have to talk to his number two, then."

"That would be Peter Collins. I've dealt with him a couple of times."

Freeman called his banker, talked for a moment, then hung up. "All Gunn's accounts are temporarily frozen," he said to Stone. "No transferring any funds into or out of accounts, and no trading."

"That may be a good thing," Stone said.

Freeman's secretary knocked and came into the room. "You should turn on your TV to CNBC," she said.

Freeman switched on a large flat-screen TV hanging on the wall on the other side of his office. A reporter stood outside the building where Jack Gunn's offices were located. In the background officers in body armor were moving into the building and there was yellow police boundary tape everywhere.

"The latest word is that somebody has shot several people in the offices of Jack Gunn, the investment banker who was taken to the U.S. Attorney's office earlier this morning for questioning," the reporter was saying. "We have not been told who the shooter is, how many people he has shot, or whether there are any fatalities, and it may be some time before we know any of that."

Stone looked past the reporter, and his eyes widened. He saw Herbie Fisher leaving the building with his arm around his new wife. "That's my client," he said, pointing. He got his cell phone out and speed-dialed Herbie's phone.

"Hello?" Herbie said breathlessly.

"Herbie, it's Stone Barrington. I've just seen you come out of Gunn's building on TV. What's going on up there?"

"This guy who sits next to Jack's office has shot a couple of people; I don't think anybody is dead. We were down the hall in Stephanie's office when the shooting started, and we got the hell out of there."

"Who is the guy doing the shooting?" Stone asked.

"His name is Peter Collins," Herbie replied. "I just met him this morning. We were supposed to talk to him about moving my money over to the firm."

"Did you do that?"

"No, we didn't have time."

"That's good. Get Stephanie to your apartment and call me when you're there."

"Okay, Stone." Herbie hung up.

So did Stone. "The guy doing the shooting is Peter Collins," he said to Mike Freeman. "I don't think he's going to be taking any calls this morning, except maybe from a police hostage negotiator."

"Oh, swell," Freeman said. He picked up his phone. "Sally, put that conference call through," he said. "Stone, I may as well let them all know what's happening, or what we know of it."

"I suppose so," Stone said.

The call was put through, and Freeman brought his colleagues up to date, then told them he'd get back to them when he had more information. He hung up.

"I guess there's nothing else we can do except wait for more information," he said to Stone.

"I guess not," Stone replied.

6

Stone got back to his office a little after five and went through the messages Joan had put on his desk before she left for the day. Dino had called and so, to his astonishment, had Peter Collins of Jack Gunn Investments.

Stone didn't know Peter Collins. Just for the hell of it he dialed the number. It rang seven times before it was picked up.

"Hello?" a hoarse male voice said.

"This is Stone Barrington. I'm returning Peter Collins's call. Who is this?"

"This is Peter Collins."

"What can I do for you, Mr. Collins?"

"I need an attorney to represent me in a multiple-count criminal action," Collins said.

"Are you still holding hostages there, Mr. Collins?"

"Yes."

"How many?"

"Four."

"What are their names?"

Collins told him, and Stone wrote them down.

"How many are injured?"

"Just one. I accidentally shot him in the leg while herding everybody into my office."

"Where in the leg?"

"Left, outside thigh."

"So you missed the femoral artery?"

"Yes. He's been given first aid and is alert and talking."

"Good. Mr. Collins, I can't represent you in the criminal action because I'm corporate counsel to one of your clients, Strategic Services."

"I didn't know that," Collins said.

"I was appointed only yesterday. What I can do for you is represent you in your talks with the police hostage negotiator and make sure you're dealt with nonviolently and that your rights are not violated. Then I can recommend an attorney to represent you in your legal difficulties. I assume that these multiple charges are related to your work and the taking of the four hostages. Is that correct?"

"That's correct."

"All right. Are you willing to give yourself up?"

"Yes, but I have conditions."

"What are they?"

"One: that nobody shoots me. Two: that I'm not led out of the building handcuffed, and that I leave the building through the garage, sitting in the right front seat of a police car. Three: that the wounded hostage is taken out of the building first, on a stretcher. Four: that no one asks me any questions until I've spoken in person with an attorney."

"Is that it?"

"That's it."

"I don't think that's going to be a problem, Mr. Collins."

"Please call me Peter; I'm more comfortable with that."

"Peter, I'm Stone. Can you remain near this phone?"

"Yes."

"I'll call you back in less than half an hour. If anything happens in the meantime that worries you, you can call me back on the same number you called before."

"All right."

"Just be calm, and don't talk to the police or anyone else until I call you back."

"All right. You can hang up now."

"Thanks." Stone hung up and called Dino.

"Bacchetti."

"It's Stone."

"Dinner tonight?"

"I think so, but first I have to get you to patch me

through to the hostage negotiator who's handling the thing at Jack Gunn Investments."

"Why?"

"Because the guy who's holding the hostages called me and asked me to represent him in the negotiations."

"Are you kidding me?"

"I am kidding you not."

"Hang on." Dino put him on hold for about a minute, then came back. "All right, he's on the line. His name is Hank Willard, Lieutenant."

"Hello, Hank?"

"Yes, Stone. Dino has told me who you are. What can you tell me?"

"Peter Collins wants to give himself up. He has conditions, but I don't think you're going to have a problem with them."

"What are they?"

Stone read from his notes.

"That's it?"

"That's it. How are you going to handle it?"

"You have any suggestions?"

"Yes. First I'd send a stretcher and a couple of unarmed EMTs who are not cops up there and take the wounded man away. By the way, Collins says the wounding was an accident, completely unintentional."

"I can do that."

"Then I think you should allow Collins to leave his gun in a desk drawer, lock it, and take an elevator down to the garage without a sniper taking him out."

"Okay, done."

"Remember, no cuffs. It's my guess that Collins wants to leave this way so that he won't be seen on television doing the perp walk."

"Yeah, okay."

"If you treat the guy respectfully, then I don't think you'll have any trouble with him. You need to brief the other officers in the car on that. In fact, I suggest that you meet Collins alone when he gets off the elevator, and that you put him in the front seat and get into the back. When you get him to the station, walk him in without cuffs and put him into an interrogation room and give him something to eat and drink while he waits for his lawyer."

"Okay."

"I am of the impression that he *wants* to talk to you, but only with an attorney present."

"Who's his attorney?"

"I have to make a couple more calls before I can tell you that."

"Okay."

"Wait for me to call you back before you send the EMTs upstairs. Collins says the guy is stable and not bleeding."

"I'll give you half an hour, Stone, no more."

"Done. Where are you taking him?"

"The Seventeenth Precinct, on East Fifty-first Street."

Stone hung up and called Peter Collins back.

"Hello?"

"It's Stone. The police are willing to meet all your conditions. The hostage negotiator, Lieutenant Hank Willard, is going to escort you to the police station, and you won't be seen on TV as a criminal. I suggest you make yourself presentable, suit and tie."

"All right. When do we start?"

"I have to get your attorney lined up; then I'll call you back."

"All right."

Stone hung up and opened his address book to the page of lawyers' numbers he kept handy. It took him only a moment to settle on Milton Levine. Levine was short, bespectacled, and balding, and he did not look like a corporate legal eagle. He dialed his direct number.

"Who is this; tell me fast."

"It's Stone Barrington, Milt. Shut up and listen."

"I'm listening; talk."

"You know about the hostage situation in that Park Avenue office building?"

"Yeah."

"I'd like you to represent the hostage holder, whose name is Peter Collins." Stone gave him the rundown on Collins's demands and Hank Willard's acceptance of them.

"So you've done everything. What's left for me?"

"Get your ass over to the Seventeenth Precinct on

East Fifty-first, listen to the man and represent him. You'll know better than I how to handle it."

"When?"

"Right now."

"Shit. I had a hot date for drinks."

"This shouldn't take more than a couple of hours; push it back to dinner."

"Good thinking. Bye." Levine hung up.

Stone called Peter Collins.

"Hello?"

"Everything okay there?"

"Yes."

"Your attorney's name is Milton Levine. Call him Milt. He doesn't look the part but he's as smart as they come, and he'll do good by you. He's going to meet you at the police station."

"All right."

"Now, we're going to set this in motion. First, the EMTs will come and take the injured man away. Then you lock your gun in your desk or your safe and take the elevator to the garage. Hank Willard will meet you there and escort you to the station. Got it?"

"Got it."

"Remember, as soon as the EMTs have taken the wounded man away, you lock up the gun and leave. The police will come after you've gone and take the hostages out."

"Thank you, Stone. I'm grateful for your help."

"Good luck, Peter."

Stone hung up and called Hank Willard. "We're on," he said. "Collins's attorney is Milton Levine. Go."

"We're going," Willard said. "Thanks for your help." He hung up.

Stone hung up and breathed a sigh of relief.

7

Stone met Dino at Elaine's. They were on their first drink when Bill Eggers walked in, sat down, and ordered a single-malt scotch.

Stone was surprised to see him. "What're you doing here, Bill?" he asked.

"I'm not here," Eggers said, taking a tug at his drink.

"Okay, how did the meeting go that you didn't have this afternoon with Jack Gunn and Leighton Craft?"

"It went well," Eggers said. "Gunn maintains his innocence and says that Peter Collins is the probable culprit."

"I spoke to Peter Collins this afternoon, and he maintains his innocence, too."

Eggers stared at him. "You spoke to Peter Collins?"

Stone explained his conversations with Collins and the hostage negotiator.

"And everything went according to plan?"

"As far as I know. Dino, what have you heard?"

"I was about to tell you," Dino said. "They got everybody cleared out and took Collins to the One Seven."

"Nobody got hurt?"

"Nobody. Hank Willard stuck to the agreement. The guy who got shot was treated and released; it wasn't a bad wound."

"Who did you get to represent Peter Collins?" Eggers asked.

"Milt Levine."

"Good call," Eggers said. "He's probably one of the few guys around who isn't representing somebody who's involved in this thing as a victim."

"He'll do a good job," Stone said.

"Did Collins lay the blame on anybody?"

"Not to me," Stone replied. "Who are the candidates?"

"Just Gunn and Collins, as far as I know," Eggers said.

"What were your impressions of Jack Gunn at your meeting?" Stone asked.

Eggers shrugged. "Angry, but in control. He says that Collins is the only guy in the firm who could have pulled this off without his knowledge."

Stone's cell phone vibrated; he looked at the screen and saw Milt Levine's name. "Hello?"

"Stone, it's Milt Levine."

"How'd it go?"

"I met with Collins at the One Seven; then he answered every question the police put to him. I bought what he had to say."

"What was the disposition?"

"He'll be arraigned for the shooting and hostage-taking tomorrow morning, and I'll get him bailed out. He hasn't been charged with taking any money."

"Who does Collins think is responsible?"

"He says it's got to be Gunn, possibly with the help of his son."

Stone blinked. "What son?"

"Name of David."

"Hang on," Stone said. He covered the phone and turned to Eggers. "Are you aware that Gunn has a son?"

Eggers frowned. "There was no mention of a son at our meeting."

Stone went back to the phone. "David comes as a surprise to everybody I know," he said.

"Well, he's going to get talked to," Levine said. "I gotta go."

"You still got the hot date?"

"You bet your ass." Levine hung up.

Stone put his phone away. "I don't get it about the son," he said to Eggers. "I was at Gunn's daughter's wedding last night. I sat at the family table and there was no son there and no mention of one."

"It's a mystery," Eggers said.

Stone got back on his phone and called Herbie Fisher.

"Hello?"

"Herbie, it's Stone. How are you?"

"I'm okay," Herbie replied. "Stephanie is pretty upset. She talked to her mother, and she's pretty upset, too. Jack got home in time for dinner, and he's also pretty upset."

"Herbie, I just heard that you have a brother-in-law."

"David? Yeah."

"Where was he at the wedding?"

"He didn't come to the wedding or the reception."

"Was he invited?"

"Yeah, but just between you and me, I'm pretty sure his mother and Stephanie were glad he didn't show up."

"Does he work for Jack?"

"Yeah. He's the number three guy there, after Jack and Peter Collins. Jack says Peter is the guy who did the stealing."

"Herbie, will you do me a favor?"

"Sure, Stone. What do you need?"

"I need to know where David Gunn is, or when anybody in the family last saw him."

"I'll see if I can find out, Stone."

"Be subtle, Herbie; don't upset anybody. Ask Stephanie."

"Hang on, I'll ask her."

"Herbie!" But Herbie had put the phone down. He came back a moment later.

"Stone, Stephanie says David is on vacation down in the islands somewhere."

"She doesn't know where?"

"No."

"Thanks, Herbie." Stone hung up. "David Gunn is on vacation somewhere in the islands."

"Which island?" Eggers asked.

"The daughter doesn't know which one."

Dino spoke up. "Maybe one with an unregulated banking system, with numbered accounts?"

Eggers set his drink down. "I wonder why David's name didn't come up at our meeting," he said.

"Maybe Jack Gunn is in denial about his son," Stone suggested.

"Maybe Jack is in cahoots with his son," Dino said.

"Bill," Stone said, "do you think that's a possibility?"

"I would not hazard a guess," Eggers replied, "but I'm sure going to ask Jack about it in the morning."

"How did you keep Gunn from getting arrested?" Stone asked.

"Before I even met him, Jack ordered a firm of forensic accountants—one approved by the U.S. Attorney—to do an audit of the firm's books. They've already started, and they'll be working twenty-four/seven until they're done. I think that impressed Tiffany Baldwin."

Tiffany Baldwin was the U.S. Attorney for the Southern District of New York, with whom Stone had once had a brief fling that had been featured in the gossip columns.

"I'm very happy that I'm not representing anybody in this mess," Stone said, "because then I would hate to have to deal with Tiffany."

"Yeah," Dino said, "I remember you dealing with her on Page Six of the *Post*."

"Please don't bring that up again, Dino," Stone whimpered.

"Okay, but I'll sure remember it," Dino replied.

"Me, too," said Eggers.

8

Stone was at his desk the following morning when Joan came into his office. "Good morning," he said.

"And to you," she replied. "Before you got in this morning Mike Freeman called and said he'd like you to attend a meeting in his office this morning at eleven."

Stone glanced at his watch. "Plenty of time. What kind of meeting?"

"He didn't say, but he did say it was important. You should be there a little early, he said."

"Okay," Stone replied.

There was a rap on his door, and Herbie Fisher walked in. "You got a minute, Stone?"

"Just about that," Stone replied, trying not to groan.

Joan sauntered out. "You two have fun," she said.

"What's up, Herbie?" Stone asked. "I thought you were going on your honeymoon."

"Stephanie thought it would be unseemly to go," he said. "That's the word she used: 'unseemly.'"

"I guess she has a point," Stone said.

"Yeah. I'm worried about what all this stuff is going to do to my reputation," Herbie said.

Stone looked at him askance. "Reputation?"

"Yeah, my reputation."

"Herbie, I don't think your bookie is going to worry about your reputation, as long as you pay your losses. Who else would give your reputation a thought?"

"You know, people."

"What people?"

"People who know the Gunns, who know Stephanie."

"Herbie, you don't work for Gunn, and neither does your wife, yet."

"Well, you know: lie down with dogs, get up with fleas."

"You're worried about getting fleas?"

"Yeah, on my reputation, as it were."

"As it were? Where did you pick up that little phrase, Herbie? Have you been hanging out at the *New Yorker*?"

"The *New Yorker*?"

"Maybe in the cartoon department?"

"I don't get it, Stone."

"Neither do I, Herbie. Any more news from David Gunn?"

"Stephanie talked to him at breakfast time. He called."

"Where did he call from?"

"He wouldn't tell her. She told him he'd better get his ass back here to help out with this."

"And how did he reply to that request?"

"He said he'd think about it. She's really pissed off at him."

"I'm not surprised. Have you had any dealings with David?"

Herbie shrugged. "Not much. I did recommend him to my bookie."

"Swell," Stone said. "The bookie who wanted to murder you?"

"We got past that," Herbie said.

"Is David big into the ponies?" Stone asked.

"More like sports betting."

This was not good, Stone thought. "Does he lose a lot?"

"He says he wins; says he's got a system."

"A system? That means he loses. Does his being in the islands have anything to do with your mutual bookie?"

"Come to think of it, I did get a call from him asking about David, but of course I couldn't tell him anything because I didn't know anything."

"That is certainly grounds for keeping your mouth shut," Stone said. "Well, you have your reputation to think about. If I were you, I'd distance myself from David," he advised.

"He's already in the islands," Herbie pointed out. "Isn't that far enough?"

"I was speaking metaphorically, not geographically."

"Huh?"

Stone looked at his watch. "Never mind. I have to go to a meeting. Was there something in particular you wanted to see me about?"

Herbie scratched his head. "Yeah, but I can't remember what it was."

Stone got into his coat. "It'll have to wait."

"Oh, I remember: the accountants said it wasn't Peter Collins that stole the money."

Stone stared at Herbie. "Already? Who did they say it was?"

"David."

"How much did David steal?" Stone asked.

"A little over a million dollars," Herbie replied.

"Well, that doesn't sound so bad. I'm sure Jack Gunn can write a check for that."

"No, I'm sorry, it was a little over a billion."

Stone's jaw dropped. "Well, those three little zeros make a difference, don't they?"

"I guess."

"Gotta run, Herbie," Stone said, making for the door.

Stone had trouble getting a cab, and traffic was bad, so he was five minutes late arriving at Mike Freeman's office. The secretary told him to go in, and when he did he found Mike talking with someone Stone knew.

"Come in, Stone," Freeman said. "I'd like you to meet Lance Cabot."

"We've met," Lance said drily. Lance was the deputy director of intelligence for operations at the Central Intelligence Agency.

"How are you, Lance?" Stone asked, shaking his hand. He was tempted to check his wallet.

"Very well, Stone," Lance replied, sitting back down. "I'm surprised to run into you at Strategic Services."

"That makes two of us," Stone said, taking a seat.

"How do you two know each other?" Freeman asked.

Stone started to reply, but Lance beat him to it. "We've had dealings in the past," he said casually.

"Mike," Stone said, "this is a business meeting, isn't it?"

"Yes, it is."

"Well, I'm afraid I have to declare an interest."

"That won't be necessary," Lance said.

Stone ignored him. "Some time ago I signed a consultant's agreement with Lance's employer, and I've done some odd jobs for him."

Lance reddened slightly. "I don't think it's necessary to—"

"Lance, perhaps you'd better release me from that agreement if I'm going to represent Strategic Services in its dealings with you. Is that what you have in mind, Mike?"

"Yes, it is," Freeman replied.

"Well, Lance, do you release me from our agreement?"

Lance's look could have burned a hole through cardboard. "Yes, I release you—but only for the purposes of business associated with Strategic Services."

"I guess that's good enough for me," Freeman said.

It wasn't good enough for Stone, but he didn't want to make anything more of it. He had the feeling that this was going to come back and bite him in the ass.

9

Lance turned his attention from Stone to Mike Freeman. "Mike," he said, "the Agency is contemplating outsourcing some of our operations."

"Oh?" Freeman answered.

"Yes. What with Iraq, Afghanistan, and the war on terror at home, we're starting to get stretched pretty thin."

"I can understand that," Freeman said.

"The war on terror at home?" Stone interjected. "Doesn't your charter prevent the Agency from operating at home?"

Lance crossed his legs and leaned back in his chair. "Our purview is expanded to domestic when the president authorizes it."

"Does he authorize these forays in writing?" Stone asked.

"Yes, he does."

Stone sat back and let Mike continue.

"How familiar are you with our operations, Lance?" Freeman asked.

"More familiar than you might think," Lance replied.

"Do you have any questions about our operations?" Freeman asked.

"Not at the moment," Lance said. "I expect I'll have specific questions if we come to the point of hiring you."

"Are you contemplating hiring us for activities currently within our various fields of operations?"

"Possibly," Lance said.

"Why don't you tell us the sort of thing you have in mind, then," Freeman said.

Stone cut in again. "Or, perhaps *specifically* what you have in mind."

"I can see us using your personnel protection services," Lance said. "I can see us purchasing armored civilian vehicles from your transportation division. I can see us chartering your C-17 cargo jet for delivery of personnel and equipment in foreign zones."

"We would be pleased to consider projects in any of those areas," Mike said.

"Lance," Stone said, "I somehow have the feeling that you are contemplating operating in some areas where you might not want the Agency to be seen to be operating. Is that the case?"

"Quite possibly," Lance said. "Tell me, Mike, what

percentage of your operations people have former or current high-security clearances?"

"All of them," Freeman replied, "who are former military, FBI, or intelligence people. The ones who have served in similar capacities in other countries would not, of course, have American clearance status, present or former. They would amount to about twenty percent of our operations people."

"Would that include you yourself?" Lance asked.

"I am Canadian by birth but I have been a U.S. citizen for eight years now, and I have never applied for a security clearance."

"Would you object to being vetted for such a clearance?"

"Not at all."

Lance reached for his briefcase beside his chair, opened it, and produced a form and handed it to Mike. "Would you kindly complete this form?"

"Of course," Freeman said, taking the form and glancing at it. "How soon do you need it?"

"Now would be a good time," Lance replied.

Freeman took a pen from his pocket and a magazine from the coffee table for support and began filling out the form.

"Well, Stone," Lance said, "what have you been up to?"

"Work, work, work," Stone replied. "Not much else."

"Anything you can talk about?"

"I'm afraid not," Stone said. "Client confidentiality, of course."

"Of course. I understand you've recently become type-rated in the Cessna Citation Mustang."

Stone was surprised he knew. "Yes, I have. Jim Hackett arranged to have me trained in the airplane."

"Good skill to have," Lance said.

"A pleasant one." He looked over at Mike to see how he was doing on the form. He appeared to be on the last page.

Freeman picked up a phone and buzzed his secretary. "Would you come in, please?"

The woman entered the room, and Mike handed her the document. "Would you fill in the relevant spaces on past employment and residences, please? It's all in my curriculum vitae in our files."

"Of course," she replied, and left with the document.

Stone began to wonder if Mike's background could stand a background check. Freeman was not who he said he was, and Stone was, perhaps, the only living person who knew that. Freeman was, in fact, British and a former member of MI6, from which he had been forced as part of a witch hunt against him some years ago. Jim Hackett had been killed because Mike's enemies in the British government believed him to be the man they were hunting, when Mike Freeman was, in fact, that man.

"What brings you to New York, Lance, apart from visiting us?" Freeman asked.

"Nothing else," Lance replied. "I had, in fact, intended to speak to James Hackett, but of course, his death intervened. Do you know who killed him?"

"We're still working on that," Freeman replied.

"Stone, how about you? You were with Hackett when he died, weren't you?"

"Yes, but I'm unable to speak about it," Stone replied. He did not want to tell Lance why not.

"Mmmmm," Lance purred. "Client confidentiality?"

"Yes," Stone replied, hoping his curiosity would stop there.

"You did some work for Felicity Devonshire at MI6 not very long ago, didn't you?"

"If I had, I certainly couldn't comment, could I?"

"No, I expect she asked you to sign the Official Secrets Act."

The secretary reentered the room before Stone could reply and handed the form to Freeman, who looked it over, signed it, and handed it to Lance.

Lance looked it over, too. "May I use your fax machine?" he asked.

"Of course," Mike replied. He led Lance over to a bookcase and opened a panel for him, revealing the machine. Lance pressed a couple of buttons and dialed a number. "Will it send both sides of the document?" he asked.

"Yes," Freeman said, "if you select that option."

Lance sent the document, then returned to his chair

and put the form into his briefcase. "We'll have a response shortly," Lance said.

"Don't you have to conduct an investigation?" Stone asked.

"Yes, but for the moment we will compare the information on the form electronically with what we already know about Mike, to be sure there are no discrepancies."

This did not seem to worry Mike.

Lance's cell phone rang. "Excuse me," he said. He held the phone to his ear. "Yes?" He listened for a moment. "Thank you," he said, and hung up. "Well, that's done. Now we can proceed, I think."

10

Lance leaned forward in his chair. "Mike, let me outline a not altogether hypothetical situation in which you might be very helpful to the Agency and to your adopted country."

Freeman said nothing, just nodded.

"Let us say that there exists in a fairly large city of this country a financial institution which we have reason to believe has been funneling funds to an Al Qaeda subsidiary in Indonesia."

Mike nodded again.

"This institution has a virtually foolproof safeguard against outside intrusions into its computer network."

"I would be very interested to hear about those safeguards," Freeman said.

"Essentially," Lance replied, "while they use outside connections to send data, they do not receive data except on a single connection, which has not only the latest in firewall protections, but on which every incoming request for data is vetted by a human operator before it is passed on to the central computer."

Freeman frowned. "That sounds almost too simple," he said.

"Yes, it does, doesn't it? Oh, their ordinary office computer system accesses and downloads from the Internet, but their system for transmitting and receiving secure data is discrete from that."

"You want us to supply you with people who can hack into their computers?" Freeman asked. "I should think the National Security Agency could better handle that."

"Of course," Lance replied. "Unfortunately, the bulk of their personnel are not available to us . . . on-site, let us say."

"You mean they won't do a black bag job for you?" Stone asked.

"To put it crudely," Lance said drily.

Freeman spoke up. "Am I to understand that you want us to put our people *inside* this institution for the purpose of sacking their computer system?"

"At our present level of expertise, that is the fastest way for us to gain access to their secure data."

Freeman had not stopped frowning. "You want us to carry out an illegal entry into their offices and steal their data."

"We would, of course, provide umbrella protection from prosecution to your people," Lance said.

Stone spoke up. "I'm sure that Richard Nixon offered the same protection to the Watergate burglars."

Lance blinked. "Well, perhaps so."

"I'm sure I could find personnel in our organization who would be enthusiastic about such an operation," Freeman said, "but I am not sure I could furnish someone with a sufficient level of computer expertise to break into a secure system within a matter of a few hours, which is what you are talking about."

"I understand," Lance said. "That is why your people would take an NSA operative along with them."

"I think that would make a great movie," Stone said, "but a bad business story in the *Wall Street Journal*. I have to tell you, Mike, that you would be putting your company at great risk at a level all out of proportion to the reward to be gained."

Lance bristled. "The reward, as you put it, Stone, is to destroy the enemies of your country."

"By breaking the laws of my country," Stone pointed out.

"I think I sense your position on this, Stone," Freeman said. "Lance, I will have to discuss this matter with some of our people, then get back to you with a decision in principle, not having details of the actual operation."

"Perfectly understandable, Mike," Lance replied. "I'm at the Lowell, and here's my cell number." He handed Freeman a card.

Freeman stood up. "Thank you for coming to see us, Lance." They shook hands and Lance left.

Stone and Freeman sat down again.

"Well, Stone, what do you *really* think?"

Stone laughed. "I think that Lance Cabot is someone who can never be completely trusted, and I would not want to see the reputation of Strategic Services in his hands."

"Is that the only reason you're against it? I mean, dealing Al Qaeda a serious blow is an attractive goal."

"Mike, if this job were as easy as Lance makes it sound, he'd have his own people do it. The Agency is not short of people with the requisite skills for such an operation, so why doesn't he use them? And I very much doubt that the president would ever put his signature to a finding on such an operation. That might very well be grounds for impeachment."

"Good points, all," Freeman said.

"Mike, I can see you're attracted to this. Why?"

"For personal reasons, I suppose. I've always believed that the greatest benefits derive from operations with the greatest risks."

"Then, if you were a poker player," Stone said, "you'd always try to fill an inside straight."

"Not always," Freeman replied, "but sometimes."

"If you gamble for thrills, that's a good position to take," Stone said. "But if you have to make a living playing poker, you'd soon find yourself on the street, broke and hungry."

"What you say about poker is true," Freeman replied. "But in this kind of operation you make your own odds."

"You'd need to know everything to make your own odds, and with an operation like this you can never know everything; you'll only know what Lance wants you to know. Also, Mike, if you undertake this, you'd be dabbling in politics, and that's a dangerous arena for a business."

"All valid arguments," Freeman said, "and I'll take them all into consideration." He smiled. "I wouldn't mind having Lance Cabot in my debt; that might come in useful sometime."

"Mike, I've had considerable dealings with Lance, and I can tell you it can be profitable to deal with him. But you must remember that, in any situation, the safety of Lance's ass is Lance's most important priority, and any benefits from dealing with him will come only after Lance has first benefited, if then."

Freeman took an envelope from his desk and handed it to Stone. "Here's the check for your old airplane," he said. "I trust it's correct."

Stone glanced at the check. "Entirely acceptable," he said.

Freeman handed him another envelope. "These are the sales documents and the request to the FAA to keep your old tail number. The process will take a few weeks."

Stone signed in the relevant places and handed the papers back to him. "Fly it in good health," he said. "It's always served me well."

Freeman handed him another envelope. "And these need your signature for your new airplane," he said.

Stone walked home with a spring in his step, the check burning a hole in his pocket.

II

Stone hired a driver and went to pick up Adele Lansdown at her apartment at 71 East Seventy-first Street. He knew that this was the side door for a more famous address, 740 Park Avenue, said to be the most prestigious in the city.

The doorman on duty called up, then directed him to the elevator. Stone knew the building because he knew a woman who lived there, in her parents' apartment.

A houseman in a white jacket admitted him, led him to the living room, and poured him a drink. Stone spent his waiting time looking at the pictures in the room.

"Are you interested in art?" Adele's voice said from behind him.

Stone turned to watch her come toward him. "I enjoy looking at it, but I'm not in the market at this level," Stone said. "My mother was a painter, and we always had good pictures in our house."

"Would I know her?"

"Perhaps. Her name was Matilda Stone."

"I know her work very well," Adele said. "I have standing orders at two galleries for her work, should it ever become available."

"I've heard that before," Stone said. "People who acquire her work seem to hold on to it."

"Do you have anything of hers?"

"I have four of her oils—New York scenes."

"I envy you those. May I see them sometime?"

"Of course," Stone said. "They're in my bedroom."

Adele laughed. "And I've already turned down one invitation to tour that site."

"Perfectly understandable, on short acquaintance."

"Perhaps on my next visit to your house. Shall we go to dinner?"

"Certainly. My car is downstairs."

"Where are we going?"

"I thought the Four Seasons would be nice."

"Always."

They arrived at the restaurant and were immediately seated in the Pool Room, a reference to the pool, not the game. They ordered drinks, then dinner.

"How are things in your family?" Stone asked.

"Difficult," Adele replied.

"I understand Jack hasn't been charged with anything."

"That's correct, and it's the only thing that lets us hold our heads up around town."

"Have the accountants finished their work?"

"Their report is due in a day or two," she said.

"Did Jack invest your money?"

"Some of it. I put the proceeds of my husband's estate in his hands, but I continued to manage my own funds. I started a cosmetics business years ago, and I sold it before the recession, so I have means of my own to support me."

"An enviable position to be in," Stone said. "Has anyone heard anything from David?"

She gazed at him over her martini glass. "You're very well informed. What do you know about David?"

"That he's . . . on vacation."

"Well, yes."

"And that he's suspected of being the real culprit—or, at the very least, Jack's coconspirator."

"Suspected by whom?" she asked.

"Just about everybody, I gather."

She shrugged. "I honestly don't think Jack is capable of stealing his clients' money. For one thing, he's always made plenty of his own. He was a top man at Goldman Sachs; only went out on his own when he was passed over for CEO there. He left with a very large bundle, which he used to establish his own business, and that has done extraordinarily well."

"And how do you feel about David?"

"I love the boy. He's always been the perfect young man, you know—top of his class, everybody's choice to succeed." She made as if to continue, but stopped.

"But?"

"But I don't understand his generation; they are all so different from the way we are, used to having everything so early in their adulthood."

"You think he might have cut corners?"

"A billion dollars' worth of corners?" she asked. "It hardly seems possible."

"I guess we'll know when the accountants are done," Stone said.

When they were back in the car Adele said, "Now I'd like to see your mother's pictures."

Stone mixed them a drink in the living room, then took Adele upstairs in the elevator and switched on the lights that washed the wall where the four pictures hung.

Adele went and stood before them, gazing intently at one after the other. She turned and put her hand on her breast. "They take my breath away," she said.

"They still do that to me, too," Stone replied.

"If you should ever—"

Stone held up a hand. "Never. They'll go to the Metropolitan Museum—eventually—to hang with her other work there. The museum shop is already selling reproductions that are somewhat smaller than the originals."

Adele sipped her drink and looked around the room. "You've done this quite well," she said. "Who was your designer?"

"I was," Stone replied.

"I'm not at all uncomfortable in your bedroom," she said, "but I'd like to take one more look at your pictures and then be taken home."

"As you wish," Stone said. He waited until she was finished, then took her empty glass and led her to the elevator.

"Did you ever marry?" she asked on the way down.

"Never," Stone lied. There had been a marriage, with the daughter of a friend, but it was terminated after only a few weeks. He had never felt married.

"Do you have something against the institution?" she asked.

"No, I always assumed I would be married someday; it just hasn't happened."

They left the elevator and walked to the car.

"Have you ever come close to marrying?" she asked as he opened the door for her.

"Yes, but I've managed to stay out of serious trouble."

She laughed. "A bachelor would look at it that way."

"It was just a joke," he said.

"I wonder," she replied.

"I'll have the driver take you home, if that's all right."

"Of course," she said. She reached up and put her

hand on his cheek, then kissed him in a meaningful way. "I hope you'll ask me out again."

"What are you doing this weekend?" he asked.

"I'm perfectly available."

"I'll pick you up at nine on Saturday morning, then."

"Where are we going?"

"A surprise," he said. "Bring country clothes and some good boots for walking and a warm coat."

"I'll be ready," she said.

He kissed her again, then put her in the car and sent it on its way. Now he had something to look forward to.

12

Stone was having breakfast in bed the following morning while doing the *Times* crossword puzzle with the TV on. He was distracted from the puzzle by the mention of Jack Gunn's name and turned his attention to the TV.

"A moment ago," the reporter was saying, "the forensic accountants who have spent the past days combing through the business records of Gunn Investments made the following statement."

A man in a pin-striped suit appeared on-camera: "After a thorough inspection of the books and computer systems of Gunn Investments, we have concluded that no money is missing, and no wrongdoing has been committed by anyone in the firm. We did find and have corrected an anomaly in the firm's computer software that incorrectly transferred some of the firm's general fund to three of its foreign accounts. Those funds have been returned to the New York account, and the books now balance. We have recommended to the Securities and Exchange Commission that the firm's customer accounts be unfrozen, and we have recommended to the U.S. Attorney for the Southern District of New York that no charges be filed against any member of the firm."

The camera returned to the reporter. "There you have it. Gunn Investments has been given a clean bill of health, and Jack Gunn is scheduled to make a public statement in about an hour. We'll have that for you. In the meantime, David Gunn, Jack Gunn's son, has returned to Miami after a week-long sail in the Caribbean." The camera showed a handsome young man in sailing clothes being mobbed by reporters at a marina.

"I knew nothing about all this until we sailed into the harbor this morning," he said. "I've been at sea and out of touch for a week, and I'm returning to New York today to be of any help I can in sorting this out."

Stone turned the volume down and went back to his puzzle, but he couldn't concentrate. Herbie had told him that David Gunn had spoken to his sister, Stephanie, a day or two earlier. Now he was saying he'd been out of touch for a week?

But Stone had other things to think about. He put down the puzzle, called the caretaker of the Maine house, and asked him to get the place in order for guests and to meet him at the airstrip on Saturday morning; then he called Mike Freeman.

"Good morning, Stone. Did you hear the good news about Jack Gunn?"

"Yes, I just saw it on TV," Stone said.

"That's a great relief," Freeman said.

"I'm planning to use the Mustang on Saturday and Sunday," Stone said, "if you don't need it. I'll be back no later than noon on Monday."

"Fine. Enjoy yourself."

"Have you heard anything more from Lance Cabot?"

"No. I think he's expecting me to call him today. I'll do that, and I'll say, while we are interested in doing work for the Agency, we don't want to participate in the sort of mission he mentioned."

"I think that's a good move, Mike."

"Let's have lunch next week sometime."

"I'd like that," Stone replied. They said good-bye and hung up.

Stone was already at his desk when Milton Levine called.

"Morning, Milt."

"And to you, Stone. Thanks for the referral of Peter Collins."

"You're very welcome. How did it work out?"

"We're pretty much squared away. Turns out Collins had a permit for the gun, and the man who was shot agreed it was an accident. I pleaded him to one count of unlawful discharge of a firearm and he got probation and community service."

"Nothing for the hostage-taking?"

"None of the people involved wanted to press charges, and the hostage negotiator testified to Collins's cooperation, so the whole thing pretty much went away. He's back at the office this morning."

"I'd like to be a fly on the wall at the first meeting between Collins and Jack Gunn," Stone said.

"So would I, but my guess is they'll put it behind them, and it will be business as usual. I owe you a good dinner for the referral."

"Anytime, Milt," Stone said, and they hung up.

Stone felt a sense of relief that all the problems that had cropped up in the past few days seemed resolved. Now he could leave for the weekend with nothing on his mind, and he relished that prospect.

"Hi, Stone."

Stone looked up to see Herbie Fisher leaning against the doorjamb.

"Good morning, Herbie."

"I hear you and Adele hit it off last night."

"We had a very pleasant evening," Stone replied.

"And I hear you're off to some surprise place this weekend, too."

Stone frowned. "You certainly hear a lot, Herbie."

"The women in the family are constantly talking to one another," Herbie said. "Don't tell one of the family, unless you want them all to know. Where are you taking Adele?"

"I'm going to take your advice, Herbie, and not tell you. Otherwise, it won't be a surprise, will it?"

"You heard that Jack is off the hook? David too?"

"I heard."

"Jack's spending the day calling clients and telling them everything's okay."

"Good idea."

"Say, Stone, would you like to invest some money with Jack? He doesn't take a lot of new clients, but Stephanie could have a word with him."

Stone thought about the unaccustomed large chunk of cash sitting in his accounts, from his Woodman & Weld bonus and the sale of his old airplane to Strategic Services. "That's an interesting idea, Herbie. Let me get back to you on that, will you?"

"I'm putting everything with Jack, myself," Herbie said.

"Everything?"

"Sure, why not? Stephanie will be watching over it for me."

"It's a good idea to put her in charge of your money, Herbie. She probably doesn't have a bookie."

Herbie found that very funny. "No, she's a lot more conservative than I am."

"*Everybody* is a lot more conservative than you are, Herbie."

"Well, yeah, I guess."

"Anything else on your mind?"

"No, I was just passing by," Herbie said.

"When are you off on your honeymoon?"

"In a few days. We're rebooking everything."

"Have a good time," Stone said, turning back to his work. Investing with Jack Gunn seemed like a pretty good bet, he was thinking.

13

On Saturday morning Stone picked up Adele and drove to Teterboro Airport, to Jet Aviation, where the Mustang sat out on the apron, waiting for them.

Adele showed an interest in the airplane, so, after loading their bags in the forward luggage compartment, Stone took her along on the preflight inspection; then he hooked up the battery, and they prepared to taxi. Stone got his IFR clearance, then worked his way through the long checklist, started the engines, and asked ground control for permission to taxi. Shortly, they were lined up on runway one with a takeoff clearance. Stone did his final, brief checklist, then pushed the throttles all the way forward and held the brakes on while the engines spooled up. He released the brakes, the airplane accelerated quickly down the runway, and Stone rotated, then retracted the landing gear and flaps. At seven hundred feet, he switched on the autopilot and began flying the

Teterboro Six departure, but shortly he was given a vector to the Carmel VOR, then a moment later, direct to Kennebunk.

Adele had been listening on her headset from the copilot's seat. "Kennebunk? That's in Maine, isn't it? Are we going to Maine?"

"We are," Stone replied. "To an island in Penobscot Bay called Islesboro and a village called Dark Harbor."

"It sounds wonderful," she said.

The countryside was mostly white beneath them and got whiter as they flew east and north. Stone showed Adele Islesboro on the chart; then he ran through his descent and landing checklists, to stay well ahead of the airplane. They had only just reached their cruising altitude of thirty-three thousand feet when Boston Center started their descent.

Soon Stone could point out Islesboro and the landing strip.

"The strip looks awfully small," Adele said.

"It will look larger as we approach," Stone replied, "and the airplane is very good at short field work. Now, excuse me, I have to concentrate on landing."

His checklist called for a final approach speed of 88 knots, and he concentrated on reaching and holding that speed while extending the flaps and landing gear. He put the airplane exactly where he wanted it and right on the speed number, then applied the brakes.

"Very good brakes," Adele said. "I didn't think we'd be able to stop so quickly."

"There's Seth Hotchkiss," Stone said, pointing at the restored 1938 Ford station wagon parked beside the runway. "He and his wife, Mary, take care of the place."

"How long have you owned the house?" Adele asked.

"I don't own it. It was built by my first cousin Dick Stone, who died a while back. He left me lifetime use of the house, and on my death it will go to a foundation he set up."

"That was very nice of him," she said.

"It was indeed," Stone agreed.

Seth greeted them and put their bags into the back of the wagon, while Stone installed the engine plugs and pilot covers and disconnected the battery. Then they drove away.

"Are you having a quiet winter, Seth?" Stone asked.

"Quiet as usual," Seth replied. "We got some snow last week."

"It's very pretty," Adele commented as they drove through the village.

At the house, Mary greeted them, and Seth took their luggage upstairs.

"I've got some clam chowder on the stove," Mary said. "Would you like some?"

They agreed and had a good lunch in the kitchen, then moved to the living room.

"What's that sound?" Adele asked.

Stone listened. "Phone," he said. He took his house

key and opened the locked door that concealed Dick Stone's study. Dick had been about to be promoted to the job now held by Lance Cabot at the CIA when he, his wife, and daughter had been murdered, but Stone didn't want to tell Adele that they had been killed in the house.

Stone picked up the phone. "Yes?"

"Good afternoon, Stone."

"How on earth did you know I was here, Lance?"

"Stone, are you forgetting where I work? I always know everything. I thought you knew that."

"I keep forgetting," Stone replied. He had told his secretary where he was going, but she wouldn't have told Lance.

"A bit chilly up there, isn't it?"

"Yes," Stone replied.

"You don't sound very happy to hear from me," Lance said.

"Why should I be happy to hear from you, Lance? It's a weekend, and I'm away from my office."

"Ah, yes; I forgot that you are a nine-to-five office worker."

"What do you want, Lance?"

"Well, Stone, first of all I want to tell you how unhappy I was with your performance in my meeting with Mike Freeman."

"Performance? What the hell does that mean?"

"I expected you to take the Agency's position in our conversation."

"I'm counsel to the company," Stone said. "I take their position in all meetings, with you or anybody else."

"Stone, you've been on the Agency's payroll for some time now."

"I'm not on your payroll," Stone said. "You pay me when I work for you, like any other client. It's not like I'm on salary."

"Still."

"Lance, perhaps it would be better if you just released me from my contract with the Agency."

"Oh, no, I don't want to do that. There are times when I need your particular talents."

"Well, don't try to employ them when I'm representing Strategic Services."

"Mike called me yesterday and declined to be involved in the situation I outlined to him."

"Good. That was my advice."

"Actually, that situation was entirely hypothetical, designed to test Freeman's willingness to be involved with us. I expect we'll find other ways for him and his company to be useful to us."

"You were never able to get Jim Hackett to play ball with you, were you, Lance?" Stone was guessing now.

"That was a different time. Jim is gone now."

"Well, you should expect Mike Freeman to treat your offers with equal skepticism."

"I certainly hope not, Stone, for your sake as well as his."

Stone was rendered speechless by this remark, and by the time he recovered himself, Lance had hung up. Stone went back to the living room.

"You don't look very happy," she said.

"I had a business phone call at a time when I didn't want one," Stone replied. "How about a walk? I'll show you around."

Adele went to get her coat and boots, while Stone tried to put Lance Cabot out of his mind.

14

They walked along the water, carefully picking their way over rocks on the shore. The harbor was empty of boats, and the Tarratine Yacht Club was closed and shuttered.

"It's beautifully desolate, isn't it?" Adele said.

"Well-chosen words."

"I like it that you brought me up here," she said. "Most men would have taken me south to someplace warm."

"I wanted you all to myself," Stone said. "Up here I don't have to compete with your friends and the tourists and the shops for your attention."

"You have my undivided attention," she said, squeezing his hand.

They were gone an hour, and when they returned Mary made them hot buttered rum, and that warmed them up.

*　　*　　*

At dinnertime Mary had managed to produce lobster Thermidor, and they ate it with a bottle of good white Burgundy from Dick Stone's cellar.

Back in the living room, Adele stood at the window and watched the moon rising. "Are these windows tinted?" she asked. "The moon is a funny color."

"Let me tell you about the house," Stone said. "My cousin Dick was a lifelong employee of the Central Intelligence Agency, something I didn't know until shortly before his death. Dick finally got the job he'd wanted all his life, deputy director for operations, but he died before he could assume the office. When he built the house, the Agency, in consideration of Dick's importance to it, added many security features, among them thick, armored glass in all the windows. That's why the moon's color may seem a little odd."

"Dick Stone was from your mother's side of the family?"

"Yes, he was her brother's son."

"How did he die?"

"He was murdered, along with his wife and daughter."

Adele looked shocked. "Was this in connection with his work?"

"No, it was a family matter. Say, can I show you the bedroom?"

She laughed and kissed him. "I'd love to see it," she said.

He led her upstairs, and they helped each other undress, then plunged under the eiderdown duvet and clung to each other for warmth.

"I'm glad we're not in Palm Beach," she said, throwing a leg over his.

"I'm glad, too," Stone said; then he turned his attention entirely to her needs.

After lunch the following day, Stone left the house alone and drove out to the airfield. There had been a little snow in the night, and he wanted to see if he was going to have an icing problem with the airplane.

The sun was well up, though, and what snow there may have been on the airframe had melted. Stone was about to get back into the old Ford when suddenly there was a helicopter over the runway. It was black, and he noticed that there was no registration number on the fuselage.

The chopper settled slowly; then a rear door opened and someone beckoned for him to approach. Stone walked over to the helicopter, and Lance Cabot leaned forward from a rear seat and offered his hand. Stone shook it; then other hands grabbed him and hoisted him aboard the aircraft. The door slammed, and the chopper rose straight up, then banked and turned south.

"What the hell is this?" Stone shouted over the noise of the rotor.

Lance pointed at his ear and mouthed, "Can't hear

you." Then he motioned for Stone to sit back in his seat, and another man buckled his seat belt.

They flew south for ten minutes across Penobscot Bay; then the helicopter descended and set down on a small island. The engines were cut, and the rotor spun down; then Lance and his two aides, along with Stone, got out and walked toward a large house fifty yards away.

"What is this place?" Stone asked. "And what the hell am I doing here?"

"I thought we'd have a chat," Lance said as they climbed the steps to the front porch. They shed their coats in the entrance hall and Lance led Stone to a paneled library overlooking a rocky beach. He poured them both a brandy, and they sat down.

"Whose place is this?" Stone asked, grateful for the warmth of the brandy.

"It's a rental, sort of," Lance replied. "Belongs to an alumnus of the Agency. We use it for various tasks in the off-season. Right now there's a Chinese agent upstairs in one of the bedrooms, being turned, I should expect."

"Is this where you called me from?"

"Yes. As we flew in yesterday, I saw Jim Hackett's little Mustang at the Islesboro field, so I knew you were here."

So Lance was not all-knowing, after all, Stone thought. "You shouldn't have told me that," he replied. "I was terribly impressed with your knowledge of my whereabouts. And, by the way, the airplane is mine now. Hackett left it to me in his will."

"You are a great inheritor of things, aren't you, Stone? Your house in New York is from an aunt, I believe."

"Great-aunt."

"Then Dick Stone's house, and now a jet airplane. You're a fortunate fellow."

"I suppose I am at that," Stone said.

"Well, if you're a nice fellow, nice things happen to you, don't they?"

"If you say so," Stone replied warily. He had the feeling something not so nice was about to happen to him.

"I expressed my displeasure with you yesterday, on the phone," Lance said. "Now I want to expand on that a little."

"You don't need to expand, Lance; I'm well aware of your displeasure."

"I thought it might help if I gave you a little background."

"All right."

"Will Lee, as you know, is now in his last term as president, and that means his wife, the lovely Katharine Rule Lee, is in her last years as our director."

Stone nodded and sipped his brandy.

"Things are always changing in the intelligence game, but because of the president's two terms and what turned out to be Kate's calming presence, we at the Agency have had a rather long period of stability. There have been blips along the way, of course, among them various problems associated with the work of outside contractors."

"Yes, I've read about those in the papers," Stone said. "Particularly about the murder trial of a few of your mercenaries."

"We do not accept that term," Lance said. "These people are patriotic Americans, not simply hired guns. They actually save us money by performing many chores peripheral to our actual missions. We don't have to train their people, you see; most are ex-military or ex-Agency or ex–something else, so they arrive with the requisite skill set."

Stone continued to sip his brandy, which had warmed him down to his fingertips by this time.

"Because of some of the difficulties raised by previous contractors," Lance said, "I am particularly interested in having Strategic Services on our team."

"Because they're clean?" Stone asked.

"Precisely. Jim Hackett has always operated in a highly ethical manner, and his reputation, and that of his company, is, as a result, impeccable."

"And Mike Freeman wants to keep it that way," Stone said.

"Of course, of course," Lance replied, "and yet it is Mike himself who is the greatest threat to the company's reputation."

Stone stopped sipping brandy. "What do you mean by that?" he asked carefully.

"I think you may already know," Lance said. "But I'm going to tell you anyway, just so all our cards will be on the table." He took a sip of his brandy, then continued.

15

Lance sniffed his brandy and took another sip. "Freeman is not his real name," he said, "or, at least, not the name he was given at birth. He was then called Stanley Whitestone."

Stone sipped his brandy and waited.

"Mike was a well-brought-up young Englishman when he was recruited for MI6, which is, as you know, the Brits' foreign intelligence service. He excelled there and many said he was headed for the top. Then he fell in love with a much younger woman. She was twenty-two or so, a student at Cambridge, and Mike was in his mid-thirties and married. Her father, who was an important member of Parliament, was not amused. He came down rather hard on the girl, who had, by this time, found herself pregnant. Mike stepped up; he left his wife and became engaged to the girl, but she decided to have an abortion. Afraid of calling attention to herself because of her father's position, she did not go to a hospital. Instead, she called on her best friend at Cambridge, a medical student, to perform the procedure. The boy was gay and the son of another important MP.

"The young man got through the procedure at his boyfriend's country cottage and left her there overnight alone. When he returned the following morning she had contracted an infection and was very ill. He got her to a hospital, but she died later the same day. Mike Freeman knew nothing of any of this at the time.

"The boy was arrested, charged with performing an illegal abortion, and did a plea bargain for six months in prison. His medical career was ruined. While in prison he was raped and murdered by another prisoner, leaving two angry and powerful fathers to mourn the two young people.

"Time passed, the two MPs rose in the political world, and when their party won the next election, the girl's father joined the cabinet as foreign secretary and the boy's father as home secretary. Thus empowered, they set out to avenge their unlucky children and destroy Stanley Whitestone.

"By this time, under pressure created by the two fathers, Whitestone, fearing for his life, had left MI6, changed his name to Michael Freeman, and vanished. Eventually, he acquired an altered face, a Canadian passport, and a slight Montreal accent. Then he met Jim Hackett, went to work for him, and rose to number two in Strategic Services. With me so far?"

Stone shrugged noncommittally.

"Then your friend Felicity Devonshire, head of MI6, at the behest of the two fathers, employed you to find Mr. Whitestone. Felicity did not know the backstory, and the fathers had fabricated charges of treason, or worse, against Whitestone. The rest you know, am I right? In fact, you were with Jim Hackett when the sniper got him. I am prepared to believe that you knew nothing of that."

"I won't confirm or deny any of your story," Stone said.

"You are so stubborn, Stone," Lance said, laughing and shaking his head. "But I respect your loyalty and your rectitude, which is why I am now formulating a new approach to Mike Freeman and Strategic Services."

"I'm sure he'll be interested in hearing what you have to say," Stone said, "as will I."

"Properly noncommittal," Lance said. "I'm going to make Mike an offer he can't refuse, as the Godfather used to say."

"I hope the content of your offer will be different from those of the Godfather," Stone said.

"Don't you worry, Stone; it will all be legal, proper, and aboveboard. Well, perhaps not entirely aboveboard, given the business we have chosen. Aboveboard is not really what we do, is it?"

"Finally, something we can agree on," Stone said.

There was a sharp rap on the door of the study.

"Come in!" Lance commanded.

The door opened and a large man in hunting clothes filled the doorway. "The gentleman has said he is ready to speak to you now, sir."

"Tell him I'll be right with him," Lance said, and the man closed the door.

"Did someone make him an offer he can't refuse?" Stone asked.

"Well, yes," Lance replied.

"I suppose that involved what you people like to call 'enhanced interrogation'?"

"His interrogation was certainly enhanced," Lance said, "but not in the way you might imagine. The offer he couldn't refuse involved a new life for himself and his family, certain protections, and a considerable sum of money. He will be a very happy ex-spy."

"More likely a double agent," Stone said.

"That, while covered by your security clearance, is on a need-to-know basis, and you most definitely do not need to know."

Lance rose. "Will you invite me to dinner tonight on your island?"

Stone stood, too. "I'm very sorry, but I have a previous engagement with someone a lot more beautiful than you, Lance."

"Rain check, then?"

"Next time you're in New York, I'll take you to Elaine's."

"Done."

The two men walked toward the door together. "The chopper awaits you," Lance said.

"And when will you make your new offer to Mike Freeman?"

"I have already done so," Lance said.

"And what did you offer him that he can't refuse?"

"I'm sure he'll tell you in due course," Lance replied. "He may even tell you about the mission we've engaged him for. That's up to him."

"I'm not going to like it, am I?" Stone asked.

"You may, or you may not," Lance replied. "Your opinion is of little consequence. Have a nice flight." They were in the entrance hall now. Lance turned and bounded up the stairs, two at a time.

Stone found his coat, hat, and gloves and walked outside. The rotors of the helicopter were already turning.

"Right this way, Mr. Barrington," a man standing next to the machine shouted.

Stone climbed aboard, found a headset to protect his hearing, and buckled his seat belt.

The copter rose vertically, banked to the north, and climbed to a hundred feet or so, high enough to pass over the mast of any unsuspecting yacht that might be out for a cold-weather sail.

Stone watched Islesboro come into view, then the airstrip, and he wondered what sort of an offer Mike Freeman could not refuse.

16

Stone got back to the house in the late afternoon, hung up his heavy coat and took off his boots, then found Adele in the living room.

"I thought you had abandoned me," Adele said, pouting.

"I'm very sorry. I got . . . swept up in a business thing and couldn't get back until now."

"A business thing? I thought nobody knew where we were."

"A business associate happened to fly over the island and saw the airplane parked at the strip, and he insisted on a meeting. Can I get you something warming to drink?"

"I'll try some of that bourbon you like," she said.

Stone poured them both a Knob Creek and sat down. They clinked glasses and drank.

"Oh, someone named Mike Freeman called and asked that you call him as soon as possible."

Stone sighed. "You'll have to excuse me for a few minutes," he said. "I'll be back in time to pour your second drink." He kissed her and let himself into Dick Stone's secure office, then called Freeman's cell.

"Hey, there," Mike said. "Sorry to interrupt your weekend, but I need to run something by you."

"Would this be the new offer Lance Cabot has made you?"

"How the hell did you know that?"

"Lance is up here on a nearby island, and he insisted on an impromptu meeting."

"So he told you about his offer?"

"He told me only that it was one you can't refuse."

Mike chuckled. "Well, he's right. Let me lay it out for you."

"I'm listening."

"Lance has a real mission to offer us this time: he wants us to extract a person from a location somewhere in Europe and return him to the U.S."

"I'll bet that's not as simple as it sounds," Stone said.

"Maybe not, but almost. In our last conversation with Lance he mentioned the C-17 cargo airplane we own, if you recall."

"I remember; I hadn't heard about that. What, exactly, is a C-17?"

"It's a four-engine, jet cargo airplane, very large. It's very good for us in some situations: we can load half a dozen armored vehicles on it and fly them to a protection mission just about anywhere in the world. It makes us look very good to our clients. The problem with the thing is it's very expensive to own and operate. Jim got an opportunity to buy it on the cheap from an African nation that had figured out they couldn't afford it. He formed an air charter corporation, Strategic Air Services, to own and operate it. The idea was that we would defray our costs by chartering it to businesses or countries that had large cargo requirements. Trouble is, what with the world economy in a slump, we've had few charterers, and the airplane just eats away at our bottom line."

"I can understand that," Stone said, "having owned a number of airplanes that ate away at my bottom line."

"Here's what Lance has offered us: he will buy Strategic Air Services from us, then charter the airplane back to us when we have a need for it, at a rate that's just about the operating costs of the aircraft."

"I can see how that offer might be hard to refuse," Stone said.

"By the way, you sold your airplane to Strategic Air Services, so he gets that, too."

"Okay by me," Stone said. "But tell me more about this extraction he wants you to do."

"Here's what we do: Lance hires Strategic Services to fly to Iraq and ferry a large cargo of matériel back from there—part of our armed services withdrawal from that country. On the way back, we stop at an airport in Europe, to be determined, and pick up the extractee, along with some of Lance's people, so when we land in the States, it looks like an ordinary cargo flight for the military. We're paid for the empty Atlantic crossing, the trip back with the cargo, and for the extraction. The profit is considerable. What do you think?"

"I think we'll want the Agency to indemnify us for any legal problems associated with any part of the mission and from any damage to the airplane while conducting it, since our insurance may not cover government contract use. If he'll agree to that, then you're right, it sounds straightforward."

"Then, as our counsel, you're not opposed?"

"No; but Mike, I don't have to tell you how complicated something like this can get, so you want a description of the mission in writing, if Lance will sit still for that, which I doubt."

"I doubt it, too, but I'll try."

"One other thing: if I know Lance, the successful completion of this mission will bring other requests for other missions for Lance, and they're likely to get more complicated and dangerous as you go along. Don't let yourself get sucked into something you don't want to do."

"That's a good point, Stone, and I'll keep it in mind, and I'll see that you get to read any contract Lance proposes."

"Mike, there's something else you should know."

"What's that?"

"At our meeting today, Lance gave me a full account of how and why you happened to leave Britain."

Mike was silent.

"You understand, he knows your whole backstory."

"That's troubling," Mike said. "How do you suppose he came by that knowledge?"

"He's the operations director for the largest intelligence organization in the world," Stone said. "He has sources."

"Yes, Stone, I suppose he does."

"I think he told me all this in the knowledge that I would tell you."

"Yes."

"Down the road somewhere, Lance is fully capable of using this information to pressure you into accepting some mission you might not want. If you're concerned about that, then you should refuse the offer you're not supposed to refuse and decline any further business from him."

"If I did that, would it prevent him from using the information in some other way?"

"You have a point, Mike. You're the only person who can say how much damage the release of that story might do. I can foresee circumstances in which public knowledge of your past might make you a sympathetic character, but no one can guarantee that. You, alone, know what you had to do in order to effect your disappearance and your identity change and what risks the wide knowledge of that might entail. Whatever you decide, I'll do everything I can to help you."

"Thank you, Stone. Let me sleep on it, and we'll talk when you're back in the city. Good night."

"Good night, Mike." Stone hung up and went back to the living room and poured Adele and himself another drink.

"Mary says dinner is at seven," she said.

"Sounds good," Stone replied, but his mind was elsewhere, trying to figure out how the possible exposure of Mike Freeman might play out.

17

Early on Monday morning they flew back to Teterboro, and Stone raised another subject that had been on his mind.

"Adele, are you going to continue to keep your money with Jack Gunn?"

"Yes, since all the hubbub seems to have been cleared up. I trust Jack."

"Herbie Fisher has suggested that I move some of my money there. I have an unusual amount of cash at the moment."

"I think that's fine, if Jack will take you as a client."

"Herbie says Stephanie can arrange it. I'm sure I would be one of his smaller clients."

"I think it's a good idea. I've had returns of between eight and twelve percent annually, which is good. It's not the sort of thing that Bernie Madoff paid, but then his company was a Ponzi scheme, and Jack's is not."

"I was a little confused about the story that some of their funds—apparently a billion dollars or so—were somehow inadvertently . . . transferred to some of their foreign accounts. They called it a computer glitch."

"I don't understand that stuff," Adele said. "I only understand that I had a letter from Jack saying that my funds were secure and that I can withdraw any part of my capital anytime I wish."

"Do you know if many people have taken him up on that offer?"

"I've heard there are some, but since nobody lost any money, most of his clients are standing pat."

"Thanks for your advice," Stone said.

They landed at Teterboro and drove back into New York. Stone dropped Adele at her apartment building, then drove home. In addition to the morning mail there was a fax of several pages from Mike Freeman, which was the agreement with Lance Cabot. To his surprise, it included all the items Stone had suggested. He called Mike.

"Good morning, Stone," Freeman said. "Are you back?"

"I'm at my desk, and I've read the agreement with Lance that you faxed me."

"What do you think?"

"I think it looks good," Stone said. "Lock it in your safe."

"We're going to close on the sale of Strategic Air

Services in a few days, but our in-house legal department can handle that. Tell me, how would you like to fly to Iraq and back on the C-17?"

"That's quite an invitation. How long would we be gone?"

"It will be a quick turnaround, so probably a couple of days. It will be an experience that not a lot of civilians have, and the airplane is more comfortable than you might imagine."

"When would this happen?"

"Perhaps as early as this weekend, perhaps a few days later."

"Let me think about it," Stone said. "Ask me again when you know your departure date."

"Okay, I'll do that."

"Mike, what are you doing about your funds that are with Jack Gunn?"

"We're leaving them with him, and we're also investing the proceeds of the sale of the aircraft charter business."

"So you feel comfortable with Gunn's accountants' statement about the audit?"

"Our CFO was comfortable with it, so that's okay with me. Finance is not my strongest suit."

"I'm thinking of putting the proceeds of the sale of my airplane with Gunn."

"Why not?" Freeman said. "I'll call you when we have a launch date for Iraq."

"Okay," Stone said, and hung up. He thought for

a little while, and then he picked up the phone to call Herbie Fisher. Then he hung up. Herbie was knocking at his door, as he often did, unannounced.

"I hear you had a pleasant weekend," Herbie said, managing not to leer.

"Yes, I did," Stone replied. "Herbie, I've thought about it, and if Stephanie can arrange for me to invest with Jack Gunn, I'll give him a million dollars to manage."

"Is that the million dollars I paid you?" Herbie asked.

"No, that's been used to pay down my debt, but I sold my airplane, so I have some extra cash for a change."

"I'll speak to Stephanie about it and get back to you," Herbie said.

"Good. Was there something else you wanted to talk about?"

"Yes," Herbie said. "I was thinking of going into business for myself."

Stone had a sudden vision of what a disaster that might be. "What sort of business?"

"I was thinking of opening a sports and horse-racing book."

"Herbie, sit down," Stone said.

Herbie sat down.

"I want you to listen to me very carefully," Stone said.

"I'm listening, Stone."

"You are aware, aren't you, that taking bets is against the law?"

"Yeah, but everybody does it. Gambles, I mean."

"Yes, but people who gamble with bookies have only their own bets to lose. A bookie, if he figures the odds wrong on a sports event, could lose everything. For instance, when New Orleans surprised everybody by winning the Super Bowl by two touchdowns over the Colts, a lot of bookies were very unpleasantly surprised. I expect they took a big, big hit on that one."

"Well, yeah, you've got to expect that, but bookies lay their bets off with people who can afford to take the losses."

"Yes, Herbie, and the people they lay them off with are called the Mafia. You've had some experiences with them."

"I remember."

"Do you remember that you're lucky to be alive after those experiences?"

"Yeah, I guess."

"Herbie, there are all sorts of downsides to running a book; taking big losses and dealing with the Mafia are only two of them. For instance, remember how you were worried about your reputation when Jack Gunn seemed to be in a lot of trouble?"

"Yeah."

"Well, I think Jack Gunn would be very worried about his reputation if it became known that he had a son-in-law who was a bookie."

Herbie thought about that for a moment.

"That might make things very uncomfortable for you with your new wife and her family."

"Maybe I should talk to Stephanie about that," Herbie said.

"If I were you, I would forget the whole thing and not even mention it to Stephanie. If she starts hearing things like that from you, she's going to start wondering if she married the right guy."

"You think?"

"I think," Stone replied.

Herbie thanked him and left.

Another disaster, hopefully, averted, Stone thought.

18

Stone was having a sandwich at his desk when Adele Lansdown called.

"How are you?" she asked.

"I'm very well, thanks; haven't changed since this morning."

"I know it's short notice, but I wonder if you could come to dinner at my house this evening?"

"Sure, I'd like that."

"Some old friends from out of town are here, and I've invited my nephew David and his girlfriend, too."

"What time?"

"Seven thirty, and don't dress up; no necktie required."

"All right."

"There's something you should know that might affect you. I'll tell you about it when we're alone."

"Sounds mysterious. I'll see you then," Stone replied, and hung up.

Stone, who was, by habit, compulsively on time, forced himself not to leave his house until seven thirty, so that he could be fashionably late. He hailed a taxi on Third Avenue, and what with traffic, he got out of the cab and crossed Park Avenue, then presented himself at the downstairs desk at seven forty-five, entering the building just ahead of a handsome couple who had gotten out of a cab. As it turned out, they were also expected at Adele's.

Stone gave his name to the doorman, who called upstairs, then turned and introduced himself to the couple.

"We're Ben and Ann Wharton," the man said, and they all shook hands.

The man in charge of the desk hung up the telephone, then dialed the number again. "I'm not getting a reply from Mrs. Lansdown," he said. "You say she was expecting you?"

"Yes," Stone replied, and the Whartons said so, as well.

The man hung up the phone again, and it rang immediately. "There she is," he said, picking up the phone. "Front desk." His face drained of color. "Right away," he said. He hung up and dialed four digits. "Emergency at seventy-one East Seventy-first Street," he said.

"We need an ambulance and the police immediately. A woman is dead and another injured. Please hurry." He answered a couple of questions and then hung up and faced Stone and the Whartons.

"What's wrong?" Stone asked.

"Mrs. Lansdown's cook called down and said . . ."

"Come on, man," Stone said, "spit it out."

". . . said that Mrs. Lansdown has been killed."

Stone took out his phone and speed-dialed Dino's cell number.

"Bacchetti."

"It's Stone. I'm at seven-forty Park, and a woman named Adele Lansdown is dead. The doorman at the building called it in. I think you ought to come, too."

"Be right there," Dino said, and hung up.

The Whartons were staring at him.

"I'm a retired police officer," Stone said. "I called the lieutenant in charge of the precinct detective squad and asked him to come."

"What should we do?" Ben asked.

"We should all stay right here and wait for the police to arrive."

"This is terrible," Ann Wharton said. "Can't we just go back to our hotel?"

"No; you must stay and give the police a statement," Stone said.

"Do you mean we're suspects?"

"No, certainly not. I saw you get out of a taxi as I

was crossing Park Avenue, and we entered the building at the same time, so we can vouch for each other."

A tall, willowy young woman walked into the building and up to the desk. "Mrs. Lansdown, please," she said to the doorman. "My name is Mia Meadow."

"I'm sorry, Ms. Meadow," the man said, "you'll have to wait here with these people."

Stone introduced himself and the Whartons to the woman. "I'm afraid something is wrong upstairs. We're waiting for the police."

"Wrong?" she asked.

Stone was about to explain when a tall, handsome young man arrived and kissed the woman on the cheek. He looked like a young Jack Gunn, so Stone assumed he was the son. "David Gunn?"

"Yes?"

"I'm Stone Barrington, a friend of Adele's, and this is Ben and Ann Wharton. Apparently, something is wrong in Adele's apartment, and we're waiting for the police." As if on cue, the noise of an ambulance and a police cruiser could be heard approaching the building.

"Wrong? What do you mean?"

Stone explained what had happened, and as he finished the lobby became suddenly crowded with uniformed and plainclothes police officers and a pair of EMTs with a gurney. Dino was right behind them.

Stone introduced Dino to the dinner guests. "I'm

glad to meet you all, and I'm sorry about the circum-stances," Dino said.

"Can you tell us what's happened?" David Gunn asked.

"I will shortly," he said. "You folks please have a seat over there," he said, pointing at a seating area. "Don't leave until a detective has taken your statements. Stone, you come with me."

Stone excused himself from the group and followed Dino to an elevator, right behind the EMTs and two detectives. As the elevator went up, Dino introduced the two detectives as Salero and Bartkowski.

Dino led the way out of the elevator, with Stone hot behind. A woman in a white chef's outfit was standing at an open doorway, holding a towel to the back of her head. "This way," she called out, stepping back to let them in. "Mrs. Lansdown is in the dining room, to your right."

An EMT stayed with her, checking her injuries, and Dino, Stone, and the detectives walked into the dining room. Adele Lansdown was lying on the floor beside an overturned chair and some scattered tableware. The detective Salero knelt beside her and held three fingers to her neck.

"No pulse," he said. He lifted her head and looked under it. "At least one to the side of the head."

"All right," Dino said, "everybody in the living room, except you," he said, pointing to the EMT. "Pronounce her and note the time. Salero, you go downstairs and get separate statements from the other dinner guests. But before you do that, call the ME."

They went back into the living room, where the EMT was applying a bandage to the back of the cook's head. "She needs to get checked out at the hospital," he said. "We'll put her in our ambulance."

Bartkowski sat in the chair next to the injured woman. "Can you answer a couple of questions?" he asked.

"Yes."

"Your name?"

"Betty Hardesty. I'm Mrs. Lansdown's chef."

"Can you tell me what happened?"

"I was standing at the stove, cooking dinner, and then, next thing I knew, I woke up on the floor with my head hurting. I got to my feet and called out to Mrs. Lansdown, and when she didn't answer, I went to look for her and found her on the dining room floor. I called downstairs, and then I went to the door to wait for somebody to come. Will somebody turn the stove off, please?"

"Stone," Dino said, "will you do that?"

Stone walked past Adele's corpse and into the kitchen, where something in a copper skillet was sizzling. He shut down the large Viking range and looked around. There was a door at the rear of the kitchen, closed. He opened it and found a back hall with a staircase and an elevator; then he returned to the living room.

The two EMTs were helping the chef onto a gurney.

"Bartkowski," Dino said, "go downstairs and help Salero with the dinner guests' statements. I'll hold down the fort here until the ME arrives. When you're done downstairs, if nobody sounds like a suspect, send them all home and come back up here."

Stone took Dino to the kitchen and showed him the service entrance.

Dino checked the door. "Unlocked," he said. "Anybody could have walked in."

"Whoever walked in was pretty businesslike," Stone said. "Took out the chef, then Adele."

The ME arrived and started his work.

19

Stone and Dino sat in the living room while the medical examiner did his work in the dining room. They had worked the apartment and found everything in perfect order, except the dining room. The criminalist arrived, did his work, and reported no physical evidence. Salero and Bartkowski came back from the lobby to report.

"Tell me," Dino said.

"They all had the same story," he said. "They arrived at about the same time, and when the doorman called up, nobody answered at first; then the cook called downstairs. They all say they were invited for dinner."

"I can confirm that," Stone said. "Adele called me about one this afternoon and asked me to dinner, then told me that she had invited a couple visiting from out of town and her nephew David Gunn and his girlfriend. The Whartons and I arrived simultaneously, Mia

Meadow a couple of minutes later, and David Gunn a couple of minutes after her."

Bartkowski scribbled all that in his notebook.

"Okay, fellas," Dino said, "get back to the precinct and start working this. Confirm all the names and addresses. I'll vouch for Barrington."

The two men left, and Dino stared at Stone. "You don't look so good, pal."

Stone sighed. "It's not every day that my dinner date gets murdered."

"How well did you know her?"

"Met her last week at Jack Gunn's daughter's wedding, and we spent the weekend together in Maine."

"You got a witness who can put you in Maine?"

"The caretaker and his wife. Oh, and Lance Cabot."

"Lance was visiting you?" Dino knew Cabot from several meetings at Elaine's.

"No, it was really weird: I hadn't told anybody where we were going, but I got a call from Lance on Dick's line to the Agency, which, I guess, is still working."

"How did he know you were there?"

"I went out to the airfield to check on whether there was any snow accumulation on the airplane, and this black helicopter shows up with Lance aboard. He practically kidnaps me and takes me to a nearby island where his people are interrogating some Chinese spy."

"Why the hell would he want you there?"

"I don't know. I think maybe he was just impressing

me with how he could keep tabs on me. Turns out, he had flown over Islesboro earlier and saw my airplane there. He invited himself to dinner, but I nixed that; then the chopper flew me back."

"So that was the first time you'd spent any time with Adele?"

"We had dinner at the Four Seasons before we went to Maine."

"Anybody you can think of has anything against Adele?"

"No. Of course, I didn't know her long enough to meet any of her circle of friends. The only nexus we had was Herbie Fisher, who was marrying her niece."

"The son, David—I read he was on a sailing trip when the blowup at his father's business happened?"

"Yeah, I saw him interviewed on TV in the marina, after he got back to Miami. Actually, I'm told he was a suspect in the missing-money scandal, which turned out not to be a scandal at all, since there was no missing money."

"Would he have anything against his aunt?"

"Not that I know of. If he wasn't on good terms with her, why did she invite him to dinner, and why did he accept?"

"Makes sense," Dino said. "What about the other couple?"

"She described them as old friends from out of town. I never even learned where they were from."

Dino checked his notes. "Chicago. Neither of them

was an investor of Gunn's. How did Adele feel about Jack Gunn?"

"She liked him, trusted him. When the mess blew over she kept the proceeds of her husband's estate with him, and recommended that I invest with him. No hard feelings there."

"Late husband?"

"Yeah, she told me that she shot him, after he had blackened her eye and broken her arm. She was never charged with anything."

"Lansdown," Dino said, thinking. "Last year. I remember the case. They ran it by me, and I didn't see any need for charges."

"You think anybody had something against the cook?" Stone asked.

"If so, he would have shot her and hit Adele over the head, not the other way around."

"Good point," Stone admitted. "You know, security is pretty good in a building like this. Makes you wonder how somebody got in through the service entrance."

The ME came in from the dining room, followed by two helpers and the corpse on a gurney. "Death by shooting, two in the head, small caliber, typical of a pro job. She'd been dead for less than an hour when I got here."

"Fax me the full report," Dino said. "Thanks, Doc."

The man left.

"I think we're done here," Dino said, "and the smell of that food cooking makes me hungry."

"Elaine's?"

"Where else?" Dino said. "Let's leave by the service entrance." He led the way out the back, where Dino had another look at the door. "Doesn't seem tampered with."

"Probably when you live in a building like this, you think you can leave your door unlocked," Stone said.

Dino rang for the elevator and it came quickly. "New elevator," Dino said as they got on. "Probably faster than the building's main elevators, unless they're new, too."

They got off on the ground floor, and Dino had a good look at the outside door and its lock. "Look at this," he said, touching the door beside the lock and rubbing his fingers together. "Mucilage; looks like the bolt was taped back."

The door from the lobby opened and a uniformed employee of the building stood there. "Oh, it's you, gentlemen. Sorry to disturb you."

"You got a camera back here?" Dino asked, looking around.

"Right up there," the doorman said, pointing to a high corner.

"Let's have a look at your tapes," Dino said, and they followed him back to the front desk.

At Dino's request, the doorman rewound the tape to seven-fifteen and pressed the PLAY button. At seven twenty-two the door opened and a man in a dark hooded sweatshirt entered, his hands in the sweatshirt's pockets. "Rewind and replay one frame at a time," Dino said.

The doorman did so.

"The angle of the camera is too high. You can't see the face," Dino said.

The doorman made a note. "I'll see to that."

"All his clothes are dark," Stone said. "I can't see anything identifying."

"Keep playing," Dino said. "I want to see him when he leaves."

The doorman played the tape forward at double speed. The man left the way he came, at seven twenty-six, and paused to pull a piece of tape off the door lock; then he was gone.

"You got an outside camera?" Dino asked.

"Not working," the doorman said. "I called it in late this afternoon, but the repairman didn't show yet."

"Bad luck," Dino said. "Let's take a look at the street." He led the way to the service entrance, and they stepped out onto Seventy-first Street. Dino pointed at a Dumpster parked across the street, and he and Stone crossed to have a look in it.

"Give me a leg up," Dino said. "You're dressed too nice."

"Sure," Stone said, cupping his hands.

"It's pretty full," Dino said from above Stone. "Somebody's renovating. Uh-oh." He held up a black sweatshirt, then handed it to Stone. "Got some latex gloves, too."

Stone held it by thumb and forefinger and checked the label. "Banana Republic," he said. "Must be thousands of them on the street."

Dino hopped down to the street, produced a large plastic bag, and stuffed the sweatshirt into it and the gloves into a smaller bag, which he placed in the larger bag. They walked around the corner to where Dino's car was waiting and got in. Dino tossed the bag into the front passenger seat. "Take us to Elaine's, then get that bag to Bartkowski and Salero at the precinct, and tell them to get it to the criminalist," he said. "Sign the chain of evidence log, and I'll do it when I get in later." Dino called the precinct and told the two detectives to expect the sweatshirt and gloves, to check the gloves for fingerprints on the inside, and to get a copy of the videotape from the doorman at the building; then he sat back in his seat and sighed.

"Feels good when you've done everything you need to do," he said. "Let's eat."

Stone agreed.

20

At Elaine's their first drink was delivered.

"It has to be a pro job," Dino said. "It's too clean for anything else—no rifling of her drawers or jewelry box, just in, slug the cook, shoot the woman, and out."

"He must have cased the rear entrance earlier," Stone said, "or the outside door wouldn't have been taped. He came through the lobby to get in."

"He could have stood around outside and waited for somebody to open the rear door, then grabbed it before it closed," Dino pointed out.

"I guess. I think your detectives ought to get all the visitors' names for the day, though, everybody who isn't a resident."

"Good idea," Dino said. "I'll send them back for that. Any other thoughts?"

"I can't help think that this had something to do

with the blowup at the Gunn company," Stone said. "That seems to be the only irregular event in the family."

"Another thing," Dino said. "She offed her husband; that must have offended somebody—his family, a friend."

"Revenge served cold," Stone said. "Maybe; I guess it's worth checking out."

"Had to be a pro."

"Or somebody who's watched enough TV to figure out how a pro works. If I'd been on time for dinner, maybe things would have been different."

"Yeah," Dino said, "maybe he'd have shot you, too."

Herbie Fisher and his new wife walked into the restaurant and approached Stone and Dino's table. "We just heard," Herbie said, and they sat down without being asked.

"Hello, Stephanie," Stone said. "I'm sorry for your loss. This is Lieutenant Dino Bacchetti. He's in charge of the investigation."

"Tell us what happened, Lieutenant," Stephanie said.

"Somebody came into the building's service entrance, having taped the lock back earlier, took the elevator upstairs, opened the service door to the apartment, which wasn't locked. The chef was at the stove, cooking. He hit her with something substantial, like a gun barrel. She fell to the floor, unconscious. He walked into the dining room, where your aunt was standing near the table, shot her in the head. She fell, he shot her again in the head, and then he left the way he came. We got a video of him at the back entrance, coming and going, but he was wearing a hooded sweatshirt, and his face isn't visible. We found the sweatshirt and a pair of latex gloves in a Dumpster across the street. They'll be checked for trace evidence. That's about it, so far."

Stephanie teared up and shook her head. "I don't get it," she said. "Who would want to hurt Aunt Adele?"

"Give that some thought," Stone said. "Anybody angry with her? Even a family member?"

Stephanie shook her head. "Everybody loved her."

"Not everybody," Dino said.

"Do you know anything about her will?" Stone asked. "Who would inherit?"

"She didn't have any children," Stephanie said.

"And her husband is dead," Dino pointed out. "Did he have any close family members?"

"His parents are dead," Stephanie replied, "but he had a brother. He's a diplomat of some sort, stationed in London."

Dino made a note of the man's name. "Anybody else?"

"A younger sister. She lives in Hong Kong. Her husband works for an American bank there."

Dino noted that, too. "Either of them in town?"

"Not that I know of," Stephanie said. "I hardly knew them. I do know that they both liked Aunt Adele better than they liked their brother. He was a bad drunk, and everybody thought he was a real shit."

"Was Mrs. Lansdown married before?"

"Once, in her early twenties. It lasted only a few months."

"His name?"

"Karl Stein," she replied. "Last I heard he was in L.A., working in the movie business."

"As what?"

"He started as a writer, but he produces and directs, too."

"Any hard feelings there?"

"I don't think so. They were young and stupid. I don't think Adele ever heard from him."

"You know who he works for?"

"Various studios. He has his own production company, Steinware Films. I read a magazine piece about him once."

"Can you think of anyone else that Mrs. Lansdown had problems with? Former employees, that sort of thing?"

"No, she was a very likable person. Her chef had worked for her for years, and they're quite good friends."

"Tell me about David's relationship with his aunt," Dino said.

"They got along fine," she replied. "I think between the two of us, he was her favorite."

"How long has he been seeing Mia Meadow?"

"The better part of a year, I think. She was on the sailing trip with him. The family thinks they might end up married."

"She and Adele have any problems?"

"No, Adele liked her."

They were all silent for a moment.

"Would you like a drink?" Stone asked.

"No," Stephanie replied. "We have to get back to Mother; she's distraught. We just wanted to know what happened." She thanked Dino and Stone, and she and Herbie left.

"This is going to be a tough one," Dino said.

Stone couldn't bring himself to disagree.

21

Stone worked through the week, clearing his desk. On Friday there was a memorial service for Adele at a small, nondenominational church on Lexington Avenue. A few people said nice things about Adele, including her nephew and niece. Stephanie was composed. David barely got through his part; tears ran down his face as he finished. A jazz quartet played a melodic, rather solemn piece, and the service broke up.

The Gunn family was lined up on the front steps, and Stone paid his respects. Herbie stood to one side, waiting for it to be over, and Stone walked over to him. "How are you, Herbie?"

"I'm okay, but everybody in the family is pretty broken up, and I don't seem to be able to do anything to help."

"Herbie," Stone said, "has anyone in the family behaved oddly?"

"How do you mean?"

"I mean, has anyone done anything out of character, something you wouldn't expect?"

Herbie thought about it. "Well, Stephanie has been pretty cold about the whole thing, and David has been crying, off and on. I would have thought it would be the other way around."

"Is Stephanie normally a very emotional person?"

Herbie thought some more. "Only in bed," he replied.

Stone went back to work.

Late in the afternoon Mike Freeman called.

"We closed on the sale of Strategic Air Services," he said. "The new company is called Airship Transport. We're meeting in my office early Monday morning. We'll chopper up to Newburgh, New York, where the company is based, on the old Stewart Air Force Base. Bring your passport and clothes for a couple of days; you won't need a necktie."

"Okay. Mike, have you put the proceeds of the sale with Gunn yet?"

"No; we'll deposit the check on Monday."

"Put it in the bank until we get back from our trip."

"Why?"

"I have some concerns about what's going on at the Gunn company. His sister-in-law, Adele Lansdown, was murdered earlier this week, and I'm not yet certain whether that had anything to do with the business. I was going to put some money with them, but I'm holding off."

"All right," Freeman said. "I'll hold off. We can talk more about this on the trip."

"See you Monday morning, Mike," Stone said.

They both hung up, and Stone went back to work.

Stone spent an idle weekend, sitting up in bed watching old movies and reading the Sunday *Times*. He didn't even feel like dinner at Elaine's with Dino.

On Monday morning, Stone packed a bag with rough clothes, put on a parka, and took a cab to the offices of Strategic Services. He walked into Mike Freeman's office and was surprised to see someone he knew well.

"Hello, Holly," Stone said, giving her a hug and a kiss.

"Hello, Stone," she replied. Holly Barker was Lance Cabot's assistant at the Agency, and they were old and close friends. "I'd like you to meet Todd Bacon, who's going to run Airship Transport."

A young man in his early thirties stood up and offered Stone his hand. He was about Stone's size, but slimmer in the waist, and had short, sandy hair. "Hello, Stone. I've heard a lot about you."

"Good to meet you, Todd," Stone said. He'd never heard anything about the guy.

"We'd better get going," Mike said. "Your luggage is already in the van."

They trooped downstairs, boarded a plain van, and were transported to the East Side Heliport, where a six-passenger twin-turbine chopper was waiting for them. They and their luggage boarded, the rotors turned, and they were on their way north. They had a spectacular view of the city as they moved up the East River, then crossed to the Hudson, north of the George Washington Bridge. They descended into what was now Stewart International Airport and landed next to the ramp before a huge hangar. The C-17 was being towed out onto the ramp, and Stone found its size overwhelming.

Stone grabbed his bag and followed the group to the rear of the giant airplane, where they simply walked up the lowered tail ramp and into the airplane. They deposited their luggage in bins as instructed, and Stone took a moment to look around. He was standing inside a cavernous space more than twenty feet wide and high. Ahead of them was an Airstream trailer, strapped down and with various cables and tubes attached. They walked past the trailer and found a dozen first-class airline seats bolted to the floor, then past that to the cockpit, which was big enough for two built-in, double-decker bunks and four jump seats behind the two pilots. The instrument panel was a maze of large glass screens, switches, warning lights, and circuit breakers. It was several times the size of the panel on Stone's Mustang.

"Preflight's all done, and we're ready to go," Mike said. "Take a jump seat next to me, Stone."

Stone sat down, buckled in between Mike and Holly,

and watched the pilots start the four engines and work their way through their checklists.

"This thing has four Pratt & Whitney engines," Mike said, "each producing more than forty thousand pounds of thrust. We can carry more than a hundred and seventy thousand pounds of cargo."

"How much runway are we going to need?" Stone asked, worried about what was available to them.

"The airplane can work out of a thirty-five-hundred-foot runway," Mike said. "How's that for short-takeoff performance?"

"Range and speed?"

"This is the ER, the Extended Range version. We can fly two thousand eight hundred miles without refueling. Today, we'll refuel at an air force base at Lajes, in the Azores, then go on nonstop to Iraq. We should have a nice tailwind, too. Cruising speed is four hundred and fifty knots."

The airplane began to taxi, with linemen at each wingtip, making sure they cleared any obstacles. Stone watched an airliner take off ahead of them and then, after a final cockpit check, they taxied onto the runway. The first officer shoved the throttles forward while the brakes were held, and when the engines reached full power, the captain released the brakes and the airplane moved forward faster than Stone would have thought possible, pressing him into his seat. They were in the air after a takeoff roll that seemed to take only seconds, and Stone put his headset on to keep out the noise.

He could hear the captain talking to the tower, then to New York approach. Shortly, they were at flight level 290 and over the Atlantic Ocean.

"Come with me," Mike said, unbuckling his seat belt.

Stone and Holly followed him to the Airstream, and he opened the door for them. Inside were four bunks, some comfortable chairs facing a large TV screen, and a galley.

"This is our rest area," Mike said. "We're flying with two crews, and the off-duty pilot and copilot can use the bunks in the cockpit." He led them out of the trailer and pointed to what looked like a hotel laundry bin with canvas sides. "Our parachutes are in there. Has either of you ever jumped?"

"Once," Stone said.

"I did airborne training in the army and got my wings," Holly said.

"Getting out of this thing is real easy, should we have to," Mike said. "All you do is strap the chute on, clip onto a static line at the rear, then just run off the lowered tail ramp. The rest is easy, depending on where you land."

Stone thought about that for a moment. "I hope we won't have to do that," he said.

22

After they had cruised for a few minutes, Stone, Holly, and Todd Bacon followed Mike Freeman from the cockpit to the Airstream trailer, where they settled into chairs and Mike gave them a choice of movies. They settled on *Casablanca*.

It was quieter in the trailer, so they didn't need headphones. A smaller screen next to the big one displayed a moving map, which showed them out over the Atlantic, with the tip of Long Island disappearing off the rear edge.

Stone hadn't seen the movie for years, and he enjoyed it as much as the first time he'd experienced it. When the titles came up at the end, Stone checked the moving map, which showed another ninety minutes of flight time to the Azores. Todd and Holly got up from their seats and left the trailer, leaving Stone with Mike.

"Tell me about what's going on with Jack Gunn's business," Mike said.

"I don't know what's going on there," Stone said. "I only know that Jack's wife's sister was murdered a few days ago." He told Mike about the aborted dinner party, the police investigation, and the people surrounding what had happened. "I can't prove that Adele's death has anything to do with the business, but I have a bad feeling about it, and I don't want my money there until we know everything about her death. That's why I recommended that you not deposit the proceeds of the sale of the company with Gunn."

"Should we remove what we have with them now?"

"Do you have any sort of business insurance that would protect your investment?" Stone asked.

"No."

"Then it can't hurt to move your funds."

Mike nodded. "I'll call the office and get the process started." He picked up a cordless phone from a credenza and called New York.

Stone dozed off in his reclining chair and only woke when the sounds of the airplane changed.

"We're descending into Lajes," Mike said. "I'm going to go up and watch our landing."

Stone followed him and they sat in the jump seats again. Through the pilots' windows he could see an expanse of blue Atlantic, gleaming in the late-afternoon sunlight, and an island came into view. Stone spotted the long runway a few minutes out and watched the pilots as they slowed the airplane's descent, then put in flaps and slats and lowered the landing gear. They landed smoothly and taxied off the runway, where a fuel truck was waiting for them.

"We'll stay on the airplane," Mike said, "to avoid having to clear local customs."

An Air Force contingent did enter the airplane and check passports, though. An hour later they were climbing out of Lajes and heading for Gibraltar and the Mediterranean beyond. Once they were at altitude again, Stone went back to the trailer and lay down on a bunk. Shortly, he was asleep. He woke in time to get a look at Gibraltar, far below; then he had a dinner prepared by a caterer before they left Stewart, along with a glass of wine. Then he went to sleep again.

He didn't wake up until Mike shook him.

"We're landing in fifteen minutes," he said.

Stone got up, washed his face and brushed his teeth, then went forward to a jump seat. The sun was up, and the airplane was descending at a much steeper angle than when they had landed in the Azores.

Mike spoke up. "We're making a steep descent into Baghdad International, in order to give insurgents less chance of hitting us with missiles."

"Missiles?" Stone asked. "Nobody mentioned missiles."

"It's less likely than it would have been a year

ago, but we have to treat the place as a war zone. We won't get off the airplane here, but I think you'll find it interesting to watch what happens. There are two runways here, one of ten thousand feet and one of thirteen thousand. The airport is about ten miles west of the city."

Stone couldn't believe how steep the approach was. He tried to find the rate of descent on the instrument panel, but he was too far away to read it. He reckoned that they were falling out of the sky at the rate of at least eight or ten thousand feet a minute, with everything hanging out—landing gear, flaps, speedbrakes, spoilers, if the airplane had them. He had never seen a view of an airport out the pilot's window like the one he could see now.

The airplane touched down, and immediately Stone was thrown against his seat belt as the engines were reversed. Shortly, they were off the runway, and Stone could see a fuel truck ahead of them, waiting. The airplane taxied up to the truck and cut its engines, as the tail ramp came down. Stone got out of his seat and followed Mike into the huge cargo bay. Immediately, forklifts began bringing in pallets of matériel. As soon as they were set down, the forklifts went back for more, and airmen secured each pallet with netting, cables, and rope. It was all incredibly efficient, and by the time the tail ramp had closed, the fuel truck was gone and the engines were starting. Stone noticed that the central area of the cargo bay, behind the Airstream, was empty. He followed Mike back to the jump seats.

"Where are we stopping for the extraction on the way back?" Stone asked Freeman.

"I don't know," Mike said. "Todd Bacon will tell us when we're airborne."

"What's Bacon's story?" Stone asked.

"All I can tell you is, he's one of Lance's people, he's, at least, the titular CEO of Airship Transport, and he's in charge of the extraction."

"What's Holly here for?" Stone asked.

"I get the impression that she's here to watch Bacon," Mike replied.

The airplane was already rolling down the runway, using a lot more of it than on previous takeoffs. The pilot rotated, and the airplane began to climb steeply. Stone looked out a side window and saw something flying toward them, leaving a trail of smoke. Before he could speak, someone yelled, "Missile at two o'clock!"

Stone was thrown hard against his seat belt, and the airplane picked up speed and turned first right, then left.

"Clean miss!" the copilot yelled, and they began climbing again.

"Holy shit!" Stone said. "That's the first time I've ever been shot at in the air!"

"Me, too," Mike said. "I think 'holy shit' pretty much covers it for me, as well."

"Are we safe yet?"

"Who knows?" Mike replied.

The airplane continued its steep climb, and gradually Stone's grip on the armrests of his seat relaxed.

Todd Bacon appeared in the cockpit. "Okay, everybody in the trailer," he said.

23

Stone, Mike, Holly, and Todd Bacon sat in the reclining chairs, and Todd unfolded a map. The first thing that struck Stone was that it was not an aeronautical chart but a Michelin road map.

"All right," Todd said. "We're going to land in northern Spain to extract a longtime fugitive and return him to United States jurisdiction."

"By extract," Stone said, "do you mean extradite?"

"Extradition is impossible," Todd replied.

"How come?" Mike asked.

"All right, I'll tell you the whole story," Todd said, "or at least as much of it as I know."

"We're all ears," Mike said.

"The man's name is Erwin Gelbhardt, born in Germany sixty-eight years ago, brought to the U.S. at age eight and later naturalized. His father was a German diplomat, and the child grew up as his father served in Egypt, Spain, Saudi Arabia and Iran, and the U.S., where he retired and remained. As a result the boy, who had already displayed an affinity for languages, picked up those four languages, as well as his native German and English. He learned French in school."

"A bright kid," Mike said.

"Very bright. He was educated at Choate, Yale, and Harvard Business School, graduating at each school near or at the top of his classes. After getting his MBA he took a little over a million dollars, inherited from his mother, and during the next decade, turned it into more than a hundred million dollars made from various businesses in North, South, and Central America. Wherever he did business he specialized in corrupting local officials, up to and including intelligence officials and heads of state. He had a lot of cash to throw around, since he paid little or no taxes in the United States, despite his American citizenship.

"Eventually, the IRS came after him in a big way. He was arrested as his private jet landed in Key West on a flight from Cuba, and as soon as that became known, people began to come out of the woodwork with information about other crimes he had committed in the countries where he operated. A line formed for extradition to half a dozen countries.

"He was held without bail, but during a lunch break at his trial, he went to the men's room and vanished. No one yet knows how he got out of the courthouse. He left the country on a cargo plane headed for Algeria, and, we think, on arrival there he had extensive cosmetic surgery to alter his appearance.

"After that he went into the arms business in a big way. He had money hidden in Swiss and other banks around the world to fund his enterprise, and, operating under various names, he supplied weapons, small and large, to third-world countries and insurgencies around the globe. In recent years he adopted the name Pablo Estancia and, using his language skills, affected a Spanish accent in whatever language he spoke, which by that time numbered ten or twelve, including Chinese, Arabic, Urdu, and various Middle Eastern tribal dialects. He moved across borders with impunity with multiple passports and IDs and made himself the indispensable man with Islamic insurgencies of all stripes, including Al Qaeda and the Taliban. You have a picture of him now?"

"Pretty much," Mike said.

"Why are you holding a road map instead of an aeronautical chart?" Stone asked.

"Because we're going to land tonight on a road."

"A *road*?" Stone asked, horrified. "No ordinary road could ever support the weight of this airplane, loaded as it is."

"That's not necessarily true," Mike said. "The load will be spread over triple-tandem landing gears, and many tires."

Stone didn't know what triple-tandem meant, but he got the idea. "And will we be able to take off, too?" he asked.

"What we will have for a landing strip will be two and a half miles of straight, newly paved, four-lane superhighway," Todd said.

"Full of construction equipment, no doubt," Stone said.

"All the equipment is being moved to the other side of the highway as we speak," Todd said, "and the beginning and end of the stretch we're looking for will be marked by cars with strobe lights. The crew has the exact coordinates and elevation of the landing end of the roadway. It is located in a fairly narrow valley, with mountains on each side, but we will have room for a long approach."

"Swell," Stone said. "I'm trying to remember why I came on this trip."

"For the fun," Holly said. "Aren't you having fun?"

"Not yet," Stone replied.

"We're refueling at an American air base in Cádiz, east of Gibraltar," Todd said. "From there, we'll head out over the Atlantic, then turn, descend into Spain. We will be on the ground for a matter of minutes, including further fueling from two trucks; then we'll be heading, nonstop, back to Stewart International."

"Where we'll all clear immigration and customs?" Stone asked.

"Nearly all of us," Todd replied. "We'll be at the extraction point just after midnight, local time." Todd left the trailer.

"I told you it would be an interesting trip," Mike said.

"I hope we're all alive to tell about it," Stone said.

Holly spoke up. "Lance Cabot would be very unhappy if you told *anyone* about it," she said.

Stone had a meal, then stretched out for a nap. He was awakened in time to strap himself into a jump seat for the landing at Cádiz. They were on the ground for nearly an hour, then took off again, heading west and climbing.

"When do we turn around?" he asked Todd.

"As soon as we're out of radar range of the coast," Todd replied. "Not too long. We'll follow a civilian flight from the Azores to La Coruña, on the northern coast of Spain. We'll be flying closely enough behind it so that, together, the two airplanes will make only one primary target on coastal radar."

"Will the other airplane know about this?" Stone asked.

"No. Civilian airplanes don't have radar that can paint other aircraft, only their transponders, and ours will be off. Before the airplane reaches La Coruña, we'll break off and head for our landing area."

"We have only a twenty-eight–hundred-mile range, is that right?"

"Yes, and that's plenty."

They cleared the coast of Portugal, and Stone saw

the copilot reach up and turn off some switches. He looked out the window and no longer saw the wingtip strobe and nav lights.

Stone put on his headset again.

"Other aircraft sighted," the copilot said, checking his radar; then he looked out the windscreen and pointed. "Two o'clock and three miles," he said, "at our altitude."

The C-17 entered a steep bank to the right, and Stone tightened his seat belt.

24

Stone watched from his jump seat through the pilots' windows as the big aircraft turned into position behind the airliner, then began to catch up. Gradually the airliner grew larger in the windscreen, until Stone thought they would ram it from behind.

Stone unbuckled his seat belt and moved up behind the copilot. "How do you know when the other airplane will slow down?"

"We don't, exactly," the man replied.

"Swell," Stone muttered.

"Don't worry; we're trained for formation flying for in-air refueling. The second he begins to slow, we'll pop our speedbrakes, and that will keep us apart."

"Good luck," Stone said. He returned to his seat and strapped in tightly. He thought about fetching a parachute from the bin in the cargo bay, but he figured if they rammed the other aircraft, he wouldn't have an opportunity to use it before he was hamburger.

Stone was still sitting rigidly in his seat when suddenly he felt the aircraft slow down, with the attendant turbulence of extended speedbrakes. The airliner grew larger in the windscreen, but only for a moment, and he saw the speed indicator tape on the pilot's instruments begin to wind down for the approach into La Coruña. The lights of a big city were ahead. They would join the Instrument Landing System momentarily, he knew.

Then, as the airliner banked to join the approach, the C-17 banked in the opposite direction. Stone figured they were at around three thousand feet, and he knew there were high mountains, the Pyrenees, to the southeast. They flew in that direction for a few minutes, climbing a few thousand feet; then the airplane banked left again, then leveled its wings and began flying northeast and descending.

Stone stared through the windscreen, willing something to happen that would tell them they were on course for landing. They were descending rapidly now, and Stone could see the stars disappearing behind mountains on either side of them. They were in the valley. Then, miraculously, he saw a pair of strobe lights ahead of them on the ground—red on the left, green on the right.

Todd spoke over the headset. "If either light goes out, the pilot will know we're off course and he'll correct."

It didn't sound like any landing system Stone had ever heard of. Then he noticed that on the flat glass instrument panel, a picture of the ground had appeared. The airplane was equipped with synthetic vision, a computer-generated map of the earth's surface, showing major features. A road appeared on the screen, and a moment later the flashing strobes disappeared underneath them and the airplane touched down.

"Yeah!" Todd yelled.

Stone yanked off his headset, his ears ringing from the shout. Engines were reversed and brakes applied, and the aircraft came to a halt. Immediately, two fuel trucks appeared ahead of them, rushing toward the airplane. They were wearing red flashing beacons on top, like an airplane. The pilots shut down the engines and refueling began. It didn't take long, but where was the extractee?

As the fuel trucks pulled away Stone heard the whine of the tail platform lowering. He got up, walked back to one side of the trailer, and looked aft. A car was racing up the highway behind them, toward the airplane. With a screech of brakes, a black Mercedes drove up the tailgate and stopped behind the trailer, and the ramp began to close. Simultaneously, the engines began to start, one by one. Stone went back to his jump seat and strapped in.

The copilot shoved the throttles forward, and the engines began to spool up for takeoff, but above the noise came a sound Stone had not expected to hear: the firing of automatic weapons.

The pilots released the brakes and the airplane surged forward, and the sound of gunfire was left behind. But out the pilots' windows Stone could see the flashing red beacons on the two fuel trucks, still ahead of them on the road, and the airplane was catching up fast.

"The trucks have to get to an exit to get off the highway," Stone said aloud to nobody in particular.

"Pray they do," Mike replied over the headset, "and soon."

The trucks were, no doubt, unaware of the airplane behind them, but then the copilot switched on the landing lights and they were illuminated. The aircraft had reached a point where Stone could read the license plates on the trucks when the pilot rotated, barely clearing the two highly flammable vehicles.

"Now all we've got to worry about is the mountains," Todd said.

"Yeah?" Stone asked. "Why don't we worry about what the people shooting at us might have hit?"

"Okay, that, too," Todd said.

The airplane rose rapidly, and Stone could see the shadowy mountaintops being left behind. He began to breathe again.

The copilot unbuckled and began to walk aft in the airplane. "Come on," he said, "let's look for damage."

Stone unbuckled and followed Todd and Mike aft. Holly was right behind.

"It's hard to see bullet holes with no sun outside," Mike said.

"Maybe," Stone replied, pointing, "but you can see them in the Mercedes." There were two holes in the left front fender.

Todd jerked open the rear door of the car. "Everybody okay in there?" He apparently heard what he wanted to hear. The driver got out of the car, and Todd helped a man out of the rear seat.

He was a little over six feet tall, about 180, Stone reckoned, with thick, longish salt-and-pepper hair, a straight nose, and a firm jawline. He looked very fit, but he was moving in a shuffle, since his hands and feet were shackled to a thick leather belt around his waist.

Todd led him to the trailer, and Stone followed, curious about the man. He was allowed to use the toilet; then he came out and shuffled toward one of the big reclining chairs.

"Okay," the man said, stopping, "I'm aboard. Can we shed all this hardware now?"

Todd shrugged, came over, and removed the shackles.

"Good evening, Mr. Gelbhardt," Stone said.

The man looked at him with a small smile. "Call me Pablo," he said. "It has been a long time since anyone called me anything else."

"Have you had a pleasant journey?" Mike asked.

"There are no involuntary pleasant journeys," Estancia replied. "I thought my bladder would burst." He took a seat.

"Tell me, Pablo," Stone said, "was the shooting directed at us or at you?"

Estancia smiled broadly, revealing excellent dental work. "A good question," he replied.

25

Pablo Estancia was dressed in tan slacks, a yellow silk shirt, and a nicely tailored dark blue blazer with brass buttons. He seemed perfectly at ease as he surveyed his new companions.

"Now, let's see," he said. "The young gentleman is so CIA that he might as well have the letters tattooed on his forehead."

Todd seemed to blush.

"You, sir," he said to Mike Freeman, "are too old to be CIA and on this particular mission. I think you are a retired intelligence officer, but considering your accent, not from the United States." He turned to Holly. "This very attractive woman is mature, yet still involved in Agency activities, probably in a supervisory position."

They all laughed; then Estancia turned toward Stone and appraised him carefully. "You, sir, are a little too polished-looking, even in those clothes, to be CIA, or even FBI."

Stone laughed. "So who am I?"

"You are a lawyer," Estancia said, "but an unconventional one."

"Not a bad guess for a cold reading," Stone said.

Estancia chuckled. "This airplane is not military, but CIA," he said. "No one aboard is in uniform. Where, may I ask, are we heading?"

"To the United States," Holly replied.

"And where will we land?"

"Not too far from the coast."

"And then I will be transported to a safe house for interrogation?"

Holly shrugged. "Perhaps."

"Well," Estancia said, "allow me to make you a promise: I will answer your questions truthfully, in return for immunity from prosecution for myself and my household."

"Your household?" Todd asked.

"My wife, children, their children, my mistress, and my domestic staff, numbering twelve."

"We can talk about that," Holly replied, "once we are settled at our eventual destination."

"This is a very impressive airplane," Estancia said. "May I look around?"

Todd looked at Holly. "Why not?"

Mike led Estancia out of the trailer and into the cargo bay.

"Astonishing!" Estancia enthused. "I could ship anything in this aircraft, and as much of it as anyone could buy!" He looked into the cockpit. "Amazing avionics," he said. "Complete situational awareness at all times. Tell me, did you pick me up at an airport, or on a road?"

"On a road," Todd replied.

"I thought so." Estancia stepped forward and peered at the very large multifunctional display in the center of the instrument panel, and at the moving map displayed there. "And I see we are headed for—what is the name of that airport? It used to be an air force base."

"Stewart International," Todd said.

"Ah, yes, at Newburgh, north of New York City."

"Correct," Todd replied.

"Well, thank you so much for the tour," Estancia said. "May I return to that very comfortable chair in the caravan?"

"Sure," Todd replied.

They all trooped back into the trailer. "A nice television," Estancia said. "Do you have movies? I love movies."

"Yes," Mike replied. "What would you like to see?"

"Do you have *Singin' in the Rain*?" he asked. "That is my favorite movie. I love Gene Kelly, and Debbie Reynolds is very cute."

"I think we can manage that," Mike said. He found the DVD and inserted it into the machine. He also turned on the smaller screen to show the moving map.

"Very nice," Estancia said. "I enjoy watching our

progress. I am very impressed with all the trouble you have gone to, just to get me to the United States. You should have just invited me, and I would have taken my own airplane."

"What do you fly?" Stone asked.

"A Gulfstream Five," the man replied. "Very fast, excellent range, very comfortable. Do you have an airplane?"

"Yes, I have a small jet, a Citation Mustang."

"Isn't it fun to fly yourself?" Estancia said. "I have my private, my instrument rating, my multi-engine rating, and three jet type ratings. I enjoy being in the left seat."

The movie started, and Estancia watched it, rapt. Eventually, everyone but Stone moved out of the trailer for one reason or another, leaving him alone with the extractee.

"May I ask your name?" Estancia asked.

"I'm Stone Barrington."

The two men shook hands.

"Where do you practice law?" Estancia asked.

"In New York City."

"Do you do criminal trial work?"

"Sometimes."

"I think I may be in need of a lawyer quite soon," Estancia said, obviously aware of his understatement. "Do you have a card?"

Stone dug a card from his wallet and handed it to the man.

Estancia gazed at it, seeming to memorize the information; then he stuck it into a jacket pocket and settled down to watch the movie.

Later that night Mike, Todd, and Holly returned to the trailer and got into their bunks.

"We'll be arriving around four or five a.m., local time," Holly said to Stone as she pulled up a blanket.

Estancia glanced at his watch, then returned to the movie. He turned down the volume so as not to disturb the others.

Stone woke around four a.m., Eastern time. He had never changed his watch. The others were still in their bunks, but Estancia wasn't there. He must be back in the cockpit, Stone thought to himself. He glanced at the moving map and saw that they were off the tip of Long Island and were descending through eighteen thousand feet. He splashed some water on his face and left the trailer, taking his jump seat in the cockpit for landing. They were now descending through ten thousand feet over Long Island Sound, approaching the coast. He could see the lights of the towns out the window, and to the south, the glow of New York City.

The others filed in and took their seats.

"Where's Estancia?" Todd asked.

They all looked around and realized their prisoner was not in the cockpit.

"He must be in the john," Mike said.

Then a roar began to fill the cockpit, growing louder, and the aircraft seemed to be striking turbulence. Papers in the cockpit were flying around.

"The rear platform is lowering!" the pilot yelled over the noise, and Stone couldn't hear what he said next over the roar of air.

Everybody got out of the seats, in spite of the turbulence, and moved into the cargo bay, looking for Estancia. Todd looked in the trailer and came back. "He's not in the john."

"Good God!" Holly yelled, pointing.

Stone stepped to the other side of the cargo bay and saw the interior lights of the Mercedes on and Estancia at the wheel. He ran toward the car, followed by the others.

Before any of them could reach the car, it reversed, sped down the ramp, and disappeared into the dark night.

Everybody was stunned into silence. Mike recovered first. He walked aft in the airplane, found the switchbox, and closed the rear ramp.

Relative silence returned to the interior of the airplane.

"He committed suicide?" Todd asked.

"No," Stone said. "He was wearing a parachute."

26

Fred Holland, a successful cosmetic surgeon, lay sound asleep in his Rye, New York, home when he was shocked awake by something like an explosion. He lay there for a couple of minutes, afraid to get out of bed, wondering if another explosion was on the way.

Finally, mustering his courage, he went to the bedroom window, which overlooked the gardens leading down to Long Island Sound, and peered through a small opening. It was dark outside, but the security lighting was on for some reason. It must have been a clap of thunder, he thought, since the walk around the swimming pool was wet with rain. He closed the curtains and went back to bed.

A couple of miles west of where Dr. Holland was trying to go back to sleep, Pablo Estancia looked down at the rapidly approaching ground for a place to land.

It was his thirty-first parachute jump, a hobby of his youth.

Ahead and slightly to his left he saw a school, the grounds lit with streetlights. Estancia pulled on the left side of the harness to correct course and aimed for the darkened soccer field.

He touched down, buckled his knees, and rolled as he had been taught; then he was on his feet, gathering in the billowing chute. He could not believe his luck. He carried the chute to the sidelines of the field, then walked past the bleachers and found a large oil drum, used as a wastebasket. He set down the chute and took some old programs out of the drum, then stuffed the chute into it and put the trash back on top. Then he started walking.

He had seen some railway tracks as he floated down, and he headed that way. When he found them he thought about it, then started walking south along the tracks. After half a mile or so he could see a train station ahead of him, and he made for that.

A sign on the station proclaimed the stop to be Rye, New York. Estancia hoisted himself onto the deserted platform and looked around. A schedule on the wall told him the first train of the morning would be arriving at five-ten. He checked his pockets for money but found only euros. He went into the station men's room and urinated, then pulled out his shirttail and took out some dollars, replacing them with the euros from his pocket. He also removed an American passport. He put everything in his pockets, then tucked in his shirttail and buckled his belt.

He went back to the platform and sat on a bench; then he used his cell phone to call his home in Spain. His wife answered.

"Hello?"

"Listen carefully," he said. "Plan B." He waited while she thought about that.

"I understand," she said.

"All is well," Estancia said, then hung up.

Plan B meant that she was to immediately pack up the children, most of their clothes, put them and all the staff into four vans, drive to Gstaad, Switzerland, and occupy their house there.

A man walked onto the platform pushing a hand trolley loaded with a high stack of newspapers and began filling a row of coin-operated newspaper dispensers. Estancia didn't have any change, but he negotiated the purchase of a *New York Times* for twenty dollars, the smallest bill he had; then he settled himself on a bench and waited for the train.

The C-17 settled onto the runway at Stewart International, braked, and taxied to the lighted ramp in front of the airplane's hangar. The copilot went aft and lowered the rear ramp, then started releasing the cables holding the pallets in place. Two forklifts rolled up the ramp and began removing the pallets to waiting trucks.

Mike Freeman stood behind the trailer, looking at

the sides of the airplane. "I count eight bullet holes," he said to Todd. "You'd better get your maintenance people on that right away. They'll either have to be patched or the panels replaced."

Todd produced his cell phone. "I've got to call Lance Cabot," he said.

Holly put a hand on his arm. "I think you'd better let me do that," she said. Leaving Todd to speak to the maintenance crew, Holly, Stone, and Mike walked into the offices of Airship Transport and sat down in the lounge. Holly dialed a number on her cell phone.

Stone sat next to her, and he could hear both sides of the conversation.

"Cabot," a voice said loudly.

"It's Holly. I hope I didn't wake you."

"Don't be ridiculous. Where are you?"

"Back at Stewart."

"I got your text message," Lance said. "Congratulations on a successful extraction."

"The extraction went perfectly," she said. "Todd did an outstanding job of planning it."

"Then why do you sound so down?" he asked.

"As we were approaching the coast we lost Estancia."

"You *lost* him? How the hell did you do that?"

"He lowered the rear ramp of the airplane, then got into the Mercedes that delivered him, started the engine, and backed out of the aircraft."

"Backed out of the aircraft? Onto the tarmac?"

"We hadn't landed yet."

Lance digested that for a moment. "You were still in the air?"

"Yes."

"Estancia committed suicide?"

"Maybe not. Stone says he was wearing a parachute."

"I saw the shoulder straps," Stone said, leaning into the phone.

"Where the hell did he get a parachute?"

"There was a binful stacked right outside the cockpit."

"Let me get this straight," Lance said. "Estancia put on a parachute, got into the Mercedes, and drove it off the airplane into thin air?"

"Exactly," Holly said.

"My God," Lance said. "I hope it didn't land on somebody's house. We'd never hear the end of that."

Fred Holland's gardener arrived for work shortly after dawn, and on going to the rear of the house saw that the swimming pool's water level was down by a foot. He got a hose, turned it on, and walked to the edge of the pool and dropped the hose into the water, then he looked down and saw a black automobile sitting on the white bottom. *"Jesus H. Christ!"* he said aloud to himself. "That must have been some party!"

Pablo Estancia got onto the five-ten train and took a seat. He bought a one-way ticket from the conductor and then got out his cell phone and dialed a number.

"Gelbhardt residence," a sleepy woman's voice said.

"Helga, this is Mr. Gelbhardt," he said in German. "I'm sorry to wake you but I'm arriving in New York soon, and I should be at the apartment in about an hour."

"Yes, Mr. Gelbhardt," she replied. "Would you like some breakfast?"

"Yes, please: two scrambled eggs, bacon, toast, orange juice, and coffee."

"I will look forward to seeing you," she said.

"Good-bye, Helga." Estancia hung up. He had owned the New York apartment for more than twenty years. It was in his wife's maiden name, and the IRS had not discovered it when his difficulties arose. He had not visited it for more than a year, but Helga and her husband, Fritz, kept it in good order, ready for his arrival on short notice.

Estancia opened his *Times* to the Arts section and began to do the crossword.

27

Stone woke a little after nine, but he was not ready to get up yet. He ordered breakfast from his housekeeper, and she sent it up with the *Times*. He switched on the TV, which was tuned to the *Today* show.

He listened idly to the news as he scanned the front page, then something caught his ear.

"Matt," a young female news reader was saying, "I have a mystery for you this morning. Let's go to our local reporter in Rye, New York."

Another young woman holding a microphone appeared on the screen. She was standing next to a large swimming pool in a lush garden.

"Matt, this is the garden of a surgeon who lives in Rye, and his garden runs all the way down to the beach of Long Island Sound. The doctor awoke this morning to find something in his swimming pool." The camera crane moved high and over the water, pointing down.

"That," the reporter said, "according to a police diver, is a nearly new Mercedes 550 sedan. It has Spanish license plates and has two bullet holes in the left front fender, and no one is inside. Neither the doctor nor anyone else has the slightest idea how it got there."

The camera switched to a shot of the reporter and the doctor, with his back turned to the camera. "Tell us what happened," she said.

"Well," the doctor replied, "I was wakened at four thirty or five o'clock this morning by a very loud noise, like an explosion. I got out of bed and looked out the rear window and saw nothing. I figured it must have been thunder, since the area around the pool was wet with rain, and I went back to bed. Later this morning, the gardener found the car and we called the police."

The camera switched to a uniformed police officer wearing a chief's insignia. "We've looked all over the area," he said, "and there was simply no access to the pool that would have allowed the car to drive into it. The only way it could have gotten into the pool was to have been dropped from the air."

The camera switched back to the reporter.

"Regina," Matt Lauer said, "has anyone reported a car missing from an airplane?"

"Not as far as we know, Matt," the woman replied. "We've called every cargo transporter in the phone book, and they're as baffled as we are."

"Keep us up to date on this story," Lauer said. "I'm dying to know what happened."

The phone rang. "Hello?" Stone said.

"Stone, it's Lance. What the hell happened last night?"

"It's all as Holly said," Stone replied. "I watched a movie in the trailer with Estancia, and I got sleepy and went to bed. When I woke up Estancia wasn't there. Then we heard the rear platform open and all ran aft. I saw Estancia at the wheel of the car, and I could see the shoulder straps of a parachute. Mike had briefed us earlier about where they were stored. Estancia started the car, put it in reverse, and disappeared into the night. There was just a story on the *Today* show about the car landing in somebody's swimming pool in Rye, but there was nobody in it."

"I saw that just now," Lance said. "Thank God it didn't fall on a school or hospital."

"Looks like you've bought Estancia a very expensive airline ticket to the United States," Stone said. "Are the police looking for him?"

"Ah, no," Lance replied.

"Why not?"

"To call in the FBI or the police would attract too much notice. We can hardly put out an APB on him."

"Doesn't he owe the IRS millions? Let them find him."

"I don't want to wrestle the IRS for possession," Lance said. "We'll have to find another way."

"Well, good luck," Stone said. "Good-bye, Lance." He hung up.

*   *   *

Pablo Estancia had arrived at his Park Avenue apartment, had breakfast, showered and shaved, then phoned his barber and made an appointment for midmorning.

The man arrived at ten o'clock, set a dining chair in Estancia's dressing room, and had a look at his head. "The usual?" the barber, who had not seen him for more than a year, asked.

"I'd like it shorter, please, and I'd like to lose most of the gray."

"Of course," the man said, and went to work.

After the barber left, Estancia looked in the mirror and thought he looked ten years younger. He looked in a dresser drawer and came up with a box containing various bits of false hair. He selected a couple of pieces, brushed them carefully, and applied a thin coat of rubber cement.

Holly Barker sat next to Todd Bacon in Lance Cabot's office at the Agency's Langley, Virginia, headquarters and let Lance vent.

"This is a total fiasco," he said. "I thought you had this extraction planned down to the last detail."

"We did," Holly said, "but in our planning we somehow missed the possibility of the extractee driving a car out of the airplane and into a Rye, New York, swimming pool. I think Todd and I now realize that was an oversight," she said wryly, "but I have to point out that, in approving the extraction, you didn't spot that flaw in the plan, either."

Todd wisely kept his mouth shut.

Lance stared out the window and smiled a little.

"What are you thinking?" Holly asked.

"I was just thinking that this would make a wonderful story for my memoirs, but the Agency's censors would never allow it to be published."

Stone was at his desk in the late morning when Joan buzzed him. "There's a gentleman to see you," she said. "He won't give his name, but he says you know him."

"Oh, what the hell," Stone said. "It's a slow morning; send him in."

A man Stone had never seen before appeared in his office doorway. He appeared to be in his mid-fifties, was dressed in a well-tailored suit, and wore a dark mustache and goatee and heavy, horn-rimmed glasses.

Stone stood up as the man walked toward him with his hand out. "I don't believe I've had the pleasure," he said.

The man laughed and took a chair. "I am Erwin Gelbhardt," he said, "but you can call me Pablo."

28

Stone stared at the man for a moment, got it, then laughed, too. "You must have had an interesting morning," he said.

Pablo gave him an account of his movements since departing the C-17; then he held up a hand. "Before we continue this conversation, I would like to retain you as my attorney."

"For what purpose?" Stone asked.

"To conduct negotiations with the people who so kindly transported me to this country. I wish to reside again in this country without fear of kidnapping and what the loony right wing like to call 'enhanced interrogation.'"

"What have you to offer them?" Stone asked.

"Will you represent me?"

Stone thought about that for a moment. There was the matter of his consultant's contract with the Agency, but since he was not currently employed by them, he figured he could tap-dance his way around that.

"If, once I've heard your story, I can believe that your objective has a good possibility of coming to fruition, then yes, I'll represent you. Otherwise, we'd just be talking about a plea bargain."

"What will your retainer be?" Pablo asked.

"One hundred thousand dollars," Stone replied without hesitation, "payable in advance from a legal source, against an hourly rate of seven hundred dollars, plus expenses."

"Agreed," Pablo replied. He took an alligator-bound checkbook from his inside coat pocket and began to write. "This is drawn on a New York City bank account containing only legally derived funds," he said, handing the check to Stone.

Stone buzzed Joan. "Please type up a representation agreement," he said. "A retainer of one hundred thousand dollars, against seven hundred dollars an hour." He hung up the phone and looked at the check. "How is it you have funds in the U.S. that have not been attached by the IRS?"

"I settled with the IRS years ago," Pablo replied, "and I've filed a proper return every year since then."

Stone smiled. "That's very good news," he said, "and, if it's true, it's going to make our negotiating position much better."

"Let me explain something to you going in, Stone. In my dealings with you and the Agency I will tell you only the truth. However, if I feel that my answering a question will place in jeopardy my family or some other innocent person, I will decline to answer rather than lie."

"Good, that saves my making the standard speech," Stone replied. "Let's begin by you telling me how you accomplished a settlement with the IRS."

"It was remarkably simple," Pablo replied. "After leaving the United States I gave my tax position a great deal of thought, and I concluded that I did not wish to spend my life as a fugitive from the most powerful nation on earth. So I simply telephoned a deputy director of the IRS, introduced myself, and asked him what would be required to straighten everything out. He told me to call him back in twenty-four hours, and when I did, he said that thirty million dollars in cash and a written agreement to regularize my tax filings in the future would eliminate the problem." Pablo shrugged. "That was about three million more than I figured I owed him, but what the hell. He faxed me an agreement, and I signed it and wired him the money the same day. As a result, I now have a document, signed by the director of the IRS, stating that the United States government has no claim on any of my funds or property in this country or elsewhere as of that date, provided I file accurate returns from that date."

"I'm going to want a copy of that," Stone said.

Pablo reached into a coat pocket, produced a folded sheet of paper, and handed it to Stone.

Stone read it. "Remarkable," he said, "given the circumstances."

"There is one circumstance you don't know about," Pablo said. "I escaped from U.S. custody in Miami at the conclusion of my trial, while the jury was still out. After I arrived at my first stop, in Algeria, I learned that the jury had acquitted me. That made everything else simple, except possibly a charge of escape."

"I should think we can work that out," Stone said.

"Now, I have a question for you before we go any further. I would like to know how you came to be on that flight that I . . . deplaned from last night, and exactly what your relationship is with the CIA."

"Of course," Stone replied. "Some years ago I met Lance Cabot in England, while representing a client there. I won't trouble you with the subsequent nature of our relationship; suffice it to say that the following year I signed a consultant's contract with the Agency, and, on a number of occasions, I have assisted Lance with various problems. That will not be a conflict of interest with your case because they are not currently employing me."

"And your presence on the airplane?"

"I represent Strategic Services, who previously owned the airplane. They recently sold it to the Agency, along with the attendant charter company, then undertook to make a flight to Iraq, picking you up on the way back. I simply went along on the flight for the experience, which turned out to be very interesting, indeed."

"All right," Pablo said, "now let me tell you a few things."

"I'm all ears," Stone replied.

"Since I settled with the IRS I have taken care not to violate U.S. law. I have, in the course of my business dealings, tiptoed around all sorts of other national laws, but I have never been arrested or charged in any of those countries. I have avoided that, mostly, by conducting all of my business from Spain, by telephone or e-mail or through intermediaries."

"You are aware, are you not, that U.S. law requires you to register all of your bank accounts outside the country?"

"I am, and I have done so," Pablo replied. "All I want is what I have already told you."

"That is certainly a reasonable goal," Stone said, "if I can convince them that you will give them the information they want."

"That may be more difficult than you think, Stone, which is why I so readily agreed to your outrageous retainer."

Joan brought in the retainer agreement and handed it to Stone. He looked it over and handed it to Pablo. "Joan, this is . . . Pablo. What name are you going to be using henceforth?"

Pablo accepted the agreement. "I will revert to my original name, Erwin Gelbhardt," he said. "I have a valid passport in that name."

"Joan, this is Mr. Gelbhardt," Stone said.

"How do you do, Mr. Gelbhardt," Joan said, and they shook hands.

Gelbhardt signed both copies of the agreement and handed them back to Stone. Stone signed them both, handed one back to Pablo and the other to Joan for filing.

"But I prefer to be called Pablo," Gelbhardt said.

"Pablo it is," Joan replied, and left the office.

"Now, Pablo," Stone said, "what sort of information will you supply to the CIA, in return for being left alone?"

Pablo thought for a moment. "Well, how about the longitude and latitude of the current location of Osama bin Laden?" he replied.

29

Stone stared across the desk at his new client. The man did not exhibit any sign of insanity. "You actually have that information?" he asked.

"I do," Pablo responded.

"Who knows that you have it?"

"No one. I came across it quite by accident, and the person who gave it to me died almost immediately after telling me."

"Is there anyone who *believes* you have that information?" Stone asked.

"Not to my knowledge," Pablo replied.

"Then let's keep it that way for the time being."

"I should have thought you would want to dangle it before Lance Cabot and his colleagues as an incentive."

"Do you have any reason to believe that bin Laden might move to another location?"

"No."

"Then let's first dangle other information before Lance, and save that little piece until we really, *really* need to use it."

"I must tell you, Stone, that as a patriotic American, I have a moral imperative to give that information to my government."

"Are you morally impelled to give it to them today, tomorrow, or next week?"

"I suppose not."

"Then please let me choose the moment for transmitting it, so that you may derive the maximum benefit for being a patriotic American."

"I take your point," Pablo said.

"Now, what other information do you have for them?"

"I can give them the details of every arms transaction I have been involved in for the past twelve years," Pablo replied. "I should mention that I have what is often referred to as a photographic memory, although it might be more accurate to describe me as visually and audibly memory-efficient."

"Do you have documents to support your recounting of these transactions?"

"Alas, such transactions are never committed to paper, except as notes, which I have always destroyed at the conclusion of the business."

"What we very much need, then," Stone said, "is a transaction that they can confirm independently, as a means of confirming your veracity."

"I am unaccustomed to having my veracity questioned," Pablo said, "having built a reputation for truthfulness over these many years."

"You will have to try not to be offended by the disbelief of others," Stone said. "Each person you speak to will have his own very good reasons for disbelieving you, unless the truth can be more objectively confirmed."

Pablo sighed. "Ah, that is human nature, I suppose."

"It is the nature of the intelligence bureaucracy," Stone said, "where every person is responsible to those above him and must, therefore, cover his ass."

Pablo laughed. "I think you are right; I am unaccustomed to dealing with bureaucracy. In my business, decisions are made quickly, albeit with verification on both sides."

"As in 'you show me yours, and I'll show you mine'?"

"Precisely."

"Please remember, as we progress, that we are not dealing in the sale or purchase of hardware, but a trade of information in return for the safety of you and yours. What we are likely to get, if we are successful, is a sheet of paper with some writing and a signature on it."

"I understand. Tell me, Stone, do you have a very good safe in your offices?"

"I do."

"Then I must ask you to deposit there any paper on which you have written any information about me, so that, if your offices should be . . . disturbed, that information will not fall into other hands."

"I will do so," Stone replied. He looked at his watch. "Now," he said, "I think you should go to a place where you feel secure and wait there while I conduct some preliminary discussion with what we must think of as the opposition. If you will give me a phone number, I'll call you when I have progress to report, probably tomorrow."

"Please memorize this," Pablo said, then gave him the number. "Repeat, please."

Stone repeated the number.

Pablo stood and offered his hand. "I feel better now," he said. "I look forward to working with you."

"I look forward to that, too," Stone said, shaking the hand.

When Pablo had gone, Stone called Lance Cabot.

"Holly Barker."

"Holly, it's Stone. May I speak to Lance?"

"I'm afraid he's out of the office for the rest of the day," she said. "Did you get any sleep this morning?"

"I did, though not enough. Will you ask Lance to call me at his earliest convenience?"

"Sure. Anything I can help you with?"

"Not yet," Stone replied. "Bye-bye." He hung up, then called Dino and made a dinner date. He called in Joan, scribbled Pablo's phone number on a notepad, ripped off the page and handed it to her, along with the letter from the IRS. "Start a file on Mr. Gelbhardt," he said. "Keep it in the safe, along with any other material pertaining to him, and keep the safe locked at all times."

"Anything scary about this client?" she asked.

"He's a pussycat, but there might be those who wish to harm him in some way, and they may not be as nice—hence, the safe."

"Got it."

"Deposit his check and pay the taxes on it today, please."

"Got it."

There was a knock at the door, and Herbie Fisher stood there. "Hey, Stone."

"Hey, Herbie, come in."

Herbie took a seat.

"You don't look so happy," Stone said. "What's going on?"

"Well, I'm not seeing very much of Stephanie."

"Why not? You still live together, don't you?"

"Of course, but she leaves the apartment at seven in the morning and misses dinner a lot of the time."

"Well, she's just started a new job, hasn't she?"

"Yeah, I guess."

"Are you still going on your honeymoon?"

"Eventually, when Stephanie can take a break from work."

"What, exactly, is she doing at Gunn?"

"International stuff. She sometimes gets calls in the middle of the night about something that's happening with an overseas market."

"Is she making lots of money for you yet?"

"Not yet, and not a hell of a lot for herself. She and

David only get a ninety-thousand-dollar salary each; they could do better at a bigger firm, right out of college."

"But they both will do very well indeed over the long run, right?"

"Right, I guess, when Jack decides to retire or kicks off."

"How's Jack's health?"

"He's in better shape than I am," Herbie replied.

"More time at the gym, Herbie," Stone said. "Now, if you haven't got anything specific to bring up, I have to get back to work."

Herbie stood up. "Yeah, sure; I'm just glad to know you're here, representing me."

"That's very flattering, Herbie. See you soon."

Herbie shambled out, and Stone got busy making notes for when Lance returned his call.

30

Stone and Dino arrived on the sidewalk simultaneously, then walked into Elaine's together. Their drinks were on the table almost as soon as they sat down.

"Have I got a tale to tell you," Stone said.

"People been telling me tales all day," Dino replied. "Did you know that criminals lie all the time?"

"I seem to remember that they do," Stone said. "But you always catch them at it, don't you?"

"Most of the time," Dino said. "Now, tell me your tale."

Stone began with the story of the sale of Strategic Air Services to the CIA, then continued with the trip to Iraq, the extraction from Spain, and, finally, Pablo's short drive out of the airplane and his subsequent hiring of Stone.

"You're shitting me," Dino said when he was done.

"About which part?"

"The whole thing. You made it up out of thin air, didn't you?"

"I swear, every word is true."

"*You* were in Iraq?"

"Well, not so's you'd notice it, but even if my feet didn't touch the ground, I was there—and in the Azores and Spain, too."

"You know, I did see something on TV about a Mercedes found in a swimming pool in Rye."

"That's the one. How else could it have gotten into that guy's pool?"

Stone looked up to see Lance Cabot walking into the restaurant. He shucked off his coat, hung it up, and pulled up a chair. "You rang?" he said to Stone.

"I did, but a return phone call would have done."

"I was in town anyway," Lance said. "Good evening, Dino." They shook hands.

"How you doing, Lance?"

"I'm not sure yet; that depends on what Stone has to say to me." He ordered a drink, made a toasting motion, and took a gulp. "Well?" he said to Stone.

"You might want to wait until your second drink," Stone said.

"Why? Is your news that bad? I presume you do have news of some sort, or you wouldn't have called me."

"The news is quite good, if you're willing to be flexible."

"Uh-oh, what's the deal?"

"I have a new client: Erwin Gelbhardt, aka Pablo Estancia. And he wants to make a deal."

Lance froze, just sat and stared at Stone. "You have a conflict of interest," he said finally. "You're under contract to me; you can't represent both sides."

"First of all, I'm not currently in your employ, and second of all, this is not, strictly, a legal matter. All it requires is some conversation about terms, then the signing of a letter; then my client begins to talk."

"You're representing a man who is a fugitive from justice."

"He's not a fugitive from justice, Lance, just from you."

"He's wanted by the IRS."

"Let's not characterize the IRS as justice."

"What does he want?"

"He wants you off his back—also, the backs of his family and personal staff."

"And in return?"

"He's willing to tell you, in detail, about every arms transaction he has made for the past twelve years. Then he just wants to retire peacefully to this country and live out his life. He is sixty-eight, after all, past retirement age."

"Can he document what he's going to tell us?"

"Pablo, as he likes to be called, points out quite correctly that such transactions do not take place on paper. However, he purports to have an astonishing memory for detail."

"Okay, I'll hear what he has to say, and then we'll talk."

Stone shook his head. "Nope."

"You want something up front?"

"Yes. I want his deal in writing, and when he's finished talking I want a letter from you confirming that he has kept his word and that you have no further interest in interrogating him. I also want a letter from the attorney general stating that the United States has no interest in prosecuting him for any of his actions over the past twelve years."

"When can he surrender himself?"

"He's not going to surrender himself," Stone replied. "He's going to meet with you for three eight-hour days at a place in New York of his choosing. You may record video and audio of the meetings."

"Twenty-four hours of interrogation?"

"Three days of conversation. You won't need more than that; he talks fast."

"Five days."

"Four, and not a minute longer."

Lance picked up a menu. "What's that big chunk of veal with the polenta called?"

"Osso buco."

Lance snared a passing waiter and ordered, then sat very still, apparently thinking hard, while waiting for Stone and Dino to order.

"Where do you want to meet?" Lance asked when the waiter had gone.

"I'll give you a choice: a conference room at Woodman & Weld, or the dining room at my house."

"Well, let's see," Lance said. "The Woodman & Weld venue has the advantage of the Four Seasons right downstairs."

"Are you really going to put four days of lunches at the Four Seasons on your expense account, Lance?"

"You have a point," Lance said. "The boys in accounting tend to get itchy about that sort of largesse."

"Tell you what: my housekeeper is an excellent cook; I'll spring for lunch every day, if you do it at my house."

"I'll have to send people in to sweep the place," Lance said.

"I'm okay with a free sweep of my house," Stone said, "but I want two simultaneous recordings of the proceedings, and you leave one with my client, just so we won't have to worry about who said what at some later date. Also, the recordings will never be seen on television or outside the intelligence apparatus of the government while my client is still alive."

"You mean that if I want to put all this on *60 Minutes*, I'll have to shoot Pablo first?"

"You will never lay a hand on Pablo, neither figuratively nor literally."

"If I get the feeling that I'm being had, I'm going to be very, very angry," Lance said.

"Pablo's wish is not to have you, but to tell you everything he can. And, if you and your people behave yourselves and treat him like the gentleman he is, you may get a bonus or two when we're done."

"What sort of bonus?" Lance asked.

"That remains to be seen, doesn't it?"

Lance held out his hand. "Deal. One thing, though: I am not going to get between Pablo and the IRS. Life is too short. Any deals with them will have to be separate from our arrangement."

Stone pretended to think about that. "You're sure you can't help him with the tax people, even a little?"

"Not even a little," Lance replied.

Stone shook his hand. "Deal. You're a hard man, Lance."

"We start Monday morning at nine?"

"Good."

"I'll have my people stop by to sweep and install the recording equipment."

"Good."

Lance was looking very smug by the time his osso buco arrived.

31

Lance dropped by Stone's office the following after-noon, and Stone was ready for him. Joan got them both a drink, and Stone handed him an agreement to read.

Lance read it quickly, but apparently thoroughly. "This seems to reflect our discussion of last evening," he said, then signed two copies and handed one to Stone.

"Here is your letter to Pablo," Stone said, handing him a single sheet of paper. "You can have it retyped on your letterhead."

Lance read it. "This is a little stronger than I had conceived it."

"That won't cost you anything, Lance."

"Oh, all right."

Stone handed him another sheet of paper. "This is the letter to be signed by the attorney general."

"You really do have a lot of balls, Stone," Lance said, reading the letter. "You presume to write the attorney general's correspondence for him?"

"If he objects, the president can sign instead—on the proper letterhead, of course."

"I'll put it to the general."

"You'd better put it to him right away and get his signature, because I want all these documents signed and sealed before the start of our fourth day together."

"Or what?" Lance asked insouciantly.

"Or you won't get the bonus."

"Ah, I see; you're saving the best for last."

"Something like that."

"Give me a hint."

"It's something you want, and nobody else can give it to you."

Lance thought; then he chuckled. "Surely you're not talking about—"

"I'm not talking, period," Stone said. "This conversation is at an end."

"Oh, all right. I'll see you Monday morning at nine. Will you be offering breakfast, as well?"

"If you can ask questions while chewing. Who are you bringing with you?"

"Holly will be here, and at least one person who may remain anonymous. Also, there'll be a court stenographer with his little machine."

"As long as they'll all fit at my table."

"Will you have anyone else there besides Pablo? If so, they'll have to be cleared."

"Just the two of us," Stone said. "Occasionally, Pablo and I may have to consult privately, and as our agreement states, I can instruct him not to answer, if necessary."

"Ever the lawyer, Stone," Lance said. He shook hands and left.

Joan came in when he had gone. "So that's the elusive Lance Cabot?"

"Elusive? Why do you say that?"

"Well, I've heard you talk about him for years—usually disparagingly—but I've never seen him until now. He's very good-looking and beautifully dressed, too. It's strange having two of you in the office at once."

"I'll introduce you next week."

Joan left, and Stone called Pablo.

"Hello?" He sounded relaxed, but alert, as he always did.

"Mr. C. has just left my office. We have concluded arrangements, and I'd like to tell you what they are."

"Please do, I'm dying to know."

"He's going to have four eight-hour days of your time to interview you. He'll be bringing several of his people to sit in, and the entire interview will be recorded with video and audio, two copies. You get one; he gets one. That way there can be no later dispute about who said what to whom."

"All right, but I don't want our discussion about you-know-who recorded—audio or video."

"That's fair. We're going to get all the signed documents—including a letter from the attorney general—before we introduce that subject. It will be the very last thing on the agenda."

"Good. I will need a large-scale map of the border area between Afghanistan and Pakistan."

"I'm not going to ask him to bring that; it would tip him off. Visit a map store. There's one on West Forty-third Street, just east of Sixth Avenue."

"As you wish," Pablo said.

"Pablo, now would be a good time to move your family," Stone said.

"I have already done so," Pablo replied. "My family and my staff have moved to my house in—"

"I don't need to know that," Stone said.

"My wife called me last night. They are safe and comfortable."

"I'm glad to hear that."

"It will be a great relief for her when this business is concluded."

"I'm sure it will be."

"You will have to come and visit us, Stone. I live in very nice places. You'd like Marbella."

"That's on the coast of Spain, isn't it?"

"Yes, a lovely spot."

"It would be very pleasant to come and see you, Pablo."

"Stone, I would like you to draw a new will for me."

"I'd be happy to, as a courtesy."

"I'll messenger over a list of my bequests, so you can have it ready to be executed when I see you."

"Pablo, do you have a residence in Florida?"

"I do, in Palm Beach."

"I'm going to get a document for you to sign declaring Florida as your legal residence."

"Is there a tax or some other advantage?"

"Yes; you'll avoid paying New York State and City income taxes. In Florida you'll pay a small intangibles tax on your investment holdings—stocks and bonds."

"That would be acceptable," Pablo said.

"What address have you filed your tax returns from?"

"My Marbella address."

"Is there anything else I can do for you?"

"Can you recommend a trustworthy private detective?"

"I can, but I need to know what you have in mind. I don't want to screw up our deal with these people, either before or after our meeting with them. You're going to have to promise to be a law-abiding citizen."

"Then let's wait until we meet to discuss that."

"Certainly."

"Do you need any other local referrals?"

"A good shoe repair shop," Pablo said.

"Jim's Shoe Repair, East Fifty-ninth, between Park and Lex."

"Thank you so much, Stone."

"They'll be here at nine sharp on Monday morning," Stone said. "I suggest you come here at eight for breakfast, so we can have a little time to talk."

"I'll be there at eight sharp," Pablo said.

"Good day, then." Stone hung up. This was going to be either fun or absolute hell, depending on how Lance conducted himself, and Stone knew he could do little about that.

32

Stone was nearly done for the day when Joan buzzed once again. "Stephanie Gunn Fisher for you on line one."

Stone thought that sounded like the name of a substantial heiress and socially prominent woman, which, of course, she was.

He pressed the button. "Good afternoon, Stephanie."

"Hello, Stone," she said cheerfully. "How are you?"

"I'm very well indeed, and I hope you and Herbie are, as well."

"We're very well, too."

Stone hoped that, since the health of everyone involved had been established, she would get on with it. She did.

"Herbie has told me of your interest in investing with the Gunn company, and I'm happy to tell you that

I've discussed it with Jack, and he has agreed to accept you as one of his investors."

Stone thought as fast as he could. "That's certainly good news, Stephanie, but since speaking with Herbie about the investment, there have been some changes in my financial setup, so I won't be able to avail myself of that opportunity at the present moment."

There was a long silence. "Something I can help with, Stone? A loan or a line of credit, perhaps?"

"I don't think that will be necessary," Stone said. "I just have a few things to sort out before I can make the commitment."

"I see," she said, and there was a cool edge to her voice.

"I'm very grateful for your speaking to Jack about me, and I will certainly understand if he wants to change his mind, but I just can't do it right now."

"Would you care to mention a time when we should talk again?"

"I'll be in touch as soon as things have calmed down a bit."

"Tell me, Stone, are you in any way connected to the security firm Strategic Services?"

"Yes, I'm their outside counsel and a member of their board."

"Are you aware that they have submitted a request to withdraw their investment from our company?"

"They consult with me mostly on legal matters, not

financial ones, and since I've only recently been appointed, I haven't attended a board meeting yet."

"I see. I hope the recent flare-up of publicity hasn't played a part in their decision, because everything at Gunn Investments is in apple-pie order."

"I'm glad to hear that, and I'll be happy to convey your assurances to the CEO when next I see him."

"Thank you, Stone, and I wish you a pleasant week." Stephanie hung up.

Stone sighed, relieved that he had avoided telling an outright lie to get through that conversation.

Joan buzzed again. "Pablo for you."

"Hello, Pablo," Stone said.

"Stone, I have just learned from a reliable source that my passport and those of my family have been flagged by the State Department and thus may not be used to enter or leave the country."

"That's not good news, Pablo. I'm sorry."

"You must get back to Mr. C. and tell him that these flags must be lifted at once, or I will be unable to speak with him and his people next week."

"I'll do the best I can, Pablo, but we have a signed agreement with him that does not include this problem. I'll speak to him; perhaps he will be of help."

"Thank you. I'll wait to hear from you."

Stone hung up and looked in his book for a cell number for Lance, then dialed it.

"Yes?"

"It's Stone. Something disturbing has come up."

"How sad. What do you want?"

"The American passports of Pablo and his family have been flagged, preventing them from entering or leaving the country."

"Well, I suppose you'll have to take that up with the IRS, Stone," Lance said. "It's their beef."

"No, it's not; it's the State Department who has flagged the passports. Will you look into this, please? I know that the Agency has a close working relationship with State, and I don't want to see Pablo struck mute by this easily solved problem."

"Clearly, you have never dealt with the State Department, and I resent your suggestion that Pablo might violate our agreement."

"That is not his intention, Lance, as I'm sure it was not your intention to have Pablo and his family inconvenienced in this manner. I hope we can sort this out to prevent any dissension among us."

"Well, I'll be happy to phone someone at Foggy Bottom, but I can't make any promises."

"I'm sure when your contact there learns of the great value of Pablo to national security, he will see the light."

"May I have the numbers of the passports, please?"

"I don't think that will be necessary, Lance: we both know your contact will have those at the tap of a keyboard."

"Perhaps," Lance said. "We'll see. I don't know if he'll still be in his office at this hour, but I'll leave a message if he isn't, and I'm sure he'll get back to me in due course."

"I would think that you would be able to reach him now, just as I was able to reach you, and he will be able to instruct the proper person to remove this obstacle before the weekend."

"Where is Pablo at this moment, Stone?"

"I don't know, Lance. He has visited me here, but most of our communication has been telephonic. He could be anywhere."

"I hope he doesn't have it in his mind to scamper; perhaps you should relay to him the difficulties such an action could visit upon him."

"Lance, you've recently kidnapped the man from his home, snatched him off a highway in Spain, and forced him to enter the U.S. illegally, without proper extradition, and then threatened him with torture. I don't think there's anything I can tell Pablo about your methods that he doesn't already know."

"I hope you're not going to be difficult about this, Stone. I'm beginning to feel just the tiniest bit stressed by your client's wavering."

"Lance, it is within your power to resolve this matter within hours, if not minutes, thereby restoring your monkish state of serenity. We will look upon your immediate actions for a sign of your good faith."

"Once again, Stone, I must point out that if this has anything to do with the IRS, that's beyond my purview."

"I'm sorry, Lance, but I forgot to mention in our previous conversations that Pablo resolved all issues with the IRS years ago and we have in our possession a letter from that agency's director confirming that, as far as it is concerned, Pablo has been, since that time, an upstanding citizen. All that remains is for you to straighten out the State Department, so that we may independently confirm that the flags have been lifted and will not be reinstated."

There was a brief silence. "I'll get back to you," Lance said, then hung up.

Stone called Pablo. "I've spoken to Mr. C. and he has agreed to call his contact with the State Department. He'll get back to us."

"God, I hope so," Pablo said.

"It's important, Pablo, that you take no action in response to this matter. Are we clear about that?"

"All right," Pablo said, then hung up.

Stone rested his forehead on the cool, glass top of his desk and whimpered.

33

Stone arrived at Elaine's to find Woodman & Weld's managing partner already seated with Dino and already drinking.

"Evening, Bill, Dino," Stone said as he slid into a chair only slightly behind the Knob Creek that had been placed on the table.

"Evening, Stone," Eggers said.

Stone looked at Bill for signs of pleasure or displeasure, but he wore his usual, very effective poker face.

"Anybody hungry?" Stone asked, picking up a menu.

"Sure," Dino replied.

"I haven't decided yet," Eggers said.

"Well," Stone said, "I hope your digestion improves quickly, because I'm starved." He wasn't about to ask if something was troubling Eggers.

Eggers fingered the menu, then set it down. "I have heard a rumor, Stone, that you may *somehow* be connected with a Mercedes automobile that *somehow* found its way into a Rye swimming pool."

Stone looked at him askance. "You think I've been running around Westchester County, driving expensive automobiles into swimming pools? I assure you, my Mercedes is cozily tucked into my garage at home and has not been out for days."

"I saw something about that on TV," Dino said innocently.

"There's all sorts of strange stuff on TV these days," Stone replied. "Probably some reality show gone wrong."

"I've heard it was a different kind of show gone wrong," Eggers said. "And I'm concerned that my firm's putative next partner might be associated with such a stunt. Dr. Holland, owner of the pool in question, is a client of the firm, and he is not as amused as everyone else in the country to find a large chunk of twisted steel in his pool. He is having to remove extensive plantings in his garden in order to get a crane in position to hoist the thing onto a flatbed truck, and there are questions as to whether his insurance covers falling German hardware."

"Bill, please tell me exactly what you have heard about my alleged connection to this event and from whom you have heard it."

"I have told you all I can."

"Then I will have to decline to comment on apparently baseless charges and rumors promulgated by anonymous individuals."

"It was Lance Cabot," Eggers said.

"Ah, then you must know that, in the extremely unlikely event I had any connection whatever to this weird occurrence, my relationship with Lance's employer would prevent me from either confirming or denying such an allegation, and Lance must know that, too."

"All right, Stone," Eggers said, "take a moment to muster all your lawyerly command of the language to craft a statement that will place you at a sufficient distance from my client's perfectly understandable curiosity about the origins of this event, something I can repeat to him."

Stone thought for a moment. "All right, you may quote me as saying that I have not now nor have I ever caused an automobile to fly through the air and into your client's swimming pool, nor have I had any opportunity to prevent such a happening. And, when you have finished telling your client that, you may tell Lance Cabot, in the nicest possible way, to go fuck himself. If I should see Lance before you do, I'll tell him myself."

"I'll have the spaghetti carbonara," Eggers said to the hovering waiter.

"Make that two," Dino said.

"I'll have Barry's secret strip steak, medium rare, with fries and haricots verts," Stone said. "And bring us a bottle of the Mondavi Cabernet that you are always out of."

"We're out of that," the waiter replied.

"Then make it the Phelps Cabernet."

"We've got that," the waiter replied, then departed.

"So, Stone," Eggers said, "what beautiful woman are you seeing these days?"

"The last beautiful woman I was seeing was murdered in her own home not very long ago," Stone said, "and my desire to see another has not yet overcome that circumstance."

"Murdered by whom?" Eggers asked.

"Ask Dino; he's the cop at the table."

"Dino?"

"My money's on her nephew or his girlfriend or both," Dino said.

"You have any evidence to back that up?" Stone asked.

"They were the last two people to arrive for the dinner party, and the nephew had access to the building through his aunt and could have entered the back hall from inside the building, taped the door latch, and later let himself in to perform the killing, then out again."

"That's a reasonable conjecture," Stone said, "but I take it you have no hard evidence."

"You could put it that way," Dino said.

Stone turned to Eggers. "How is it you are having ex parte communications with Lance Cabot?"

Eggers allowed himself to look uncomfortable for a tiny moment. "He called me; I didn't call him."

"He called you for the sole purpose of spreading rumors about my personal conduct?"

"That may not have been the only reason," Eggers said. "I can't say any more."

"On what grounds? National security? Attorney-client confidentiality? As I recall, Lance is *my* sometime client, not yours or the firm's."

"Look," Eggers said, "when a high official of the intelligence community calls and asks for some informal advice, I consider it my duty to my country to help if I can. Isn't that why you and Dino are under contract to Lance?"

"It is, or was," Stone said. "Not speaking for Dino, I find that Lance calls on me when he wants to make my life miserable or, at least, worse, and I'm getting tired of it. I've tried to resign my consultancy, but he says I can't."

"He seems to make my life more interesting when he calls," Dino said. "I like that spook stuff."

"You stay out of this," Stone said petulantly.

"Were you on that airplane that the Mercedes departed from?" Eggers asked.

"Yes, I was, and at the invitation of the firm's client, Mike Freeman, of Strategic Services, who was in the employ of Lance at the time. That doesn't mean that I caused or failed to prevent the car from taking flight. And I would suggest to you that if our work for Strategic Services somehow infringes on the gardening rights of Dr. Holland, then the good doctor should be told to take a hike, since Mike Freeman is demonstrably the more important client."

"I don't question that," Eggers said.

"Then deal with Dr. Holland however you like, and leave me out of it, okay?"

"Okay," Eggers said, uncharacteristically chastened.

34

Stone awoke the following morning, still a little steamed at Eggers, and switched on the *Today* show. Moments later the screen was filled with the image of a battered black Mercedes being lifted by a crane from a swimming pool, water pouring from every orifice, and it had some new orifices.

"Dr. Holland tells me that nearly a hundred mature plantings have had to be removed temporarily to allow the crane access," the reporter was saying, "and he wants to know who's going to pay for that. As for the Mercedes, all the glass in the car was shattered on impact, and there isn't a body panel on the car that isn't bent. The vehicle appears to be a total loss for whoever owns it, and that's not even counting the two bullet holes in the left front fender."

"Misty," Matt Lauer said, "we've had confirmation that the registered owner of the car is a Spanish corporation with the rather bland name of Overseas Info. I don't know what that is in Spanish, but our correspondent in Madrid tells us that the company is widely viewed in that country as being a front for an American intelligence agency, which shall remain nameless."

Stone switched to *Morning Joe*, which had the same footage of the car. "The question here," Joe Scarborough was saying, "is first of all, how can the CIA afford to buy very large and expensive Mercedes automobiles, and second, why are they tossing them out of airplanes, or the space shuttle, or wherever they launched the car from? And now we're getting a report that a school custodian a little distance from the Holland mansion has discovered a discarded parachute in a trash can at the school's soccer field. This seems to indicate that somebody was actually flying the Mercedes before bailing out."

The people around the show's table roared with laughter.

Stone's phone rang. "Hello?"

"It's Lance."

"Good morning, Lance," Stone said. "How is it you are discussing with Bill Eggers my presence on the C-17 the other night and, apparently, blaming me for the loss of your Mercedes?"

"I deny that," Lance replied.

"I figured you would. Tell me, have you seen the latest film of the car on the morning TV shows?"

"I have."

"Have you heard the mention of a company called Overseas Info, which is said to be a front for an unnamed American intelligence service?"

"I have."

"How is that going down upstairs at the Agency? Is everybody just pleased as punch?"

"I don't need this abuse," Lance said. "I called to give you some good news, but if you don't want to hear it . . ."

"There is nothing I would like to hear more," Stone replied. "Shoot."

"Would that I could," Lance said. "I have persuaded people at the State Department to remove the flags on Pablo's and his family's passports. I am told that will be accomplished by noon today. Are we all right on that score now?"

"We will be the moment the flags are gone," Stone replied. "As far as I'm concerned, we're still on for Monday morning."

"My people will be at your house this afternoon to sweep the place and begin installing their video and audio equipment."

"Fine."

"I should tell you that the video and audio feeds will be transmitted to Langley, where a number of analysts will be watching and listening to corroborate your client's statements. I assume there will be no objection to that."

"None from me. I'll speak to my client about it."

"Good. Now, if you will excuse me, I have more important work to do." Lance hung up.

Stone called Pablo.

"Hello?"

"I've just heard from Mr. C. that the State Department will remove the flags from your passports by noon today," Stone said.

"It has already been done," Pablo replied. "My source just phoned me."

"Also, Mr. C. wants to feed your interview back to his offices so that some of his colleagues can watch and listen, in order to substantiate the factual nature of your interview. Any problem with that?"

"None whatever," Pablo replied.

"Did you find the maps you need?"

"In fact, such a map is being FedExed to me from another country as we speak, a map that has been annotated by my source. I think Mr. C. and his colleagues will find it very interesting."

"Good. Do we need to rehearse what you're going to say in the interviews?"

"No," Pablo replied. "But you may feel free to stop me if you think I am incriminating myself beyond the terms of our agreement with Mr. C."

"I have drawn the agreement to be all-encompassing," Stone said, "so I don't think we have to worry about that. With any luck at all, by this time next week you will be free to move about as you please, and your family can join you."

"We'll see. They may wish to remain where they are for a time, and I may join them."

"Will you feel secure in Europe and other places after your interviews?"

"My assumption is that no one will know what I have said."

"That is my assumption, too," Stone replied, "but we are dealing with human beings, here, who might have a tendency to leak. You should keep that in mind."

"I will do so."

"Have you seen the television reports of the recovery of the Mercedes from the swimming pool?"

Pablo chuckled. "Yes, I have. I've been very much enjoying them."

"You should know that Mr. C. does not share your amusement, and it would be unwise to bring up the subject when you meet, and if he should bring it up, be humble and contrite. We don't want him angry."

"I understand, and I'll try my best not to needle him."

"If he needles you, remain calm."

"Remaining calm is one of the things I do best," Pablo replied.

"Mr. C. has asked about your whereabouts, and since I don't know, I've given him a truthful answer. I don't think there is anything to be gained by letting him know where you are residing during your stay in New York."

"I entirely agree," Pablo said, "and as soon as I feel free to travel, I may relocate elsewhere."

"I guess that couldn't hurt," Stone said.

"Flexibility of travel has always been very important to me," Pablo said. "Tell me, do you know if Mr. C. knows about my airplane?"

"I don't know, but I wouldn't be surprised."

"I must give that some thought," Pablo said.

"I'll see you Monday morning," Stone said. "Call me if you need anything."

"Now that my shoes have been repaired by Mr. Jim, I need nothing," Pablo replied. "Good day." He hung up.

35

Stone was at his desk when Mike Freeman called.

"Good morning, Mike."

"Good morning, Stone. I spoke to Lance Cabot a few minutes ago, and he was hinting that Strategic Services should pay for the hard landing his Mercedes experienced. He and I had only a verbal agreement about the trip we made for them, except for the charter agreement, which is in writing."

"Does the charter agreement say anything about responsibility for equipment belonging to the charter company?"

"No," Mike replied.

"Good. The other thing to look at is the terms of your verbal agreement. Did anything in your conversation with Lance mention your being in charge of the extractee or any cargo aboard the aircraft?"

"No, there was no mention of it. He told me that

two of his people would be aboard the aircraft and would take charge of Pablo."

"Then it appears that you have no liability for Pablo's actions. The cargo, including the Mercedes, was government property and was put aboard by government employees, so no liability there, unless you actually caused damage to it, which you did not. I think you're in the clear, and that's certainly the attitude you should adopt in dealing with Lance."

"Good. I feel better already."

"Nor should the gentleman in Rye who owns the pool have any claim against you."

"Even better."

"If Lance gives you a hard time, just refer him to me."

"I'll do that. Lance hinted that Pablo did not escape his clutches."

"Pablo did escape his clutches, but he will be speaking to Lance and his colleagues soon."

"Voluntarily?"

"Yes, and under mutually agreed-upon terms."

"So we have an ultimately successful conclusion to our mission?"

"It would seem so, but let's wait until everything is concluded before feeling relief. Your portion of the mission would seem to be complete, though, unless there's something else you agreed to with Lance that hasn't been done."

"No, our mission was to pick up the cargo in Iraq,

the extractee at a specified location, and deliver them to Stewart International."

"Well, I'll handle the final delivery of Pablo part, except for the car."

"The stuff on TV has been hilarious," Mike said. "I've had trouble keeping a straight face when talking to Lance."

"Hang on to that straight face, Mike; Lance is not amused."

"Will do."

"By the way, I had a call from Stephanie Gunn Fisher, and she mentioned that you had withdrawn your funds from the Gunn company."

"Yes, and it's safe elsewhere. Did you take your money out?"

"I never put it in, fortunately."

"I'm relieved to have ours out. What's going to happen there?"

"Who knows? They seem to have come through their audit in good shape, though."

"Talk to you later," Mike said, and hung up.

Joan buzzed him. "Dino is holding on two."

Stone pushed the button. "Hey, Dino."

"It was fun last night watching you and Eggers go at it."

"I'm glad you enjoyed yourself."

"Something you said struck me."

"What was that?"

"When he asked you who you were going out with."

"Well, yeah."

"First time I've ever known you to be without at least one woman on the available list."

"It's certainly a dry spell," Stone admitted.

"You want a date tonight?"

"You mean with somebody besides you?"

"I've been seeing this assistant DA lately."

"You sly dog; you never said a word."

"Her name's Doris Trent."

"Sounds like an old soap opera."

"Maybe, but she's pretty nice."

"Are you offering me your girl, Dino?"

"Certainly not. She has a friend."

"Uh-oh."

"I hear she's all right. What the hell, you might like her. Her name is Willa Crane."

"Oh, all right. Where are we dining?"

"I thought maybe the Park Avenue Café."

"Sounds good."

"I thought we'd come to you at seven for a drink, give you a chance to impress the lady with your good taste, then dine at eight."

"All right. I'll get Helene to do us some of her hors d'oeuvres."

"See you then."

Later, Stone showered and got into a suit and necktie, because he knew that's what Dino would wear; then he went downstairs to the library.

Helene, as requested, had laid out some things to nibble on and had placed a bottle of Veuve Clicquot Grande Dame champagne in a silver ice bucket. Stone removed the plastic wrap from the tray and tossed it, then got some champagne flutes from the bar cabinet. At ten past seven, the doorbell rang. Stone picked up the phone and pressed the electric unlock. "Come in," he said.

He walked to the living room and waited for the elevator to stop, then open. Dino emerged with two women: one was very small and cute; the other was tall and, Stone had to admit to himself, drop-dead gorgeous, with long, straight black hair, dressed in a black-and-white sheath that reminded him of a pinto pony. He held his breath while introductions were made.

"Stone Barrington, this is Doris Trent," Dino said, indicating the small one.

Stone heaved a sigh of relief. "Hello, Doris."

"And this is Willa Crane," Dino concluded.

Stone shook her hand. "Hello, Willa," he said. "Please come into the library." He led them into the next room, seated them, and began to open the champagne. "Would anyone like anything else besides champagne?" he asked.

Heads were shaken. He popped the cork and poured, then set the tray of food on the coffee table and took a good look at Ms. Crane, wondering about her.

He took a glass for himself and sat down next to her. "Willa, what do you do?"

"I'm a deputy district attorney," she said.

Deputy. That meant she was a career prosecutor and senior in the office. He supposed she was thirty-five.

"Tried anyone interesting lately?"

"Well," she said, "I thought about prosecuting a client of yours, but I haven't decided yet."

"Uh-oh," Stone said. "I hope we're not headed toward a conflict of interest here."

"You can hope," she said, sipping her champagne.

36

The subject somehow got changed, and eight o'clock was approaching, so they were on their first course at the Park Avenue Café before they came back to Willa's work.

"Aren't you curious about which of your clients I'm considering prosecuting?" she asked. "Want to guess?"

"Willa," Stone said, "so many of my clients are teetering on the brink of prosecution that it could be an injustice to even mention a name."

Willa laughed, a healthy sound. "All right, it's Herbert Fisher."

Dino began laughing.

"What's funny?" Willa asked.

"Herbie is always on the brink of prosecution," Dino said, "often for something he didn't do."

"You're acquainted with Mr. Fisher?"

"Yes, he's been in my holding tank a few times."

"An habitual criminal, then?"

Stone spoke up. "An innocent man who seems to have a gift for being in the wrong place at the wrong time. However, he was married a short time ago, and the experience seems to be lending stability to his existence. Which of the patently false charges against Herbie are you considering pursuing?"

"How about murder?" she asked.

"In what degree?"

"Has he committed more than one murder?"

"Herbie has never committed a murder, although he was once required to defend his life against Dattila the Hun, whom the press liked to describe as 'a Mafia kingpin.'"

"Oh, yes, I heard about that. He walked."

"It was, as I pointed out, self-defense."

"I think he got very lucky," Willa said.

"Good luck is not something that haunts Herbie's life," Stone replied.

"Really? I think he's very lucky to be walking our streets at this moment. If not for the actions of an inexperienced prosecutor, he would be held without bail as we speak."

"Wait a minute," Dino said, "are you talking about the death of his girlfriend, who fell or jumped from Herbie's penthouse terrace a while back?"

"No, I'm talking about the girlfriend who received, at the very least, a helping hand from Mr. Fisher."

"Well," Dino said, "I happened to be in charge of that

investigation, and also present at a conference between your prosecutor and Herbie's attorney—Mr. Barrington here—and I thought, given the feather-light weight of the evidence, your prosecutor made a good call."

"Thank you, Dino," Stone said. He turned to Willa. "I was able to demonstrate, through fingerprint evidence, that the young woman in question, Sheila, opened the terrace door without assistance and disappeared over the parapet while Mr. Fisher was spending half an hour or so with a magazine, at stool."

"And how were you able to prove that?" Willa asked.

"I offered to deliver Mr. Fisher for a colonoscopy, but your prosecutor declined."

Willa burst out laughing. "That's preposterous!"

"Not so much as the allegation against my client."

"He's right, Willa," Dino said. "Listen, I like nailing murderers, but believe me, Herbie is not a murderer."

"Look, Willa," Stone said, "if you want to charge Herbie, you go right ahead, but believe me, that decision would turn out to be a major embarrassment for your office, and I know you wouldn't want that."

"I might enjoy the trial," she said.

"So would I," Stone replied, "because I would be very well paid, and I would win. I don't think you would find a lot of pleasure in that."

"You let Mr. Fisher know that my office is keeping an eye on him, and that if he makes a wrong move I will fall on him from a great height."

"Lieutenant Bacchetti," Stone said, "will you please

note the prejudice toward my client in the deputy district attorney's words, as well as the threat."

Dino took his notebook from his pocket and scribbled something in it. "Duly noted," he said.

"Willa," Doris said, speaking for the first time, "you're outnumbered; give up."

Willa raised her hands. "Okay, okay. However, I am still considering a charge against Mr. Barrington himself."

"Oh?" Stone asked, laughing. "And what would the charge be?"

"Defacing city property," Willa said, "to wit, our conference table."

Stone frowned. "Uh-oh," he said.

"What?" Doris asked. "Tell me."

"It was at an office Christmas party a while back," Willa said. "Or so the story goes. It seems that Mr. Barrington and a highly thought of prosecutor were interrupted by other parties while locked in what might politely be described as sexual congress, on our office's conference table. I'm told the image of the prosecutor's bare ass remained imprinted on the table amid a circle of lighted candles, until the cleaners returned after the holiday."

Doris turned toward Stone. "Well, Mr. Barrington?"

"On advice of counsel," Stone said, "I must respectfully decline to answer, based on my rights under the Fifth Amendment of the Constitution of the United States of America."

Everybody laughed.

"So it's true!" Willa said.

"You may not infer guilt from my refusal to answer," Stone said.

More laughter. Diners nearby were beginning to take note.

"I can see that I'm going to have to get the details from the prosecutor herself," Willa said.

"I wouldn't advise that," Stone said, "as she is well known for her right cross, and if that isn't enough, she has four large Irish brothers who are police officers and who take offense at the slightest untoward reference to their sibling."

Willa threw up her hands. "I give up. The threat of violence will prevent me from ever learning what really happened."

"It appears you already know," Dino said.

"Thanks so much, Dino," Stone said. "Remind me never to call you as a character witness."

Stone and Willa parted company with Dino and Doris outside the restaurant.

"May I take you home?" Stone asked.

Willa laughed. "I believe there may be a double entendre couched in your question."

"Then take your pick," Stone replied.

37

Stone awoke alone, the other side of his bed unmussed. "Oh, well," he said aloud to himself, "she made her choice." He showered, shaved, and had breakfast at his desk.

Joan came into his office. "Do you need me earlier than usual on Monday morning?" she asked.

"Good idea," he said. "I've offered these people breakfast, and you could help Helene set up a buffet in time for their nine-o'clock arrival."

"Will do," she replied. The phone rang, and Joan picked up the one on Stone's desk. "One moment, please." She pressed the HOLD button. "A Willa Crane for you?"

"Thank you," Stone said. "Good morning, Willa."

"And good morning to you," she replied.

"Did you sleep well?"

"Probably not as well as I would have if I had chosen the other option," she said.

"I'll give you another chance, if you'll promise not to hound Herbie Fisher to an early grave."

"Be specific."

"If you can get off a little early today, I'll pick you up at two o'clock and bring you back on Sunday afternoon."

"And our destination?"

"That will remain a mystery, but rest assured, it will be a comfortable one."

"All right, two o'clock. Shall I meet you downstairs?"

"Perfect. Bring warm clothes." He hung up and buzzed Joan.

"Yes, my lord and master?"

"Will you call Seth Hotchkiss and ask him to meet two of us at the airfield around four thirty this afternoon, and that we would appreciate dinner around seven thirty?"

"Yes, Sahib."

"Are you wearing a turban?"

"No, why do you ask?"

"Never mind." Stone hung up.

As they were waiting to be cleared for takeoff that afternoon, it occurred to Stone that the last time he had taken a woman to Maine, she had ended up dead. A moment's thought allowed him to rationalize away that possibility.

"What are we waiting for?" Willa asked from the copilot's seat.

"For release by the tower," Stone replied.

The tower came onto the radio frequency. "November one, two, three Tango Foxtrot, cleared for takeoff. Climb to six thousand feet on runway heading, expect direct Carmel."

That amounted to a good break over the routine departure. "Tango Foxtrot, six thousand, runway heading, rolling." He lined the airplane up on the runway, pressed a button to center the heading, then pressed the autopilot heading button, switched on the pitot heat, and pressed the switch that brought up the command bars to follow after takeoff. He moved the throttles to takeoff power, let the engines spool up, then released the brakes.

"Wow," Willa said. "It accelerates!"

Stone rotated, got the gear and flaps up, and at seven hundred feet engaged the autopilot and removed his hands from the yoke. "Yes, it does," he said.

"November one, two, three Tango Foxtrot, contact departure," the tower said.

Stone switched to the departure frequency and checked in, then was given direct Carmel and eleven thousand feet. Ten minutes later he was given direct destination and his final altitude, flight level 250.

"It's so smooth," Willa said.

"Welcome to jet travel."

"Airliners aren't this smooth."

"They are when they have smooth conditions, as we do today."

"What a great way to travel," she said. "Where the hell are we going?"

"East by northeast. Air traffic control is being very nice to us today. Either there isn't much traffic or they think we're Air Force One."

Twenty minutes from destination they were given a descent to eleven thousand feet, and, once there, were handed off to Bangor approach and given five thousand. Stone canceled his IFR plan and aimed for just south of the short runway at Islesboro.

"Bangor is in Maine, isn't it?" Willa asked.

"Yes, and so is Penobscot Bay, below us, as is that long, skinny island right there, which is known as Islesboro."

"I've never been to Maine. This is exciting."

"I'm glad you think so." Stone turned final for runway one, lined up his approach, dropped the landing gear, and put in full flaps. The airplane quickly slowed to its approach speed of 88 knots, and Stone set down and braked sharply. "That's for us," he said, nodding at the old Ford station wagon as they rolled past it.

Half an hour later they had unpacked and were enjoying a hot toddy before a cheerful fire in the study.

"Well," Willa said, "you certainly know how to make a second date interesting."

"Thank you."

"How is it you chose this place?"

Stone told her the story of Dick Stone's death and his inheritance.

"That's sad," she said, "but in the end, fortunate for you."

"I can't deny that," he said.

"So, what's this I hear about this big conference at your house Monday morning?"

Stone looked at her, dumbfounded. "Please tell me exactly what you've heard," he said.

"That you're somehow involved with the CIA— they're your clients, or something, except you're representing somebody else on this occasion."

"And please tell me who told you that."

"The DA himself," she said, "when your name came up."

"And what is the DA's interest in me and my meeting?"

"He didn't say, exactly, just that he hoped to get some prosecutions as a result of the meeting."

Stone was baffled. This had to have come from Lance, but why would Lance have told a local, non-federal prosecutor, albeit the most important DA in the country, to expect prosecutions?

"Well?" Willa asked. "Is this true?"

Stone thought about the agreement he had drawn and that Lance had signed. He had neglected to insert provisions of secrecy, believing that Lance had no reason to mention it to anyone outside the Agency and that he would, routinely, keep it a secret.

"Well, since information about this thing is abroad in the land, I may as well tell you, on the condition of absolute confidentiality."

"But why, when I already know about it?"

"Okay, let's forget it and change the subject."

"Oh, all right, absolute confidentiality."

Stone gave her the background to the story.

"And *that*'s the Mercedes that ended up in that swimming pool in Westchester?"

"One and the same."

"And your client was driving . . . flying it?"

"For a short time, yes."

"That is the wildest story I've ever heard!"

"Tell me, is the DA expecting to call my client as a witness in these prosecutions he's so looking forward to?"

"That was my impression," Willa replied.

Well, Stone thought, we'll see about that.

38

Stone excused himself, let himself into Dick Stone's secure office, and called Lance Cabot's cell number.

"Yes, Stone? And why are you in Maine again on such a cold weekend?"

Stone ignored the question. "Why does the Manhattan district attorney believe that Pablo's questioning is going to result in numerous prosecutions for him and that Pablo will be testifying?"

Lance sighed. "I happened to have dinner with him at Peter Luger's in Brooklyn the evening before last. I'm afraid he may have overestimated his potential involvement in the results of Pablo's testimony."

"Were you drunk?" Stone asked.

"Now, Stone, don't make too much of this, please."

"Too much of it? Apparently, details of my client's cooperation are abroad in the land. Surely you're aware that that sort of information could endanger his life and those of his family?"

"Nonsense. Pablo has nothing to fear."

"Well, let's take a hypothetical example: Pablo tells you, on tape, that he sold X arms to X person on X date, and someone in the DA's office lets that slip to an acquaintance of X. What do you think X's reaction will be?"

"You have a hypothetical point, Stone, but don't stretch it. It won't happen that way."

"Lance, I give you notice now: if you ask Pablo a question the answer to which might put his life in jeopardy, I will instruct him not to answer."

"Stone, I'm sure our four days together will go very smoothly, and I'll do everything I can to protect Pablo's health and happiness during the proceedings."

"Thanks, Lance. I'm going to hold you to that, and afterwards, too." Stone hung up and returned to Willa.

"Problem?" she asked.

"Not anymore," he replied, hoping it was true.

They had a good dinner and retired early. Willa came to bed wearing only a short, filmy nightgown, and Stone received her wearing only boxer shorts. Shortly, neither was wearing anything.

"You have a reputation to live up to," Willa said, throwing a leg over and snuggling close, her breasts firmly against his chest.

"Oh, God," Stone breathed, but he did his best to live up to it.

When they had finished and lay on their backs, letting the ceiling fan cool their sweating bodies, Willa said, "I hope what I said about the DA hasn't disrupted anything for you."

"What you said hasn't," Stone said, "but what the DA said may, before this is over."

"He wasn't supposed to know about your meeting?"

"He was told by a participant who was indiscreet," Stone said. "I'll take steps to see that it doesn't matter."

"I hope that works out for you," she said.

"So do I."

The following morning they took a walk along the snowy shore.

"This place is more fun when we can take out a boat," Stone said.

"Last night made up for the absence of boats," Willa replied.

"That's your fault," Stone said. "You were irresistible."

"A girl likes to be irresistible," she replied.

"Tell me, what brought Herbie Fisher to the attention of someone as lofty as you in the DA's office?"

"As part of my ADA's supervision, I read a memo describing her—how shall I put it?—negotiation with you."

"And?"

"It read more like a capitulation," Willa replied. "I had a few words with her about that, and next time she encounters a defense lawyer she'll be a lot tougher."

"The young woman saved your office the expense of a prosecution that you'd have lost and the resulting embarrassment," Stone said. "Speaking as an ex-cop who enjoyed putting criminals away, I think she made the right call. So does Dino, you'll remember."

"I can't judge my people by what the cops think of them," Willa said.

"I should have thought that the cops' opinion of a prosecution would be a very important factor in judging new ADAs," Stone said. "It doesn't take any guts to bring a case to prosecution, if there's any kind of case at all, but it takes some guts and smarts to look at the evidence and see that it's not enough for a conviction."

"Maybe, but a different, more experienced prosecutor might have come to a different conclusion about the evidence."

"No," Stone said, "if I had been talking to you instead, you would have come to the same conclusion."

"And why do you think that?"

"Because in a case like Herbie's, I'm a better defense attorney than I was a lover last night."

"You think you're that good, huh?"

"As an attorney, yes."

"And if I'd tried the case, you think you could have gotten an acquittal?"

"I'm sure of it, but the greater skill lies in seeing that a case never comes to trial. Look at it this way: I did your office a favor."

"You have a high opinion of yourself, don't you?"

"I'm a good, pragmatic judge of what I can and can't do," Stone said. "If you'd had evidence that was conclusive, I'd have been looking to make a plea deal. As it was, I wouldn't have allowed Herbie to accept any offer you made short of a withdrawal of charges."

"I've probably been involved in a lot more such cases than you have," she said, "during fifteen years of prosecution, and I'm a good, pragmatic judge of what's possible in a courtroom."

"What's your conviction rate in the cases you've brought to trial?" Stone asked.

"Personally?"

"No, of the cases you've approved for trial, both yours and your subordinates'?"

"About eighty-five percent," she replied.

"That's very good," Stone said, "but in those of my cases that were tried and I felt should never have gone to trial, my acquittal rate is one hundred percent. Overall, it's about the same as your conviction rate."

"Then we're evenly matched," she said.

"We are, as long as you don't bring cases I know you can't win," Stone replied. "And I'll make it my business to see that you never lay a glove on Herbie Fisher."

"What's so special about Herbie Fisher?" she asked.

"If you knew him, you'd know how harmless he is."

"He wasn't harmless to Dattila the Hun," she pointed out.

"Like a lot of people," Stone said, "Herbie will fight like a cornered rat when his back is to the wall. Dattila put him in that position by repeatedly trying to kill him, to Dattila's cost."

They turned back toward the house.

"I think I'm going to have to go back to New York this afternoon," Stone said. "A couple of days ago I was comfortable about my upcoming meeting, but now I'm not, so I need to be there. Can we have dinner in the city tonight?"

"Sure," she said. "Anyway, I'm not so sure how much more snowy landscape I could have stood."

39

Before leaving the house that afternoon, Stone called Bob Cantor, an ex-cop who was very good with technical matters.

"Hey, Stone."

"Bob, I've got something urgent on my plate. Can you meet me at my house at six p.m., prepared to go to work?"

"With what kind of tools?"

"Bring the van," Stone said. Cantor had a van with several hundred thousand dollars' worth of equipment installed and tools for everything.

"Will do," Cantor said, then hung up.

The flight back was uneventful. Stone dropped Willa at her building, and they agreed to meet at Elaine's later. As Stone pulled into his garage he saw Bob Cantor's van parked outside.

The two men shook hands, and Stone let them into the house and turned off the alarm that Cantor had installed; then he led Cantor to the dining room.

"Hey!" Cantor said, looking around at the cameras and cable. "Looks like you're doing *Good Morning America* from here."

"Here's the deal," Stone said, pulling Cantor into the powder room and closing the door, then turning on the water. "A client of mine is being questioned here for four days, starting Monday morning. Their techs have installed all this stuff and God knows what else."

"You mean you think they might have overdone it a bit?"

"That's what I mean. I want you to sweep the whole house for bugs. If you find something, don't disable it, but put yours alongside it. You can do that without wires, now, right?"

"Right. It will all be recorded in the van."

"My deal with the questioners is that they will make two copies of the video and audio of the meetings and give me one."

Cantor thought for a moment. "I only saw one recorder."

"I'm not surprised," Stone said, "so I want my own recordings of the sessions."

"I can do that," Cantor said.

"Go to it." They departed the powder room and went their separate ways.

*   *   *

Cantor and a helper were hard at work when Stone left for Elaine's.

Dino and Doris Trent were already at their table when Stone arrived, and Willa arrived a moment later.

"You know, I've heard about this place, but I've never been here," Willa said. "It's too far uptown for my crowd."

Stone introduced the women to Elaine, who sat down for a minute. "So?" she said.

"Life is interesting," Stone said.

"As bad as that, huh?"

"Maybe not."

"Gotta go," Elaine said, rising to greet another table of regulars who had just sat down.

"So that's the famous Elaine," Willa said.

"The one and only," Stone replied.

"How's the food?" she asked, fingering a menu.

"Better than you've heard," Stone said. "The food critics get pissed off because they can't get the good tables that are reserved for the regulars."

A waiter appeared and took their drink order.

"Ah," Stone said, looking toward the front door, where Herbie and his new wife were entering. "And now you get to meet the dangerous and deceptive Herbert Fisher."

"You're kidding," Willa said.

The couple stopped at the table, and Stone made the introductions.

"I'm glad you can afford to eat out, Stone," Stephanie said, "in your reduced circumstances."

"I'm investment-reduced," Stone replied amiably, "not dinner-reduced."

The couple continued to their table.

"*That* was Herbie Fisher?" Willa asked.

"You expected a wild-eyed monster, huh?"

"Not exactly, but I didn't expect a nebbish, either."

"And a nebbish who married well," Stone replied. "Stephanie is the daughter of Jack Gunn."

"So he can afford the very best representation in criminal matters," Willa said.

"I'm glad you understand that," Stone replied.

Stone took Willa home and got back to his house to find that two more men had been added to Cantor's workforce.

"Stone," Cantor said, taking a small black box from his pocket and pressing a button. "This will keep us from being overheard. There's a bug on every phone in the house, including your office and Joan's. You want me to duplicate them all?"

"Every one of them."

"How much time have I got? The video installation takes longer, if you don't want them to notice."

"Six o'clock Monday morning," Stone said.

"I can do that, probably by midnight tomorrow."

"Good man."

Cantor pressed the button again and gave Stone a thumbs-up.

Stone woke the following morning and, when he went downstairs to retrieve the *Times*, found Cantor and his crew in the kitchen, drinking coffee and eating breakfast.

"We raided the icebox," Cantor said.

"That's okay."

"And we'll be done by lunchtime."

"Great news," Stone said, pouring himself some coffee.

"The stuff these people have installed in your house leads me to believe that these people are not exactly your garden-variety industrial spies," Cantor said. "This looks more like government work, and of a high order."

"I'm glad to know my tax dollars are being spent on the best," Stone said.

"But my stuff is more than good enough to pick up what you want."

"Good. When we're all done, make two copies of everything. I want my client to have a copy."

"Easily done," Cantor said. "Keep this in your pocket; it will work from there. If you come to a point in your meetings where you don't want your image or voice recorded, just press the button. All they'll get is static and snow. When you want to let them record again, press the button once more."

Stone put the device in his pocket. "Right," he said; then he went back upstairs with his coffee, a muffin, and the *Times* and settled in for a morning of reading, watching the Sunday morning political shows, and doing the crossword puzzle.

He thought about alerting Pablo to his suspicions about Lance, but decided not to. He would be on hand to protect his client.

40

At eight o'clock sharp on Monday morning Stone's doorbell rang, and he admitted Pablo. Holding a finger to his lips, he walked his client through the kitchen and out to the back garden.

"What's up?" Pablo asked.

"The whole house is wired for pictures and sound. I wanted to talk to you for a few minutes without their seeing or hearing us."

"All right."

Stone showed him the device Cantor had left him. "I've installed my own system, parallel to theirs, and something else, as well. If I need to talk to you without being seen or overheard, all I have to do is press this button, and their system won't see or hear anything."

"I want one of these," Pablo said, fingering the device. "Can you get me one?"

"I'll see what I can do," Stone said. "I've learned

over the weekend that the Manhattan district attorney is aware of our meetings with Lance and believes he may be able to develop cases from what you have to say."

"That's very unlikely," Pablo said. "I have been very careful not to conduct business in the United States that might result in the breaking of U.S. law."

"Fine, I just wanted you to know. Another thing: I think we may want to conclude these meetings earlier than Lance believes we will. I'm thinking, before noon on Thursday."

"That's fine with me," Pablo said.

"Can you drop off the grid for a few days or weeks afterward?"

"I can."

"Then, when I decide the time is right for that—and this is after you've given them their bonus—I'll say something to the effect that I want a break, because I don't want to tire you out."

"All right."

Stone explained to Pablo what to do in that eventuality.

"Thank you, Stone; I'm grateful."

"After that, call me only on my cell phone from another cell phone, one with the GPS chip removed."

"I have such a phone," Pablo said. He took a notepad from his pocket and scribbled something. "Here is the number."

Stone entered the number into his cell phone, under

the first name he thought of, which was Willa Crane. "Okay, let's get some breakfast." They went into the kitchen, where Helena whipped up something for them.

Shortly after nine the doorbell rang, and Joan, who had been warned about the recording system, let Lance and his group in and led them to the dining room, where breakfast had been laid out on the sideboard. Pablo remained in the kitchen.

Lance, Holly, and Todd Bacon made up the CIA interrogation team, and there were two technicians with them to operate the video and audio equipment.

Everyone sat down at the table and had some breakfast.

"Where is our guest?" Lance asked.

"He will join us when we're ready to begin," Stone said.

When the dishes had been taken away, Joan brought in Pablo, seated him at the center of the table, next to Stone and directly across from Lance, who had Holly and Todd on either side.

"Good morning, Pablo," Lance said. "I believe you've met everyone."

"I have," Pablo replied. "Good morning to you all."

"Are you ready to begin?" Lance asked.

"I am."

Stone nodded to Joan, who took a seat and opened a steno pad.

"I would just like to make a comment before we start," Pablo said.

"Please go ahead."

"As I have told Stone, during my career in the arms trade I have taken great care not to violate the laws of the United States, so it will be a waste of time for you to attempt to trap me into an admission of that sort."

"I see," Lance replied.

Stone spoke up. "Do you have the documents we requested?" he asked Lance.

Lance opened his briefcase, which was on the table, and handed Stone two envelopes. "There you are. Please feel free to examine them."

Stone opened the two envelopes and found Lance's letter to him, along with the attorney general's, both retyped exactly as he had written them and both signed and notarized. Stone showed them to Pablo, then tucked them into his inside jacket pocket.

"I'll make copies for you later," he said to Pablo. "Now, Lance, we may begin."

Lance stated the date and time and recited the names of those present, for the benefit of the recordings. "During these proceedings, Mr. Gelbhardt will be addressed as Pablo, which is his preference. First question, Pablo: please tell us how you left the federal courthouse, where you went, and what you did there."

Pablo took a sip of his coffee. "After the attorneys had completed their closing statements and the jury had been removed from the courtroom, I went to the men's room on the floor below, where a briefcase had been left for me with a change of clothing and a disguise, consisting of a wig and a false beard. I changed, applied the disguise, then took the elevator to the basement garage, walked outside, took a taxi to New Jersey, where, by previous arrangement, I boarded a cargo ship which had completed its lading and which sailed as soon as I came aboard.

"I was shown to a comfortable cabin and was given a merchant marine uniform and introduced to the crew as a company inspector, along for the ride. The vessel sailed to Oran, in Algeria, where I left it and, using three taxis, went to a private clinic on the south side of the city.

"There I underwent some cosmetic surgery procedures—I had never liked my nose or my chin very much, you see—and I spent another ten days there, recuperating. I was issued a legal Algerian passport during that time and acquired other identification documents. After that I proceeded to Malta, then to Italy, and finally to Spain, where I purchased a small villa on four acres in Marbella."

"Did you do any business during your time in Algeria?" Lance asked.

"No, I devoted myself to recovery from surgery and to arranging identity documents."

"And what did you do when you arrived in Spain?"

"I had already learned of my acquittal in New York, which came later in the same day I departed, so through my tax attorney in New York, I contacted the Internal Revenue Service and negotiated a settlement for any past taxes due and a declaration that I was no longer in violation of United States tax law." Pablo took a document from his pocket and handed it to Lance. "Here is a copy of that document, signed by the director of Internal Revenue at that time."

Lance read the document aloud for the benefit of the taping system. "And so you were made clean under U.S. law?"

"Yes," Pablo replied, "and I have remained so." He smiled slightly. "Although I recognize that I may have a traffic violation to deal with in the State of New York with regard to my operation of an automobile there."

Stone allowed himself a chuckle, while everyone else looked uncomfortable. He began to relax; Pablo was doing just fine.

41

Stone listened, entranced, as Pablo related more than thirty instances of arms sales abroad, giving dates, places, and names of buyers—all without using notes. The CIA team hardly spoke, just made furious notes.

At five o'clock, Stone held up a hand. "It's five o'clock, ladies and gentlemen," he said. "We will adjourn and reconvene at nine o'clock tomorrow morning."

Lance glanced through his notes. "All right, we will do so, as previously agreed." He and his party got up and left the house, followed by the recording technicians carrying luggage with the tapes inside.

Stone showed Pablo to his library, fixed them both a drink, and sat down. "That went very, very well," he said to Pablo. "You were right; you have a remarkable memory."

"It's more a gift than an acquired skill," Pablo said.

"More of the same tomorrow?"

"Yes, I think so," Pablo replied. He stared into his drink, then tapped his ear.

Stone produced Cantor's device and pressed the button.

"I have a concern," Pablo said.

"How can I help?" Stone asked.

"I don't know that you can. This morning I walked the distance from my apartment to this house. Halfway here I became aware of a four-man team following me."

Stone sat up straight. "Might they have been foreign?"

"I don't think so. They were conventionally Caucasian and dressed in business clothes. One was a woman."

"They had to be Lance's," Stone said. "Do you know if they saw you depart your building?"

"I don't believe so," Pablo replied. "I was very careful when leaving my apartment, and I saw no sign of being followed."

"They have to belong to Lance; the four-man team is a technique they teach at the Farm, the Agency's training facility. The NYPD also teaches it, but they would have no reason to be interested in or even aware of you."

"That's what I think, as well."

"I don't think you should return to your apartment right now," Stone said, "but I think we can get you safely back later tonight. We'll have dinner first."

"All right."

Stone pressed the button again.

They took a taxi to Elaine's, where Dino awaited them.

"Dino," Stone said, "this is Pablo."

Dino shook hands. "Pablo what?"

"He doesn't have a last name," Stone said quickly. "You will have heard of his expertise in flying the Mercedes 550, though."

"Ah, my congratulations," Dino said, laughing. "How did you manage to hit that pool?"

"I did not hit it," Pablo said. "In fact, I misjudged the distance to the shore when I departed the aircraft. I had thought the car would land in the sea, and that I would continue drifting toward the land. The wind was from the east."

"How did you know that?" Dino asked.

"There was an indicator of wind direction and strength on the pilot's primary flight display," Pablo said. "I saw that on a remote unit in the trailer, on the moving map, as we were descending through ten thousand feet. However, I believe the wind strength decreased at lower altitudes. Still, I made it to dry land. Unfortunately, so did the car. I was greatly relieved to hear that it did not harm anyone."

They ordered drinks and dinner.

"I have not been in this restaurant for many years," Pablo said. "In fact, I had dinner here with my attorney the night before the last day of my trial."

Elaine wandered over and sat down, and Stone introduced her to Pablo.

"I know you," she said. "You used to come in here a couple of times a month, long time ago. Gelbhardt, right?"

"Elaine," Pablo said, "I have an excellent memory, but you astonish me."

"Larry Gelbhardt, the writer, was in here a lot at the time, so your name was easy to remember. Pablo, huh? I like that."

"It's a nickname I picked up during many years of living in Spain."

"What brings you back to New York?" she asked.

Stone interrupted. "I'll tell you later."

"Whatever," Elaine replied, then got up and joined another table.

They had a leisurely dinner; then Elaine bought them an after-dinner drink.

"Dino," Stone said, "we need your help."

"Okay," Dino replied.

"Pablo needs a ride home, but I don't want him to be followed."

"I've got a good driver right now," Dino said. "How you want to work this?"

Stone told him; then they finished their drinks, and Stone signed for dinner.

Dino led the way out of the restaurant and got into the rear seat of his car, then slid across to the other side, leaving the door open. Stone, in the meantime, hailed a cab, which drew up behind Dino's car. Stone got into the cab; then Pablo jumped into Dino's rear seat and slammed the door. The car moved out.

"Stay close behind the car ahead," Stone said.

"That a cop car?"

"It is." He explained what he wanted the cabdriver to do.

At the next corner, Eighty-seventh Street, Dino's car turned right and accelerated. Stone's cab pulled into the intersection and stopped, blocking traffic that wanted to turn right.

There was a cacophony of car horns behind them, and a black SUV with darkened windows pulled alongside the cab, paused, then took off down Second Avenue, unfortunately getting caught at the next light.

Stone gave the driver his address and told him to continue downtown at his own pace. When they reached his house, he added a twenty-dollar tip to the fare, then got out of the cab.

As the taxi drove away the black SUV pulled up to where Stone stood, and the front-seat passenger window slid down. Todd Bacon sat in the car.

"That was cute," he said.

"Following my client around wasn't part of the deal," Stone said. "Tell Lance that if he does that again, Pablo will develop severe memory loss."

Bacon stared at him for a moment; then his window slid shut and the SUV drove away.

Stone let himself into the house feeling better.

42

At nine the following morning the group sat down. Stone spoke first, to Lance. "I sent you a message last night. Was it delivered?"

"It was," Lance replied.

"Do we have an understanding that all this nonsense will end as of this moment?"

Lance didn't speak right away.

"Or we can shut this down right now," Stone said.

"Pablo won't be followed," Lance said.

"I don't know what else you're cooking up, Lance, but I can tell you right now, I won't tolerate it."

"All *right*," Lance said through clenched teeth.

"Pablo," Stone said, "you may continue."

Pablo began recounting details of further arms sales. After a few minutes, Lance stopped him.

"The name you just gave us is not in our databases," Lance said.

Stone assumed that whoever was watching at Langley was running names through their computers and communicating with Lance through an earpiece.

"Often my buyers employ noms de guerre," Pablo said. "I do not always know their names."

"Describe the man you just mentioned," Lance said.

Pablo immediately gave a detailed description.

"Thank you," Lance said. "Proceed."

Pablo took up where he had left off.

At the end of the day Lance called Stone aside. "My technical people tell me that we are having gaps in the video and audio sent from your house," he said.

"Any of these gaps occur during Pablo's testimony?" Stone asked.

"Not so far."

"I am entitled to privacy in my own home and in my consultations with clients," Stone said. "Neither Pablo nor I signed up to have our private conversations recorded by your people."

"All right," Lance said, "but when this is over I am going to want to know how you did it. My people are driving me crazy."

"We'll see," Stone said.

On the third day of Pablo's testimony, the CIA team began asking a lot more questions, many of them very pointed, but Pablo always responded immediately and smoothly. At the end of the day Stone took Pablo into his library and employed Cantor's device.

"Pablo," Stone said, "are you beginning to withhold information in your answers to their questions?"

"I am not," Pablo said.

"I'm beginning to get the feeling that the people listening to us back at Langley have information about your activities that disagrees with your account of events, and they are communicating their doubts to Lance and his team."

Pablo shrugged. "Is it not common for those participating in events to have different versions of what happened?"

"Of course it is," Stone said. "I just want to be sure that you are not coloring events or altering them in such a way that the Agency is having doubts about your truthfulness."

"I can only tell them what *I* remember," Pablo said, "not what other sources may have told them."

"Quite right," Stone said. "Tomorrow, remember to bring your maps."

"There is only one map," Pablo replied.

That night at Elaine's, as Stone and Dino were having dinner, Bill Eggers of Woodman & Weld walked in and sat down.

"Good evening, Bill," Stone said, and Dino nodded.

"I am getting reports," Eggers said, "that doubt is

being cast on your client's veracity in the discussions you and he are having with Lance Cabot and his people."

"My client and I have sensed that belief in Lance and his people," Stone replied.

"Stone, it would not reflect well on Woodman & Weld if this project of yours turned out to be an embarrassment."

"Bill, I don't know how something you were never supposed to know about could possibly turn into an embarrassment, but let me tell you this: to the best of my knowledge, my client has answered truthfully every question put to him, and he intends to continue to do so."

"I hope you're right," Eggers said.

"Would you kindly explain to me how you and the firm became involved in this event?" Stone asked.

"We did not ask to be involved," Eggers replied. "Lance, for reasons of his own, decided to tell me certain things."

"For reasons of his own, indeed," Stone said. "What he is attempting to do is to put pressure on me, through you, to give him what he wants."

"Well, why don't you just give it to him?" Eggers asked.

"I and my client are giving Lance exactly what we told him we would, and for reasons of his own, as you put it, he is somehow dissatisfied. Or maybe he's just using the pressure from you as insurance. I would be grateful, Bill, if you would just tell Lance that you have every confidence that I am keeping my word."

"I have already told him that," Eggers said, "but he does not seem to be satisfied."

"I think that, after tomorrow, his level of satisfaction may rise," Stone said.

"Why do you think that?" Eggers asked.

"Because tomorrow, Pablo is going to give Lance a bonus, one that he is unlikely to want to discuss with you."

"And what is the bonus?"

"I can't tell you that, Bill; only Lance can, but don't expect him to."

"All right, Stone," Eggers said, rising, "but I have to tell you that Lance is a valued source of business referral to us, and I don't want you to do anything to queer that."

"I have no intention of doing so," Stone said, "but I have to say I'm surprised that Lance is sending you business."

"Rain is made from all parts of the sky," Eggers said, then left.

"This gets weirder and weirder," Dino said.

"I can't disagree with you."

"Are you doing something to make Lance think you and your client are lying to him?"

Stone shook his head. "Not deliberately, but Lance's

people have wired my house for sound and pictures, and Bob Cantor has seen to it that I have some control over what he sees and hears."

"I'm not sure I want to know what that means," Dino said.

43

Early the following morning Stone got a call from Bob Cantor.

"How's my little scrambler working out for you?" Cantor asked.

"I'll tell you how beautifully it's working," Stone said. "It's driving the Agency people absolutely nuts. They want to know how I'm doing it. Do you want me to tell them?"

"Funny you should mention that," Cantor replied. "My attorney is filing a patent this morning on two versions. You've got one; the other has two buttons: one for the frequency range of most bugs and one for the cell phone frequency range."

"Sounds great."

"It is, believe me. You tell the Agency people to get in touch with me, and I'll sell them preproduction units for twenty-five thousand bucks a pop, minimum order of twelve."

Stone whistled. "What will you sell the production models for?"

"We're aiming at thirty-five hundred bucks and going after the professional market first. Later, we'll market a consumer version for fifteen hundred. Tell the Agency people that the preproduction units I'm offering will allow them to adjust the frequency range on the bug scrambler. You can keep your copy, but don't give it to them; they'll just cannibalize it and clone it."

"Right," Stone said.

"How much longer are you meeting with these folks?"

"Today's the last day."

"Okay, I'll put everything on DVDs and have two copies for you ready tomorrow."

"Thanks, Bob."

Pablo was late arriving, only a couple of minutes ahead of Lance and his group. He was carrying a cardboard mailing tube under his arm.

"Here's how I want to work this," Stone said. "We'll give them the morning to continue grilling you; then immediately after lunch, we'll hand them their bonus. Once you've answered all their questions, excuse yourself to go to the john and get out the back way."

"Sounds good," Pablo said. "I'm going—"

Stone interrupted him. "I don't want to know where you're going or how," he said. "Wait a day or two, or when it's convenient, and give me a call. I'll bring you up to date on anything that's happened."

"There's something I should tell you," Pablo said. "The name they called me on—Mohammed X—the one they couldn't find in their files?"

"Yes?"

"He's the one who gave me this map." He held up the tube.

"Then please tell them that," Stone said. Joan buzzed him and said that everybody was waiting for them in the dining room.

Stone and Pablo went in and sat down at the table.

Lance began. "Pablo, let's revisit your mention of the nom de guerre Mohammed X."

"I'll tell you more about him after lunch," Pablo said, "but not until then."

"Why not until then?"

"You'll understand after lunch."

Lance sighed. "All right, but you're not getting out of here until I know everything you know about him."

"You will," Pablo said.

Pablo was now up to date on his recitation of events, so the questions fired at him before lunch were all about his previous statement, mostly clarifications.

Lunch was served where they sat, sandwiches and soup; then, when the dishes had been taken away,

Lance called the group to order again. "Now tell me about Mohammed X," he said to Pablo.

"Mohammed X is an underground arms dealer who claims to have excellent contacts inside the upper ranks of Al Qaeda and the Taliban, among other groups," Pablo replied.

"Have you sold him arms in the past?"

"No, I had met him on two occasions before . . . ah, accepting your invitation to come to the United States."

"When was the first time?"

"About three weeks ago. We had a long and alcoholic dinner in Mijas, a village up the mountain from my home in Marbella, and he dropped many heavy hints about his contacts."

"What did he tell you?"

"He told me that he had actually met Osama bin Laden, face-to-face, but he wouldn't tell me when."

"What else did he tell you on that occasion?"

"He told me that Al Qaeda and the Taliban were planning a large acquisition of small arms and antiaircraft missiles, which they intend to use against your unpiloted drones that are raining down Hellfire missiles on them. He asked if I would bid on their order. I told him I would need a detailed list of what they wanted, when and where they wanted it, and what they were prepared to pay."

"Did he give you the list?"

"He gave me that on the second occasion we met."

"When and where did that take place?"

"At my home, at lunch, on the day your people kid-napped me."

Pablo reached inside the mailing tube at his side and extracted two sheets of paper. He separated them and handed the smaller one to Lance. "This was his order. I had planned to fax it to your station chief in Madrid."

Lance looked at the list, then held it up to a camera for transmission to Langley. "And you expect me to believe that?" he asked.

"It's immaterial whether you believe it or not," Pablo said. He gave Lance a telephone number. "That is the fax line for your station chief."

"Did you bid on the weapons?"

"No. I told him I would, in due course, but I never had any intention of selling him the weapons. I think he believed I needed further convincing, so he gave me a very interesting piece of information."

"And what was that?"

"The longitude and latitude of the redoubt of Osama bin Laden."

The room became absolutely silent.

"Would you like to write down the coordinates?" Pablo asked.

Lance grabbed a pad. "Yes, please go ahead."

Pablo recited the numbers.

"My God," Holly Barker said.

"What?" Lance asked.

"It's Tora Bora, where he was almost caught before," she replied.

44

Lance looked skeptical. "That's just not possible," he said. "He wouldn't go back to the place where we nearly caught him."

"Well," Holly said, "certainly that's the last place we would look for him."

Pablo unrolled the map and weighted its corners. "Please look at the markings Mohammed X made on the map."

Lance and his party stood up to look, and a camera moved in on the map for a close-up.

"Mohammed made those markings. They're meant to outline roughly a series of caves in the mountains that have been joined over the past year. He says generators and heating equipment have been brought in, and they have made the place quite comfortable. He says bin Laden moved in several weeks ago."

"That is nonsense," Lance said. "Al Qaeda and the

Taliban have no helicopters or aircraft capable of making big drops into those mountains. There are no roads, only footpaths; and you could never get vehicles in there that could move that kind of weight."

"That's what the Johnson administration said about the Vietcong bringing supplies along the Ho Chi Minh Trail, using bicycles," Holly said.

"They have something much better than bicycles," Pablo said.

"Tell me," Lance replied.

"They have mules."

"Mules?" Lance asked. "Mules couldn't carry loads like that for any distance."

Todd Bacon spoke up for the first time. "I'm from West Virginia," he said, "and I can tell you something about mules. One animal can carry three hundred pounds all day, and they're more surefooted than any other animal."

"Mr. Bacon is quite correct," Pablo said.

"But we would have spotted them with satellites," Lance pointed out. "We can see things a lot smaller than mules."

"They cover each animal with camouflage material," Pablo said, "designed to blend in with the rocky terrain. The women in the nearby villages dye the cloth."

"And where would they get mules?" Lance asked.

"From us," Todd replied. "Back when Congressman Charlie Wilson was funding the Agency to arm the Taliban against the Russians, we flew in hundreds of mules, and they have long working lives."

"Mr. Bacon is correct again," Pablo said. "What's more, the Taliban have a breeding program to supply new animals."

"This is preposterous," Lance said, but he didn't sound very sure of himself.

"No, Lance," Holly said, "not only is it not preposterous, it's perfectly feasible, and it's just the sort of thing the Taliban would do."

"Let me tell you a little more of what Mohammed X told me," Pablo said. "There are half a dozen entrances to these caves, some of which he has marked, and dozens of air shafts for ventilation and escape. Fires are permitted only at night, when the smoke would not be detected. The caves are very deep, some leading more than a hundred feet below the mountains. They even have electric generators for powering lights and equipment."

"And on what fuel do they run?" Lance asked.

"Propane gas, transported in canisters by the mules. They have a large stockpile of them, bought in Pakistan."

"I want this Mohammed X found and brought in," Lance said.

"I'm afraid that won't be possible," Pablo replied. "I learned after arriving here that Mohammed X was run down by a hit-and-run driver in Marbella and killed instantly, shortly after our lunch that day. By that time I was on the way to meet your airplane and didn't know about it."

"Are you saying he was murdered?" Lance asked.

"I don't know, but it hardly matters, does it? Murder or accident, he's still dead."

"I want that checked out with the Marbella station of the national police," Lance said to no one in particular.

Pablo, who was standing, put a hand on his abdomen. "Will you excuse me for a moment, please?" he asked.

"There's a powder room off the kitchen, downstairs," Stone said, and Pablo left the room.

Lance had a hand on one ear, apparently listening to someone through an earpiece. He sat down, looking a little dazed.

"Something wrong, Lance?" Holly asked.

"On the contrary," Lance replied. "Our Afghan/Pakistan desk at Langley is saying that everything Pablo has told us is entirely feasible. The director has already ordered a satellite moved to the area."

"If Pablo is right," Holly said, "the satellite is not going to see very much. Apparently, they've been working on those caves for some time without being noticed."

"We'll see," Lance replied. "Where is Pablo?" he asked. "I have some more questions for him."

"I'll see," Stone said, then left the room. He went down to the kitchen and closed the door to the garden, then came back. "I'm afraid Pablo has left us," he said to Lance.

"Left us? What do you mean?"

"I mean he's no longer in the house. He has apparently decided to be somewhere else."

Lance pointed a finger across the table. "*You* did this, Stone. You set this up."

"I set up everything," Stone said, "but Pablo, naturally, has a mind of his own and your actions during the past few days have hardly filled him with confidence in you."

Lance turned to a technician. "Shut down video and audio," he said, then waited while the man flipped switches and disconnected cables.

"What are you so upset about, Lance?" Stone asked. "Pablo has given you an extraordinary amount of information this week about underground arms sales, and if he's right about Tora Bora, he's given you the greatest intelligence coup since missiles were found in Cuba."

"That remains to be seen," Lance said, gathering papers and packing his briefcase. He turned to Holly. "I want a chopper at the East Side Heliport in fifteen minutes," he said. "Full fuel. I'm not driving back to Langley, and I'm not taking the train, either. Holly, you come with me. Todd, you get yourself back to Newburgh and tend to your new charter business. I want a report soonest on the repairs to the C-17."

"Oh, Lance," Stone said, "I almost forgot. You asked about the jamming of your audio and video signals?"

"Yes?"

Stone held up the device. "This did the trick, and a

patent application was filed this morning. The inventor tells me he is able to furnish preproduction models that will also block cell phones at a cost of twenty-five thousand each, minimum order of twelve. He expects to be in production in about a year."

"Tell him I want two dozen," Lance said, then walked out the dining room door.

"Have a nice flight home!" Stone called after him.

45

Stone went downstairs to his office and flopped onto the sofa, drained. He was grateful that the marathon questioning of Pablo was over, and he doubted if he would hear from the man again. He took a deep breath and closed his eyes.

There was a rap on the door, followed by a familiar voice.

"Hey, Stone."

Stone didn't open his eyes. "Not now, Herbie, *please*."

"I think you're going to want to know this, Stone."

"All right," Stone said with a whimper, "tell me."

"The DA is investigating me."

Stone opened his eyes. *"What?"*

"No kidding. An investigator with the DA's office has been questioning my doorman about my comings and goings."

"Do you have any idea why they're interested in your comings and goings, Herbie?"

"No, and I don't understand it."

"Herbie, without giving me any details, have you been involved in anything that might even remotely resemble an illegal activity?"

"No, Stone," Herbie replied, sounding wounded. "I'm just living my life, that's all."

"Herbie, I'm going to tell you a secret that will transform your life, if you will only believe it."

"What's that, Stone?"

"If you're an honest man, you don't have to worry about being investigated. The DA can't find anything incriminating about you if you haven't done anything incriminating. Does that make any kind of sense to you?"

"Well, yeah, I guess."

"Do you believe what I just said?"

"Well, it's logical."

"No, Herbie, you have to believe in your heart that you are innocent, and then you will feel better. Work on that."

"Okay," Herbie said. "See you later."

"Please, God, no," Stone whispered to himself, closing his eyes again.

There was another rap on his office door. "Stone?"

"What is it, Joan?"

"One of those technicians from upstairs wants to do something to our telephones."

Stone thought about that for a moment. "Send him in, please." He tucked a pillow under his head and waited.

A man wearing a tool belt came in. "Mr. Barrington, I need to take a look at your office phones."

"Are you going to remove the bugs?"

"Well, sir, without acknowledging that there are any bugs on your phones, I would like to take a look at them. Only take a minute."

"All right, go ahead," Stone said.

The man went to Stone's desk and used a screwdriver to take the plastic top off the phone. There was a snipping sound; then he put the phone back together and repeated the process with the phone on the coffee table.

"Don't forget the secretary's phone," Stone said.

"Yes, sir."

"Did you do all the ones upstairs?"

"Yes, sir, all the way to the top of the house. The kitchen, too."

"Thank you."

The man went away, and Stone closed his eyes again and took a deep breath. The phone rang, and Joan came on the intercom. "A Willa Crane for you."

Stone picked up the phone. "Good afternoon, Willa."

"You sound tired," she said.

"I've just finished a four-day, ah, deposition," Stone replied.

"Oh, the one with the CIA?"

"I will not confirm or deny that."

"I will consider it confirmed, then."

"I'm afraid your boss is not going to make any cases from what transpired—unless he has extended his jurisdiction to Europe and the Middle East."

"He will be very disappointed to hear that," she said.

"In that case, you shouldn't tell him, but let Lance Cabot explain."

"Good idea. You free for dinner?"

"Sure. I should have recovered my health by then."

"Can we go to Elaine's?"

"Oh, you liked it there, did you?"

"It wasn't bad; I enjoyed the crowd."

"Okay, eight thirty at Elaine's?"

"See you there," she said, and hung up.

Stone closed his eyes and lay back. After what seemed only a moment later Joan spoke. "It's six thirty; I'm leaving."

Stone opened his eyes. "Six thirty? You're kidding."

"You've been out like a light."

Stone struggled to a sitting position. "I certainly have."

"A cold shower will bring you around."

"Brrrr," Stone said.

46

As Stone was leaving the house the phone rang. "Hello?"

"It's Dino. I can't make dinner; work."

"I'm devastated," Stone replied. "Have you gone off me?"

"Long, long ago," Dino replied, then hung up.

Stone walked into Elaine's to find his table uncharacteristically vacant. He sat down and accepted his usual Knob Creek, which the bartender had begun pouring as he was getting out of the cab.

Elaine came over and sat down. "So, where's Dino?"

"He's not going to make it tonight."

"Is he in the hospital? We could send flowers."

"He *says* he's working."

"That means he's eating somewhere else. If it's at Elio's, I'll kill him." Elio's, a rival restaurant down

Second Avenue, had been started by an old headwaiter of hers many years before.

"How would you know?" Stone asked, forgetting for a moment that Elaine always knew everything.

"I have spies."

"You are conducting a spying campaign against Elio's?"

"I don't have to; people tell me things. You tell Dino to watch himself." She got up and moved to another table.

Willa had not yet arrived, so Stone got out his phone and called Dino.

"Bacchetti."

"If you're at Elio's, you're a dead man."

"So that's what she thinks?"

"She says she has spies."

"I'm at work."

"You'd better have witnesses." Stone hung up, chuckling.

Willa breezed through the door wearing a long sheepskin coat. A waiter hung it up for her. "Whatever he's having," she said to him, then sat down.

"What good taste in whiskey you have," Stone said, kissing her as her drink arrived.

"Same to ya," she said, raising her glass and knocking half of it back.

"Tough day at the office, huh?"

"You could say that," she said with a deep sigh. "How about you? You sounded wasted when I called."

"Last day of my, ah, deposition. A lot of tension had built up, for various reasons. I was letting it all out when you and half a dozen other people interrupted my sweet reverie."

"Sorry about that."

"One of those who interrupted was a client of mine, name of Herbie Fisher. He says your office is investigating him."

Willa appeared to choke on her bourbon. "Listen," she said hoarsely, coughing and clearing her throat, "I am *not* investigating Herbert Fisher."

"In that case, you should tell your investigators to be more subtle when questioning the doormen in his building."

"Stone, I tell you again, *I* am not investigating Herbert Fisher."

"Ah, then it's some other enthusiastic but judgment-impaired law-school dropout in your office, is it?"

"I cannot comment on that. I can tell you only that *I* am not investigating Herbert Fisher, and neither, to the best of my knowledge, is anyone else in my office."

Stone peered at her narrowly. "That sounded like an almost complete denial," he said. "Let's discuss that 'to the best of my knowledge' part."

"It means what it says," she replied, sinking the rest of her drink.

Stone waved for another for both of them. "Somebody in your office is investigating Herbie?"

"To the best of my knowledge, no."

"Stop saying that! You're a deputy DA. Don't you know *everything* that goes on in your office, or are you pleading incompetence?"

"I am *highly* competent," she replied through clenched teeth, "but I do not know *everything* that goes on in our office *all the time*. Is that clear enough for you?"

"As through a glass, darkly," Stone replied. "Let's take this down a level to the rumor category. What have you *heard* about one or more ADAs in your office investigating Herbie Fisher?"

She took a gulp of her second bourbon and faced him. "Let me ask you another question, and please give me a *precise* answer."

"Shoot."

"Are you now representing or have you ever represented *anyone* in the immediate or extended family of Herbert Fisher?"

Stone thought for a moment about what that question might mean. "You're investigating his *wife*?"

"Answer my question, if you want to go on talking about this."

"No, I am not now nor have I ever represented anyone in the immediate or extended family of Herbie Fisher."

"Yes," she said.

"Yes, what?"

"Yes is the answer to your question."

Stone struggled to remember what his question was

and finally remembered. "Investigating his wife for what?" he asked.

"I warn you, this is the last question on this subject I will answer. Got that?"

"Got it."

"Here's my answer: I cannot tell you."

"What kind of answer is that?" Stone asked.

"An honest one. Please accept it."

"I accept it."

"And please know that this conversation is entirely confidential."

"Wait a minute," Stone said, "you can't say that after the fact; it has to be before."

"I am not a newspaper reporter interviewing you and promising to keep your name confidential."

"That doesn't matter."

"Let me put it this way," Willa said. "This and any other conversation you and I have had on the subject of Herbert Fisher or any member of his immediate or extended family is *entirely* confidential. Got that?"

"But—"

"Either you've got that, or I'll pay for my two drinks and leave immediately, never to be heard from again. And you'd better not take too long to think about it."

Stone thought about it instantly. "Got it. Would you like another drink?"

"I haven't finished my second one," she said. "Are you trying to get me drunk? Because if you are, I should tell you that three drinks isn't going to do it, since I'm not driving, and drinking will have no effect on my memory of the details of our conversation."

Stone handed her a menu. "Let's order dinner," he said.

47

Stone awoke suddenly. He was in a strange bed, completely disoriented, his head throbbing. He sat up on his elbows and looked around, trying to remember the evening before.

He needed to go to the toilet badly. He swung his legs over the side of the bed and fell out, having missed the set of steps provided for the purpose. Was the bed a foot higher than standard, or was he hallucinating?

He got to his feet and saw a note on the bedside table.

Some of us have to go to work. There's coffee made.

Stone made it to the john, peed, and splashed water on his face. He avoided looking in the mirror and went back to the bedroom to get dressed. This involved a scavenger hunt for the various items of his clothing. One by one he located everything but one sock, which was nowhere to be found no matter how hard he looked.

He put on his shoes and stumbled into the kitchen. There was a brown liquid in an electric coffeemaker on the kitchen counter, but he didn't like the smell. Must be decaf, he thought. He needed the high-test. He switched off the coffeepot, found his overcoat on the living room floor with his necktie in a pocket, and let himself out. A woman on the elevator smiled brightly at him.

"Good morning!" she said with enthusiasm.

"Good," he replied, trying to smile. "Good morning."

Her smile faded. "Do you have flu symptoms?" The city was in the grip of rumors of a new strain of the virus.

Stone thought about that. "No, I have hangover symptoms."

She fled the elevator at the first opportunity.

Stone stepped out of the building into sunlight like a thousand strobe lights. Shielding his eyes with a forearm, he stepped into the street and was nearly run down by a cab.

"You looking for a ride, buddy, or just suicide?" the cabbie yelled through his open window.

Stone struggled into the backseat and gave him the address. "What street are we on?" he asked.

"East Seventy-ninth," the cabbie replied. "It's the big one with all the cars."

As the cab neared his house, Stone took mental inventory of the previous evening's events. He seemed to remember some sort of drinking contest with Willa, which he had, apparently, lost. How many drinks did it take to make him feel this way?

He stuffed money into the pass-through of the driver's bulletproof shield and spilled himself into the gutter in front of his house. He looked at the front steps and decided against, instead taking the steps down to his office door.

"Good morning!" Joan said from her office as he passed.

"No need to shout," Stone said as he stumbled toward his own office. He decided to rest on his sofa for a moment before trying to find the elevator.

Joan shook him awake. "It's ten thirty," she said. "Are you working or doing anything at all today?"

Stone sat up. He found he was still wearing his overcoat.

"Mr. Herbert Fisher to see you," Joan said.

Stone got to his feet. "Tell him to come back tomorrow, and tell Helene to send some toast and coffee upstairs." He looked around for the elevator door.

"Why are you wearing only one sock?" Joan asked.

Stone raised a hand. "Not now."

"I don't think I saw that recommended in the Styles section of the *Times*," she said.

Stone got into the elevator. "I don't want to hear from you before one o'clock," he said. "Maybe not even then." The elevator doors closed, and he pressed his back against the wall to steady himself.

He got to his dressing room, emptied his pockets, and stuffed all his clothes into the two bins, one for laundry, the other for dry cleaning. He hung up his overcoat and his necktie.

He stood under a hot shower for two minutes, then got into a terry robe and made his way to the dumb-waiter, where his toast and coffee awaited; then he put the electric bed into the sitting position, ate and drank and pulled the *Times* into his lap and tried to read the front page.

"Stone." Joan's voice came from the speakerphone. "It's one thirty; you asked me to wake you."

Stone jerked awake, still in a sitting position, with a sore neck from sleeping with his chin on his chest. He pressed the button on the phone. "Forget I asked you," he said.

"Nighty-night," she replied, and switched off.

Stone pressed the FLAT button on the bed's remote, shucked off the robe and crawled under the covers, brushing aside the unread newspaper.

The phone began ringing, and nobody was picking it up. He reached for the TALK button. "Hello."

"You sound like shit," Dino said. "Are you sick or something?"

"That's what Elaine asked about you last night," Stone replied. "At least, I think it was last night."

"Are you coming?"

"Coming where?"

"To dinner. At Elaine's."

"What time is it?"

"Nine o'clock."

"I don't think I'm going to make it. Remember me to Madame."

"You want a doctor? I know a guy who makes house calls."

"Not unless he can bring along a new head," Stone said. "Gotta run." He hung up. Suddenly he was ravenously hungry, but Helene was gone for the day. He got into his robe and slippers and made his way downstairs to the kitchen.

The refrigerator was oddly bare, containing only a box from Domino's, which held three slices of desiccated pizza. He sprinkled some water on them and put them into the microwave for two minutes, while he looked for something to drink. There was, mercifully, a single Heineken in the refrigerator door shelf. He drank half of it in a gulp, burped, and attacked the pizza.

He went back upstairs and found that he was now wide awake and surprisingly un-hungover. The phone rang.

"Hello?"

"I found your sock in the bed," Willa said.

"Where in the bed?"

"Down at the bottom under the covers. I didn't know you wore cashmere socks."

"Hang on to it for me, will you?"

"I may hang it on the wall, like a pelt."

Stone managed a chuckle.

"You know, after a wild night of sex, a girl is supposed to get a phone call from the guy, thanking her."

"I am remiss," Stone said. "Thank you so much."

"You're welcome. I'm surprised to find you at home."

"I think I'm supposed to be having dinner with Dino. He called earlier."

"You slept all day, didn't you?"

"Uh, most of it."

"Did you get any dinner?"

"Leftover pizza and a beer."

"Ugh."

"Did you do any better?"

"A greasy hamburger and some cheap wine in the conference room. Standard work-late fare. Are you still hungover?"

"Oddly, no."

"A hangover never lasts past dinner. Want me to come over?"

"Yes, please."

And she did.

48

Stone woke at his usual hour with Willa's head on his shoulder. He disengaged from her as gently as possible, then performed his ablutions in the bathroom. When he returned, Willa was sitting up in bed, bare-breasted, with the TV on.

"Breakfast, if you please," she said.

"Of course. May I take your order?"

"Whatever you're having," she replied.

"You're becoming more and more agreeable," he said.

"About the bourbon—after yesterday I think I would throw up if I even smelled it again."

"Too much of a good thing?"

"Way too much."

"I hope you don't feel the same way about scrambled eggs, bacon, and English muffin," he said.

"I love all of them."

Stone called Helene, and she sent breakfast up on the dumbwaiter.

Then the TV screen went dark, and the words BREAKING NEWS appeared.

"This just in to NBC News," a young woman was saying. "American air forces are engaged in heavy bombing in the Tora Bora region, southeast of Kabul, in Afghanistan. Sources tell NBC that thousand-pound penetrating bombs are being dropped on what may be a network of caves in the mountains there, and there is speculation that the target may be Osama bin Laden." She began to relate the history of U.S. action in that region of the country.

"You think they got him?" Willa asked, taking a bite of her muffin.

"I hope so," Stone said.

Joan buzzed him. "Pablo for you."

Stone picked up the phone. "Pablo?"

"Yes," he replied. "Have you seen the news?"

"I'm looking at it right now."

"So am I," Pablo replied.

"Do I want to know where you are?"

"Just as well not, I think."

"If this works, you could be a hero."

"Nonsense. If it works, my name will never be mentioned. At least, I hope not."

Suddenly an old photograph of Pablo appeared on the TV.

"Sources at the CIA are telling us that this man,

Pablo Estancia, was the source of the intelligence placing Osama bin Laden at Tora Bora. Born Erwin Gelbhardt, in Darmstadt, Germany, he acquired the nickname 'Pablo' as an international arms dealer. We are also told that agents of the CIA interviewed him for four days earlier this week and that he provided a map of the cave network where bin Laden is supposedly hiding."

"Oh, shit," Pablo said. "Did you hear that?"

"Apparently, we're both watching NBC," Stone said.

"Yes, I suppose we are. Why on earth would Lance Cabot air this information?"

"I suppose they must be very confident that bin Laden is there," Stone suggested.

"But why bring me into it?" Pablo asked plaintively. "Now they've pinned a big target on my back."

"I have no idea," Stone said.

"It's some sort of revenge," Pablo said.

"Revenge for what?"

"I've no idea," Pablo said. "I have to go, Stone. My family is arriving this afternoon, and I have to get them to somewhere safe."

"Is there anything I can do to help, Pablo?"

"No, I don't think so. Don't blame yourself for this, Stone." He hung up.

"Well," Willa said, "that was a very interesting conversation—at least, your side of it."

"Try and forget you heard it," Stone said.

"That was your man, huh? Your client?"

Stone nodded. "He's been royally screwed, and I don't know what I can do about it."

The phone rang again. "Hello?"

"It's Holly. Have you seen the reports?"

"Right now," Stone said. "Has Lance lost his mind?"

"He's losing it right now," Holly replied. "I know you won't believe this, but Lance didn't do this. I think it's somebody at the Agency who has it in for Lance."

"I would imagine their numbers are legion," Stone said.

"Lance is more popular here than you would imagine," she said. "Somebody's head is going to roll for this."

Stone had an idea. "Listen, I think you ought to offer Pablo protection, find him a hiding place and put guards on him."

"That's an idea I wouldn't argue with, and I don't think Lance would, either, but he'd have to go to the director for funding; he doesn't have that kind of discretion. Between you and me, I was astonished when Lance ordered two dozen of those jammers at twenty-five thousand a pop. And the kind of protection you're talking about would cost hundreds of thousands."

"Talk to Lance and get back to me."

"Are you in touch with Pablo?"

"No, but he's in touch with me. He called five minutes ago, having seen the news reports. His family are arriving today at wherever he is, and of course he's very concerned about their safety."

"I'll talk to Lance," she said, and hung up.

Willa was staring at him. "This is like being in the middle of a spy novel."

"I want your word you will not speak of this to anyone," Stone said.

"Do you think I'm an idiot? I don't want to be involved; I'm just fascinated to hear about it."

"Don't you have to go to work?"

"It's Saturday," she pointed out, "but if you want me out of here, say the word."

He kissed her on the neck. "No, I don't want you out of here."

"Who's going to call next?" Willa asked.

"I've no idea."

The phone rang. "Hello?"

"It's Herbie."

Stone was silent.

"Are you feeling better?"

"Yes, thanks, and I can't talk right now," Stone replied.

"Okay. Can I call you later?"

"Make it Monday," Stone said, and hung up.

"And who was that?" Willa asked.

"A client, unrelated to anything on the news."

Willa set her tray on the floor and cuddled up to him. "Let me take your mind off all this."

"I don't think you can," Stone said.

But she could, and did.

49

Joan buzzed again, and Stone picked up the phone. "Why are you in on Saturday morning?" he asked, panting from his exertions with Willa.

"Never look a gift horse in the mouth," she replied. "Holly Barker on line one."

Stone picked up the phone. "Yes, Holly?"

"I figured out who gave Pablo's name to the press," she said.

"And who would that be?"

"Todd Bacon."

"Your acolyte? The new CEO of your new air transport company?"

"One and the same."

"Why would he do such a thing?"

"I think he's angry at Pablo over the thing with the flying Mercedes. He had planned the whole operation;

then, at the moment it was about to come to fruition, Pablo ruined it for him."

"Have you confronted him?"

"Lance is doing that right now, and he's better at those things than I."

"I hope he tears a strip off his hide," Stone said.

"I think he'll do more than that," Holly said. "I think Lance is angry enough to fire him. Hang on a minute, will you?"

Stone hung on.

"More spy stuff?" Willa asked, brushing her mussed hair out of her eyes.

Holly came back on before Stone could reply. "Okay, it's done. Todd Bacon is off immediately to man a radio listening post in the Aleutian Islands, off Alaska."

"The perfect place for him," Stone said.

"I have to agree," Holly replied. "There's a fly in the ointment, though."

"What's that?"

"I have to go up to Newburgh and get the air cargo thing running smoothly while Lance looks for somebody else to run it."

"For how long?"

"For as long as it takes," she said. "I suppose there are worse assignments, but it does take me away from the center of the action. It's Lance's way of telling me that I should have somehow prevented Pablo's automotive aviation event. This is going to drive my boyfriend crazy."

"Then you'd better get it up and running smoothly fast."

"Oh, and Lance is going to the director about funding for protection for Pablo."

"May I make a suggestion?"

"Yes."

"Hire Strategic Services; protection is what they do best."

"What a good idea! I have to go tell Lance. Goodbye!"

Stone hung up.

"Did you finish?" Willa asked.

"My conversation?"

"No, what we were doing. Did you finish?"

"Sort of, but I was interrupted."

"I didn't finish," she said.

"And that's my cue, isn't it?"

"You should be on the stage," she said, lying back and offering him access.

Stone made his entrance.

Stone and Willa appeared at Elaine's, on schedule, freshly showered and clothed. Mike Freeman was sitting with Dino at their table.

Stone introduced Willa, and they sat down. Bourbon was brought for both of them, and Willa did not pass out from the smell of it.

"I gather you spoke to Holly Barker earlier today," Mike said in a low voice.

"It's all right, Mike; Willa was there, and she's trust-worthy."

"I have a team assembled," Mike said, "but I don't know where to send them or how to transport them."

"I'm afraid I have to wait to hear from Pablo," Stone said. "This is strictly one-way communication."

"Oh, well," Mike said. "They can't blame us if somebody gets to him before we do."

Mike's cell phone buzzed, and he answered. "Freeman."

He listened for a moment. "I'm with Stone now; we have to wait for him to call. I'll get back to you." He hung up. "Holly," he said.

"Lance is nervous," Stone said.

"Let's see if we can figure this out," Mike said. "When Pablo called, did you get a caller ID number?"

"No, his phone was blocked. It was probably a cell phone, though; that's how we communicated before."

"And you don't know where he called from?"

"Now that you mention it, when he called we were both apparently watching the same broadcast on NBC, so he must be in the country. He also said that his family was arriving, so they must be coming from Europe."

"Did he say anything about an airline or an airport?"

"No, but he told me when we first met that he has a Gulfstream Five jet."

"Not that many of those in the air at a given moment," Mike said. He made a call. "I want reports on all G-Fives landing anywhere in the U.S. in the past twelve hours," he said. "I don't know how many passengers, but there would be at least one woman and some children—I don't know how many or how old. Maybe some staff and security, too. Call me." He hung up. "All right, my people are on it. Let's see if we can narrow the search."

They ordered dinner.

"Willa," Mike said, "what do you do?"

"Deputy DA," Willa replied.

"Where?"

"Manhattan."

"Ah."

"What does that mean, 'Ah'?" she asked.

"It means you're very important," Mike replied. "Not many deputy DAs."

"Four," she said. "One for admin, three others to supervise ADAs."

"I'll bet you get the juiciest cases," Mike said.

"Sometimes."

"You're awfully closemouthed," he said.

"I told you, she's trustworthy," Stone pointed out.

Mike's cell phone rang. "Freeman." He listened. "Good work," he said. "Arrange transport, four cars." He hung up.

"Did they find it?"

"Took off from Lucerne, Switzerland, this afternoon, their time. Landed six hours ago, guess where?"

"I give up."

"Newburgh, New York, Stewart International."

"So they're in New York," Stone said.

"Or its environs," Mike pointed out.

"All we need now is to hear from Pablo," Stone said.

"And soon," Mike replied. "If we can figure out where he landed, so can other people."

50

S tone and Willa were getting ready for bed when his
bedside phone rang. "Hello?"

"It is I," Pablo said.

"I'm glad you called. I need to know where you are."

"Why do you need to know?"

"Because the Agency has agreed to offer you security, in the form of contract professionals from Strategic
Services, and they need to know where to find you."

"How did you know I'm in the country?"

"It's possible to track jets, even without a tail number, if they're G-Fives. You landed at Stewart International."

"If you can know that, others can, too."

"That's very astute of you, Pablo, and all the more
reason for you and your family to be guarded as soon
as possible."

"I don't want to name my location on the phone," Pablo said.

"All right, e-mail me, and give me your phone number."

"I'll text your cell," Pablo replied.

"They need to know exactly where you are: an address."

"I'll meet them somewhere. I want to see them before I let them near my family."

"Pablo, Strategic Services is a world leader in personal security. I know the CEO well, and I recommended them to the Agency. You can trust them."

"I still want to meet them somewhere, and I'd like for you to be there, too. I don't believe I've used up the retainer I paid you."

"Pablo, give me a hint where you'd like to meet."

"All right. Litchfield County, Connecticut."

"Good. I have a house there, and that's where we'll meet."

"All right."

Stone gave him the address of his house.

"I know a house called The Rocks. Is that it?"

"Next door, much smaller house; used to be the gatehouse for The Rocks."

"What time?"

"I have to drive up from New York. Noon?"

"All right."

"Pablo, are you armed?"

"Yes."

"Don't shoot at anybody."

"You arrive first, then the others."

"That's good. Now, give me your cell number."

"There's no point. That area is a dead zone for cells."

Stone sighed. "See you at noon tomorrow." They both hung up.

"You're going up to Connecticut?" Willa asked.

"Yes. Would you like to come?"

"Yes," she replied.

Stone called Mike Freeman.

"Freeman."

"It's Stone. Pablo called, and we can meet him at noon tomorrow at my house in Washington, Connecticut."

"Good. Where is it?"

Stone gave him the address. "He wants me to arrive first, then the others. I suggest you have all four of your cars wait at the filling station in Washington Depot."

"All right," Mike said. "By the way, Lance has provided us with a safe house. It's on Lake Waramaug, in Litchfield County. Do you know it?"

"Yes. Is it Lance's brother's house?"

"That's right. Do you know him?"

"He was a client for a while."

"He's away, but there's a housekeeper."

"Sounds good."

"I'll see you tomorrow," Mike said.

"Do you want to ride with me?"

"Sure."

"Where do you live?"

"The Dakota; Seventy-second and Central Park West."

"I'll see you at ten a.m." They hung up.

"Such intrigue!" Willa said, snuggling up.

Stone stopped in front of the Dakota, a huge apartment house built late in the 1880s, and Mike Freeman came out carrying an overnight bag. Stone popped the trunk, Willa got in the rear seat, and Mike got in up front.

"Go," he said.

Stone went.

"How long a drive?"

"An hour and forty-five minutes," Stone said. "Maybe less on a Sunday morning."

Stone drove into the village ten minutes early.

"Let's go down to the Depot and make sure my people are there," Mike said.

Stone drove down the long hill into Washington Depot, and they found four black SUVs parked at the filling station, which was closed.

"God, Mike, it looks like the president's in town!" Stone said.

"You have a point," Mike replied. "Next time we order vehicles we'll go for varied colors." He got out of Stone's car, talked with one of his men, then got back in. "Okay; they'll follow us in five minutes."

"That's good," Stone said. He drove back up the hill and turned onto Kirby Road. As he turned into his driveway there was no sign of another car. "Everybody wait here," Stone said, then got out and looked around. He went to his front door, unlocked it and looked around again. Pablo was strolling through his front gate.

Pablo shook Stone's hand. "Who are the people in your car?" he asked.

"Mike Freeman, CEO of Strategic Services, whom you met on the C-17, and a friend of mine, Willa Crane. There are four cars parked down the hill; they're five minutes behind us. Where is your family?"

"At the Mayflower Inn," Pablo replied.

"How many in your party?"

"My wife, two servants, and two security. I have an appointment tomorrow morning with an estate agent to look at houses to rent."

"That won't be necessary," Stone said. "The Agency is providing a very comfortable house for you. It's well located for security. Shall we pick up your people?"

"They're packed and ready," Pablo said. "I have two rental cars."

The four black SUVs drove up and stopped in the road. "Here we go," Stone said, opening the rear door for Pablo, who got in beside Willa.

Stone drove to the Mayflower, and Pablo went inside. A moment later he and his party emerged, and porters put their luggage into two station wagons; then Stone led the way to Lake Waramaug.

Mike was on a two-way radio to his cars. "Two cars ahead of us," he said, and Stone slowed so that they could pass. "I'll direct you."

Stone noticed that Mike was searching both sides of the road with his eyes the rest of the way.

51

They drove the five miles to Lake Waramaug, a large natural lake north of Washington, and down the north side to a driveway marked only by a mailbox. The seven cars, including Stone's, filled the parking area at the house.

A man came outside from the house. "Mr. Barrington?" he asked, looking around.

"I'm Stone Barrington." He shook the man's hand.

"My name is Robert. My wife, Jane, and I run the place. Mr. Cabot is on a buying trip in Europe, but he told me to make the entire property available to you, except for the master suite and the workshop, both of which are secured." Robert looked around. "How many of you are there?" he asked.

"How many beds do you have available?" Stone asked.

"Fourteen, in seven bedrooms, including the guest-house."

Stone counted noses. "Mike, we're okay on numbers, unless you're staying."

"For a night or two," Mike replied.

"You can use my house, then."

"Thank you, Stone." He turned to his men. "Get your luggage inside; then I want a by-the-square-foot search of the property for any possible security risk." The men moved to their work.

"These people are Mr. and Mrs. Gelbhardt," Stone said to Robert. "They are the principal guests. Can you please show them to the best available room?"

"This way," Robert said, then led them into the house. Stone, Willa, and Mike followed and waited in the large living room.

"You say Barton Cabot was once your client," Mike said. "No more? A falling-out?"

"Nothing like that," Stone replied. "Our business was successfully concluded; we remain on cordial terms. Bart is an antiques dealer."

"I've researched him thoroughly," Mike said. "I think this is a perfect safe house for our purposes."

"It's quite a place, isn't it?" Stone said. "It's a pity you can't see Bart's workshop. He builds eighteenth-century American antiques out there."

Mike laughed. "You mean, like those factories in South America that turn out pre-Columbian art?"

"Yes, except Bart's pieces are handmade from old mahogany with the same hand tools that were employed at the time. The pieces are indistinguishable from the real thing, believe me."

Mike's cell phone rang. "It works here!" he said, surprised. "Freeman." He listened for a moment. "Good afternoon, Lance. May I put you on speaker so Stone can hear you?" Mike pressed a button and put the phone on the coffee table.

"Good afternoon, Stone," Lance said.

"Good afternoon, Lance."

"Is anyone else with you?"

"Yes, my friend Willa Crane, deputy district attorney in the Manhattan office."

"How do you do, Ms. Crane?" Lance said.

"I'm very well," Willa replied.

"Ms. Crane, do you have a federal security clearance?"

"I did when I worked for the U.S. attorney, some years ago."

"Please hold." Lance put them on hold for a couple of minutes, then returned. "I have authorized the reinstatement of your clearance, which had expired," he said. "I thought I might as well, because if you are where you are, you already know more than a civilian should."

"Thank you for your trust, Mr. Cabot," Willa said.

"Are you all settled in, Mike?" Lance asked.

"Happening now," Mike replied. "Within the hour

my people will have surveyed the environment and taken appropriate actions to deal with any anomalies."

"I'm pleased to hear that," Lance said. "I'm sure Barton's people will make you all comfortable."

"Pablo has brought some of his own people to help out," Mike replied.

"Lance," Stone said, "have you any news of what's happened at Tora Bora?"

"Mostly what you've seen on the news," Lance said. "But I can tell you that the cave system is pretty much pulverized. Anyone still alive there won't be for long and is beyond rescue."

"Is there any news of the principal target?" Mike asked.

"Our intelligence is conflicting," Lance replied. "Maybe there, maybe not. At the very least we've destroyed his formidable refuge."

"That's a start," Mike said.

"You might tell Pablo that."

"He and his wife are resting, I think."

"Any children?"

"They are apparently elsewhere."

"Do you have enough people there, or too many?"

"I'll know later today, and I'll report back to you."

"Your cell has captured this number, I'm sure. Call me back here." Lance hung up.

"Who is Lance?" Willa asked.

"Lance Cabot is the deputy director for operations

of the CIA," Mike replied. "Apart from the director, probably the most powerful figure there."

"Oh," Willa replied, looking impressed.

A young man entered the room. "Excuse me, Mike."

"Yes?"

"I've done a walk-around, and we're in good shape. There is a boat dock that will need covering, as will the whole of our shoreline. We're on a peninsula that juts out into the lake. We're starting our by-the-square-foot inspection now."

"Good," Mike replied, and the young man left.

"Mike," Stone said, "I don't think there's any more we can do here." He handed Mike a key. "Here's the key to the house." He gave him the security code. "We'll head on back to the city now."

Mike's cell rang again. "Yes, Lance?" He pressed the SPEAKER button.

"Mike, I wanted you to know that the NSA has detected a great deal of chatter in the air around the Middle East since the bombing at Tora Bora, and Pablo's name has been mentioned several times, and not in a complimentary way."

"Well," Mike said, "it looks as though we've made the right moves to secure Pablo's safety. That was a good call on your part."

"You may thank Stone for his insistence on that point," Lance replied. "I'll let you know if we pick up anything more specific."

"Thank you, Lance," Mike said, but Lance was gone.

52

Stone and Willa were halfway back to New York when his cell came alive. He pressed the SPEAKER button on the dash. "Hello?"

"It's Joan. I just left the house after doing some work and there are two men on the block I don't like the look of."

"Describe them."

"Young, Mediterranean-looking, very fit."

"Now, don't get all excited," Stone said, laughing.

"Ha-ha," she said.

"Please call Bob Cantor and ask him to put a couple of men at or near the house. Tell them not to shoot anybody, but I don't want the house burned to the ground, either."

"Will do. When are you coming home?"

Stone glanced at his watch: "An hour or so."

"Do you want me to wait for Bob's people?"

"No, go on home. All this weekend work of yours is beginning to worry me. Am I in some kind of trouble?"

"Usually, but not at the moment," she replied, and hung up.

"You're very fortunate to have Joan," Willa said. "Ask her if she'd like to work in the DA's office, will you?"

"I most certainly will not," Stone replied. "Anyway, she'd be bored rigid down there."

"Gee, I'm not," Willa said.

As Stone turned onto the block, he saw Willie Leahy, one of Cantor's men, on the other side of the street. He slowed and opened his window. "Any problems?" Stone asked.

"The problems have departed," Willie replied.

"Under their own steam?" Stone inquired.

"An ambulance was not necessary," Willie said. "We'll see if any other problems come to take their place."

"Thanks, Willie. Use the kitchen for your breaks."

"How long you want us on, Stone?"

"If no one has turned up by noon tomorrow, then stand down. And don't work straight through; make Bob send some relief."

"You bet your ass," Willie said, then turned back to his work.

"Do you always have armed security on tap?" Willa asked. "I saw the bulge under his arm."

"From time to time; it's not a regular thing, but

sometimes I sleep better with Willie and his brother, Peter, around."

Stone turned into the garage and closed the door behind him. "Stay for dinner," he said to Willa.

"You talked me into it," she replied.

Stone had just deposited their bags in his bedroom when the phone rang. "Hello?"

"It's Cantor. Willie got photos of the two men on your house and e-mailed them to me."

"Were you able to ID them?"

"No, but I sent them to a few people, and I just got a hit from one of them. They're Israeli."

"*Israeli?* What the hell?"

"And not just Israeli, but Mossad, their secret intelligence service. Both are attached to their UN Mission here."

"Okay, I'm baffled."

"Me, too. Have you been making anti-Semitic remarks lately?"

Stone laughed. "Of course not; I'd have you to deal with, and you're worse than the Mossad."

"Just checking."

"I don't suppose there's any way to find out why they're here."

"Well, we could ask them, but I don't think they would tell us. See you later."

"What's that about Israelis?" Willa asked.

"The two men that were watching the house are Mossad."

"This gets more exotic by the hour," she said.

"Too exotic for me," Stone replied. He dialed Pablo's cell number.

"Yes?" Pablo said warily.

"It's Stone."

"I'm surprised my phone works."

"Me, too. Two men have been spotted watching my house, and a trusted source tells me they're Mossad. You know anything about that?"

"I've done business with Israel many times, and on a few occasions with Mossad."

"Have you annoyed them lately?"

"I make it a point not to annoy my customers," Pablo replied.

"Well, they're not looking for *me*," Stone said. "I've never had anything to do with either Israel or the Mossad. It's gotta be you."

"I'll make a couple of calls tonight and see what I can come up with," Pablo said.

"Just in case somebody's listening," Stone said, "would you mention that you're not at my house?"

Pablo laughed. "Of course." He hung up.

So did Stone. "I've got some steaks in the fridge," he said to Willa, "and I make a mean risotto. Dinner here okay?"

"More than okay," she said, kissing him.

They were having dinner in the kitchen when the phone rang. Stone got up and answered it. "Hello?"

"Mr. Stone Barrington?"

"Yes."

"My name is Aaron Beck. I am with the Israeli UN Mission."

"Yes?"

"I wish to apologize for the presence of our people near your house this afternoon. I realize they must have caused you some anxiety."

"I think my friends may have caused your men some anxiety."

"I wonder if I might invite you to lunch tomorrow to discuss this situation."

"How good a lunch are we talking about?" Stone asked.

"Would the Four Seasons Grill suffice?"

"It would suffice very nicely," Stone replied. "What time?"

"One o'clock?"

"See you there, Mr. Beck." Stone hung up.

"Now what?" Willa asked.

"Now the Mossad wants to have lunch at the Four Seasons," Stone replied.

"One thinks of the Israelis as being very economical," Willa observed.

"Don't worry; I'm not picking up the check," Stone said.

53

Stone sent Willa off to work the following morning, then went down to his office.

Joan buzzed him. "Herbert Fisher on line one."

Stone sighed. "Tell him I'm busy, to call me late this afternoon."

"Right," Joan said.

Stone worked through the morning, then walked up to the Seagram Building and entered the Four Seasons. At the top of the stairway he stopped and looked around. A man at the bar to his right got up and came toward him.

"Mr. Barrington?"

"Mr. Beck?"

They shook hands, and the maître d' seated them between the tables of Henry Kissinger and the literary agent and attorney Morton Janklow.

"Good table," Stone observed. "Do you come here a lot?"

"Only when the expense account allows," Beck replied. "The table is usually occupied by our ambassador, who is away."

"I'm surprised that the expense accounts of the Mossad extend to the Four Seasons," Stone said.

Beck froze for half a second, then managed a small smile. "I must relate your observation to the Mossad, the next time I encounter them."

"Come on, Mr. Beck," Stone said, "I know who you are. This conversation will probably go better if we don't try to bullshit each other."

A captain came with the menus, and Stone ordered the Dover sole, his favorite fish. Beck ordered a large salad. Stone thought the sole must have used up most of the expense account for the day. Stone ordered a glass of Chardonnay; Beck stuck with the mineral water already on the table.

"I will not challenge your assumption," Beck said after the waiter had taken their order and left them alone.

"What can I do for you, Mr. Beck?" Stone asked.

"Please call me Aaron, and may I call you Stone?"

"Of course."

"Israelis are an informal people," Beck said.

"If you say so," Stone replied. "I don't suppose I've met more than two or three Israelis in my life."

"You've led a sheltered life," Beck said, smiling.

"Perhaps so. What can I do for you, Aaron?"

"I won't beat around the bush," Beck said. "I would like to arrange a meeting with Mr. Pablo Estancia."

"Who?"

"I thought you wished not to bullshit each other," Beck replied.

"And why do you believe I can arrange such a meeting, Aaron?"

"You arranged it for my friend Lance Cabot and his people," Beck said.

"Just how good a friend are you to Mr. Cabot?" Stone asked.

"We have a cordial working relationship."

"Then perhaps you should speak to Lance about arranging such a meeting."

"Stone, I have reason to believe that you are not ethically obligated to seek Lance's permission to arrange a meeting with Pablo."

"Oh, are you and Mr. Estancia on a first-name basis, too?" Stone asked.

"We have had occasion to meet once or twice in the past."

"Then why don't you just ring him up? I'm sure you know how to get in touch with him."

"Our usual line of communication is presently out of service," Beck said. "Thus, my meeting with you."

"Tell me, Aaron, why do you think Pablo would wish to see you?"

"As I said, we've met before and done business."

"Was the business you have done with Pablo conducted to your satisfaction?" Stone asked.

"You might say that," Beck replied.

"Is there some reason why you didn't contact Pablo
a short time ago when your line of communication was
still serviceable?"

"Circumstances change all the time," Beck said. "I
didn't need to speak to him at that time. Lance didn't
need to contact Pablo until he kidnapped him."

Stone feigned surprise. "Did Lance tell you he kid-
napped Pablo?"

Beck sighed. "I have more than one source of information."

"Aaron," Stone said, "do you wish to harm Pablo?"

"Of course not," Beck replied.

"Do you wish to invite him to Israel for a chat?"

"I would be happy to extend such an invitation."

"Do you wish to take him to Israel whether or not
he wants to go?"

"Do you really believe we are so ham-fisted as that,
Stone?"

Stone smiled. "I have formed the opinion that the
Mossad will sometimes go to great lengths to achieve
its ends. I am in mind of an assassination in an Arab
country that made the news recently, involving numerous Mossad agents carrying stolen passports. On that
occasion the Mossad was quite ham-fisted."

"Let us not revisit the past," Beck said, spreading his
hands. "Why don't we concentrate on the near future."

"Why do you wish to speak to Pablo?"

"I'm afraid that my instructions do not allow me to impart that information to anyone but Pablo."

Their lunch arrived.

"Suppose Pablo agreed to see you with his attorney present?" Stone asked.

"Stone, Pablo is not charged with any crime in Israel; why would he require an attorney?"

"He might require a witness," Stone said. "And you might be less inclined to press an invitation to your country upon him if an American citizen was present and handcuffed to Pablo."

"Handcuffed?"

"Metaphorically," Stone replied. "Let's get down to brass tacks. What have you to gain from Pablo by such a meeting, and what would Pablo have to gain from it?"

"We wish only to have the answers to some questions," Beck said. "As for Pablo, he might gain freedom from our attentions in the future."

"And how long might this conversation last?"

"I'm sure we could conclude it within the same time frame as his discussions with the CIA."

"And where do you propose that this meeting take place?"

"Perhaps at the offices of our mission?"

"You are assuming that Pablo is still in this country."

"Yes, but if he is back in Europe, his house in Switzerland would be a satisfactory meeting place."

"Pablo found his conversations with Lance and his

people to be very tiring," Stone said. "I'm not sure he would wish to endure another such session. How about a nice chat on the phone?"

"I'm afraid I must insist on a face-to-face meeting," Beck replied.

"Insist?" Stone asked. "And I thought this was going to be a friendly conversation."

"Forgive my impertinence," Beck said smoothly.

Stone put down his napkin and polished off his mind. "All I can do, Aaron, is deliver your kind invitation to Pablo, if I should happen to speak to him in the near future."

"If?"

"I have no way of knowing if he will call again." Stone stood up. "Thank you for a very good lunch," he said. "I hope they don't take it out of your pay."

Beck looked pained. The two men shook hands, and Beck handed him a card, identifying him as the agricultural attaché to the Israeli UN Mission.

54

Stone walked back to his office and phoned Pablo.

"Yes?"

"It's Stone. I've just had lunch with one Aaron Beck of the Mossad. Do you know him?"

"I do, but under a different name: Moishe Aarons. He is quite highly placed in the organization, and I'm surprised to hear that he is in this country."

"He may have come here to see you," Stone said. "He knows about your conversation with Lance and his people. He may even have heard about that from Lance himself."

"Or possibly not," Pablo replied. "Wherever there are Jews, Mr. Aarons has sources."

"If you say so."

"Why do you think he might have come to the United States to see me?"

"Because he was deeply interested in having a conversation with you, along the lines and depth of the one with Lance."

Pablo snorted. "Tell him that if he has any questions of me, Lance is in a position to answer them."

"I like that," Stone said. "Did you make inquiries about why the Israelis might be interested in you?"

"My inquiries, though oblique, lead me to believe they may think I have sold arms to the Palestinians."

"Ah."

"You may tell Mr. Aarons the following," Pablo said. "Quote: I have never knowingly sold arms or ammunition to any person or group representing the cause of the Palestinians. Unquote."

" 'Knowingly'?"

"In my business identities can be . . . flexible, but I am usually aware of with whom I am dealing."

"I will pass that on to him," Stone said, "along with your suggestion of asking questions of Lance."

"I hope that will be an end to it," Pablo said.

"I hope so, too," Stone replied. "I'll let him stew for a while, then call him tomorrow. Good-bye, Pablo."

"Good-bye, Stone."

They both hung up.

Joan buzzed him. "A Mr. Herbert Fisher to see you," she said.

Stone sighed. "Oh, all right, send him in."

Herbie opened the door, let himself in, and sat down. "Hey, Stone."

Stone noticed that he was wearing a cashmere tweed

jacket, a custom-made shirt, and that he had, apparently, found a barber who disdained gel. "How are you, Herbie?"

"Troubled," Herbie replied.

"What is troubling you, Herbie?"

"My wife."

"Well, I tried to get you to do the prenup."

"It's not that—not exactly."

"Then what is it?"

"You remember, we were supposed to go on a honeymoon in the islands?"

"Yes, I recall that."

"She won't go now."

"Herbie, women—especially women as bright and strong-willed as Stephanie—have minds of their own, and they often change them. You will come to have much experience of this."

Herbie shook his head. "It's not the changing of her mind that worries me."

"Unburden yourself, Herbie."

"You remember the business about the disappearing billion dollars from the Gunn company?"

"How could I forget it?" Stone replied.

"And you remember that David was suspected of that?"

"Again, my recall of those events is perfect."

"I'm beginning to think that it wasn't David. I'm beginning to think it was Stephanie—or maybe Stephanie and David."

Stone regarded Herbie for a moment. He did not appear to be delusional—indeed Herbie had appeared for some weeks now to be conducting himself entirely within the bounds of rationality, a sort of extended lucid interval. "What makes you think that, Herbie?"

"I've overheard snippets of telephone conversations; I've heard travel arrangements being made; I've heard mention of an island in the South Pacific called Attola."

"I've heard something about that place, Herbie, but I can't remember what."

"It's apparently a very posh place," Herbie said, "and very far from anywhere."

"Well, it sounds peaceful," Stone said.

"It also has something to do with offshore banking," Herbie said.

"Uh-oh," Stone replied.

55

Stone regarded Herbie with some sympathy. "Herbie, have you invested all your money, all ten million, with the Gunn company?"

"Not all of it," Herbie said. "Only seven million."

"Who do you deal with over there?"

"With Jack Gunn," Herbie said.

"All right, I'm going to try something; you just sit and listen." Stone looked up the number of Gunn Investments and asked to speak to Jack Gunn. Somewhat to Stone's surprise, Jack came on the line almost immediately.

"What can I do for you, Stone?"

"I'm calling on behalf of a client," Stone said. "This is very sensitive, and I must ask you not to mention this to any of your colleagues."

"All right. What is it?"

"Herbert Fisher is my client. He has seven million

dollars invested with you, and he has gotten himself into some difficulties that I believe are temporary. He therefore wishes to withdraw all his funds immediately."

Gunn was silent for a moment. "Does Stephanie know about this?"

"No, and Herbie is very anxious that she not know. It would be humiliating for him to have to explain it to her."

"What do you mean by immediately?" Gunn asked.

"I mean right now."

Again, a silence, then: "All right. I'll cut a check. Tell Herbie he can pick it up from the receptionist in half an hour."

"Thank you, Jack."

"Stephanie tells me that you declined an opportunity to invest with us."

"I'm very sorry about that, Jack, but circumstances have been difficult. I hope to have a resolution soon, and I hope I can invest with you at that time."

"I'll keep the opportunity open, then. Good-bye, Stone."

Stone hung up. "Herbie, Jack is cutting you a check right now. Go over there in thirty minutes and pick it up from the receptionist. If Jack or anyone else there tries to discuss it with you, just tell them that you can't talk, that you have to get to your bank immediately. Then take the check to the bank, get ahold of a senior officer, and ask him to clear the check immediately and deposit the funds in your account."

"All right," Herbie said. "Thanks, Stone."

"Herbie, I'd like your permission to discuss this situation with a couple of people. It might help us find out exactly what's going on."

"All right, Stone, you have my permission. Now, I had better get over there and pick up that check." He shook hands and hurried out.

Stone called Airship Transport in Newburgh, New York, and asked for the CEO.

"Holly Barker."

"It's Stone. How's the world of international business?"

"Not as boring as I thought. Actually, Todd Bacon left the place in pretty good shape. The C-17 has been repaired, and we're back in business. I may be able to get out of here and back to Langley pretty soon."

"Good luck on that," Stone said. "I need some information, and I hope you can help me."

"You can ask," she replied. "You know I can't always answer."

"Nothing like that. Have you ever heard of an island in the South Pacific called Attola?"

"Funny you should mention that," Holly said. "I first heard about it last week."

"Tell me what you can."

"The way I hear it, this was a little fleabag of an atoll, something like twelve miles by five, the sort of place we spent thousands of lives to take from the Japanese during World War Two. It has a central, extinct volcano and some glorious beaches and has failed to attract tourists because its only runway was too short, and the government couldn't afford to extend it.

"Last year, a consortium of half a dozen billionaires sort of bought the place."

"Bought a country?"

"Pretty much. The place is run by an elected president and a legislature of twelve men, and they've sold most of the island, exclusive of the capital city, its only town, in return for a bundle of cash and an agreement to rebuild the capital and extend the runway. They now have a ten-thousand-foot runway and an airport terminal building, and jet fuel is available."

"Let me guess: they have no extradition treaty with the United States."

"Nor with *any* country," Holly replied. "The new owners have also subdivided most of the island and have begun selling lots—minimum, five acres—and have funded a construction company to import building materials. They've almost completed a cushy new beach resort of about a hundred suites. And the construction company is already the island's largest employer. They've adopted a building code and everything."

"And—let me guess again—they've started a bank."

"Sorry, I should have mentioned that; it was the first thing they did. It's up and running and is a member in good standing of the world banking community."

"And it offers numbered accounts and confidential services?"

"Exactly. It already has deposits of more than a billion dollars."

"Does the IRS know about this?"

"Probably, but there's nothing they can do about it. Attola has accepted no foreign aid from the United States, so we have no leverage there, short of invasion or blockade. I understand we would like to have a naval refueling station there for both aircraft and ships, so we're being nice to them."

"This sounds like a story on *60 Minutes*," Stone said.

"It probably will be soon. Why do you want to know about this?"

"It's my turn to give you this answer," Stone said. "I am not at liberty to say."

"Gee, thanks. I spill my guts, and you tell me nothing?"

"Soon perhaps; be patient."

"Go away." Holly hung up.

Joan buzzed Stone. "Willa Crane on one."

"Hey, Willa."

"I can't talk," she said. "Dinner tonight at Elaine's, eight thirty?"

"Sure."

She hung up without another word, and Stone was left staring at a dead phone.

At the end of the day Stone decided not to let Aaron Beck stew any longer. He called the Israeli Mission and asked for Beck.

"This is Aaron Beck," a voice said.

"Good afternoon, Moishe," Stone said. "It's Stone Barrington."

"Ah, Stone."

"I have heard briefly from Pablo Estancia, and he has asked me to relay the following message to you. I quote: 'Please tell Mr. Aarons that I have not, at any time, knowingly sold arms or ammunition to anyone representing any Palestinian organization, legal or otherwise, nor do I intend to do so. Any other questions Mr. Aarons has should be directed to Mr. Lance Cabot, of the Central Intelligence Agency, who has all the answers.'"

"And where is Pablo?" Aarons asked.

"He did not mention his location to me before he hung up. Good day, Moishe, and thank you again for an excellent lunch."

Stone hung up feeling satisfied.

56

Stone walked into Elaine's to find Dino not yet at their usual table. He sat down and a drink was brought to him.

"Dino called," the waiter said. "He said not to wait dinner for him. He said you'd understand."

"I don't understand," Stone replied. "Dino never misses dinner."

"He said something about a double homicide."

"Well, that might cause him to be late." Stone took a sip of his bourbon and waited for Willa to show. That done, he reviewed his day, and considered that everything was pretty well wrapped up. He had gotten Herbie his money back; he had brushed off Moishe Aarons, and Pablo was still safe. Now he had only to pass on to Willa Herbie's suspicions about Stephanie, and then he could relax, knowing he had done his duty in full.

Willa walked in, shucked off her coat, asked for a martini, and sat down. "Whew!" she said. "What a day!"

"You sounded a little fraught when you called," Stone said. "I've never received a phone call from anyone whose first words were 'I can't talk.' What kept you so busy?"

"Work, work, work. After being mercifully quiet for a few days, the criminal classes seem to have come to life again. I spent a long day before a grand jury."

"Which indicted everybody, I'll bet."

"How'd you guess?"

"If you wrote a book about cases in which a grand jury declined to indict, it would be a very short book."

"You're a cynic."

"Let's have the grand jury argument another day," Stone said, clinking her glass against his. "Salud."

They drank.

"I have some information for you," Stone said.

"Oh, good."

"My client Herbert Fisher has given me permission to speak about this."

"Is it something I can take to a grand jury?"

"Not yet; not unless you want to add a paragraph to that book about cases they didn't indict."

"So this isn't exactly hard information."

"It is information that is hard to come by."

"Now, wait. You said Herbie Fisher told you something, and that was hard to come by?"

"It is information that would be hard for *you* to come by, without knowing me."

"Oh, that kind of hard to come by."

"Yes. Are you ready for the information?"

"Just a minute," she said, producing a notebook and pen from her handbag.

"Ready?"

"Ready," she said, pen poised.

"Have you ever heard of an island nation called Attola?"

Willa put down her pen. "I thought you were giving me information, not asking me for it."

"My question is but prelude to my information."

"All right, yes, I've heard of Attola."

"You know all about it, then, about the billionaires buying it?"

"I know all about it."

"Well, I think, from what Herbie told me, that Stephanie, possibly in league with her brother, David, is going to loot the family firm and run off to Attola."

Willa did not write anything down. "Do you have actual evidence to support that?"

"Not exactly."

Willa closed her notebook and returned it and the pen to her handbag. "I hate stuff with no supporting evidence."

"That's because you're a prosecutor and not a cop, or even an investigator. If you were an investigator you would be intrigued that Herbie heard fragments of phone conversations in which Stephanie discussed Attola and made travel arrangements."

"Fragments of conversation? You call that evidence?"

"Stop with the evidence thing. Don't you ever get a hunch?"

"Despite your opinion of grand juries, I can't get an indictment based on a hunch, not even if it were *my* hunch."

Stone handed her a menu. "Okay, what would you like for dinner?" He perused his own menu, and the waiter appeared on cue.

She regarded the menu. "Green bean salad and penne with mushrooms and Italian sausage. Do you have any other shred of information that might approach the level of actual evidence?"

"Osso buco with polenta, and a bottle of the Saint Francis Cabernet," Stone said, and the waiter went away. "This afternoon, Herbie withdrew his entire investment of seven million dollars from the Gunn company."

"On your recommendation?"

"Well, yes; he is my client, after all."

"You know, what I would really like to investigate is where Herbie Fisher got seven million dollars. Now, *that* is intriguing, because he couldn't have gotten it legally."

"Actually, he got fourteen million—after taxes and further deductions to settle with his bookie and his loan

shark and to keep his dead mistress in really sexy under-
wear, and to retain me. Now he's left with about ten
million, seven of which he invested with his father-in-
law's company."

"Stone, would it be a violation of attorney-client
confidentiality if you told me the source of Herbie's
millions?"

Stone thought about that. "No."

"Then please cough it up."

"The source of Herbie's millions is the New York
State Lottery," Stone said.

Willa took a big pull at her martini. "Do you expect
me to believe that?"

"I don't know why not; people win the lottery every
week."

"Not Herbie Fisher."

"I confess I thought that at first, too, but let me
ask you this: where do you think Herbie got the
money to buy the Park Avenue penthouse off of
which his former mistress, Sheila, fell? I mean, he
didn't pull a fourteen-million-dollar bank robbery or
win it on a horse. I'm sure if a high public official
like yourself rang up the nice folks over at the lottery,
they would confirm that one Herbert Fisher got very,
very lucky."

Willa took out her notepad and made a note. "I'm
going to do exactly that, first thing tomorrow."

"But you're not going to look into Stephanie and

David Gunn flying off to the South Pacific with a billion dollars of other people's money?"

Willa downed the remainder of her martini and waved at the waiter for another. "Call the FBI," she said. "They're pretty hunchy over there."

57

Stone lay in bed, the *Times* on his lap and the television murmuring. It was nine thirty, and he had not stirred himself. Instead, he had allowed guilt to make him slothful. Willa had gone to work, and it was time he did, too, he thought, so he showered, shaved, and went down to his office, still feeling guilty. Finally, he decided to take Willa's advice. He picked up the telephone and called an old flame, Tiffany Baldwin, who happened to be the United States attorney for the southern district of New York. He was put through immediately.

"Why, hello, Stone," Tiffany said, transmitting both surprise and interest. "Long time."

"Yes, it has been, hasn't it?" Stone replied. "I have a tip for you."

"Stone, you know I don't play the ponies."

"Not that kind of tip."

"What kind of tip?"

"A tip about the possible occurrence of a crime."

"What crime?"

"You remember the business with Jack Gunn's investment firm losing a billion dollars temporarily?"

"Yes, I was all over it. It was resolved."

"Well, it may be about to happen again, and if it does, it won't be resolved."

"Stone, I'm busy. Tell me what you're talking about."

"Jack Gunn's son and daughter, David and Stephanie, may be about to decamp to the island of Attola in the Pacific with a great deal of the firm's money."

"What evidence do you have to support this?"

"My client is married to Stephanie. He has overheard fragments of telephone conversations in which she is discussing Attola and making travel arrangements."

"Go on."

"That's it."

"That's *it*?"

"Yes."

"Stone, why are you wasting my time?"

"I thought you might want to instruct the FBI to investigate this."

"Investigate what? No crime has been committed."

"Well, not yet. Don't you investigate crimes that may be about to be committed?"

"No, we don't, and we don't ask the FBI to do that, either, not without some sort of solid evidence on which to proceed. I'm surprised at you, Stone; you know better than this."

"Okay, Tiff," Stone said, "I've done my civic duty. Now I'm going to attack the work on my desk and forget all about this."

"What a good idea!" she said, laughing. "Dinner?"

"I'm seeing somebody."

"Who?"

"Oh, no, we're not going there. Bye-bye, Tiff." Stone hung up. He felt that a burden had been lifted from his shoulders. Now he could attack the work on his desk.

Except that there was no work on his desk.

Joan buzzed him. "Lance Cabot on one."

Stone picked up. "Good morning, Lance."

"I'm afraid not," Lance said. "Pablo has disappeared."

"Lance, there are eight men from Strategic Services guarding him; he can't disappear."

"Nevertheless," Lance said.

"How did this happen?"

"His wife wanted to go to the market in Washington, and Pablo went with her. They went into the market, followed by two of Mike Freeman's men, and then straight out the back door, and they disappeared."

"You'd better check the airport at Newburgh," Stone said. "It sounds like Pablo has decided to run."

"Holly is all over that and every other airport in the area," Lance said. "Run from what?"

"Well, Lance, your very good friend and colleague Moishe Aarons has been trying to find Pablo—God knows why—but Pablo found that disturbing. Somehow—and I'm not making any accusations—Mr. Aarons found out about your meetings with Pablo. How could that have happened?"

Lance was silent.

"Hello, hello? Can you think of any way that Aarons could have found out about those meetings?"

"I'm thinking," Lance said.

"I'll just wait while you think," Stone said, then sat there silently.

"All right," Lance said finally, "he may have inferred that from something I said to him."

"Lance, we had a firm and very clear agreement that the existence of those meetings would be kept within a very tight circle of your people."

"Yes, we did."

"Did you intend that very tight circle to include the Mossad?"

"Of course not, Stone. It was just a slip of the tongue over lunch."

"It must have been a very big slip of the tongue, since Aarons knew that the meetings took place at my house and that I was in touch with Pablo."

"I have to go now," Lance said. "There are people waiting to see me."

"Lance—" But Lance had hung up.

Stone looked up to see a man he didn't recognize

standing in his doorway. He was tall, with a dark, heavy beard and black horn-rimmed glasses.

"Good morning, Stone."

"Yes? Have we met?"

The man came across the room and sat down in the chair opposite Stone. "My disguise is better than I thought."

"Pablo?" Stone said with astonishment.

"Don't make me take the beard off; it took me too long to get it right. You were talking with Lance?"

"Yes, just now."

"I heard you mention his name."

"He called to tell me you had disappeared."

"He's quite right, I have," Pablo said.

"Why?"

"Moishe Aarons wants me either in a Mossad interrogation facility or dead, and I don't think he cares very much which."

"Why do you think that?"

"Because early this morning I walked down to the lake—I take a walk every morning—and I saw a boat being driven by Moishe himself. I don't think he saw me, since I was partly behind a tree."

"Oh, shit," Stone said.

"Exactly," Pablo replied.

58

Stone tried to think of what to do. "Pablo, how did you get away from the Washington market?"

"One of my security people met us out back with a rental car and drove us here. He's gone, now, to return the car."

"Then Lance will soon find out about the rental car. What happened to the other one?"

"My other security guard returned it to Newburgh."

"Where do you want to go, Pablo?"

"To Switzerland."

Stone shook his head. "No, Aarons knows about that house; he told me so. I imagine he already has people there."

Pablo thought about that. "I have a friend who has a country house in the south of England. I have not been there for some years, so I have no noticeable connection to it."

"You're sure that Aarons isn't aware of it?"

"I can't see how he would know about it," Pablo said. "As I said, I haven't been there for a long time, and Aarons's interest in me is very recent."

"Where is your airplane?"

"At Gulfstream, in Georgia, having some avionics issues resolved."

"How soon could you get it to the Northeast?"

"Tomorrow morning."

"There's an airport near Washington called Oxford. It has a five-thousand-foot runway."

"Wouldn't Lance's people be watching it?"

Stone shook his hand. "They will check it today, but Lance doesn't have enough people around there to watch every airport. Anyway, since you have opted out of the surveillance he arranged, you have relieved him of the necessity to protect you. I've seen a G-Four take off from there, but probably not with full fuel."

"I think we would need at least six thousand feet with full fuel."

"Then have your people fly up from Georgia and land at Oxford but not refuel. That way, they won't even have to stop the engines. You can land at Gander, in Newfoundland, and top off there."

"That seems a good plan," Pablo said.

"Can you get in touch with your friend in England?"

"I'll call him now," Pablo said. He produced a cell phone and made the call. A conversation in French ensued; then he hung up. "All arranged," he said. "We can land at Blackbushe, in southern England, and he'll have us met."

A woman came into Stone's office, and Pablo introduced his wife, a petite, beautiful woman about twenty years Pablo's junior.

"I'll drive you to Oxford tomorrow," Stone said. "You two can stay here tonight."

"I think we'll be fine at our New York apartment," Pablo said. "I've never told anybody about it, and my security people will be there."

Joan buzzed. "A Mr. Aaron Beck to see you," she said.

"Quick," Stone said to the couple, "out the back. You know the way through the garden, Pablo."

Pablo and his wife hurried out of his office, and Stone asked Joan to send in Mr. Beck.

Moishe Aarons walked in, followed by two large young men.

"Mr. Aarons," Stone said sarcastically, "what a nice surprise."

"Where is Pablo?" Aarons asked.

"Are you going to start that again?" Stone asked, opening his center desk drawer and extracting a pad and pen. He left the drawer open.

"Mr. Barrington," Aarons said, "you have exhausted my patience."

"And you, mine," Stone replied.

"Search the house," Aarons said, motioning the two men forward.

Stone produced a .45 semiautomatic from his desk drawer. "Hold it right there," he said.

"You're not going to fire at us," Aarons said, but he didn't move.

"I can shoot all three of you dead before you can move, and nobody will blame me. You are intruders and I am licensed for the weapon."

"I'm licensed, too," Joan said from the door, and she racked the slide on her own .45.

The three men turned and looked at her. She had assumed a firing stance.

Aarons turned back toward Stone. "I want Pablo," he said.

"Well, you can't have him," Stone replied. "At least, not from me. Try Lance Cabot again; he seems to be a productive source for you."

"I don't have time," Aarons replied.

"And I don't have any more time for you," Stone said. "Now, hear this: from this moment I am going to consider you and your people a threat to my life and act accordingly, and I am *very* good shot." That was a lie, but he doubted if Aarons had perused his range record at the NYPD. Dino was always needling him about his mediocre shooting performance.

"Place your hands on your head, turn and walk out of the building," Stone said. "If you call again I'll hang up on you, and if you come back I'll fire on you. Is that clear?"

The three men did as Stone had ordered, and Joan locked the door behind them.

"Very good," Stone said from his office door. "I particularly liked your firing stance."

"That's what they taught me at the range," Joan said, "but I doubt if I could have hit any of them with this thing; it weighs a ton."

"Only thirty-nine ounces," Stone said.

"That's two and a half pounds," Joan pointed out, "and I'm a small girl."

The phone rang, and Joan answered. "Mike Freeman for you," she said.

Stone walked back to his desk and picked up the phone. "Hello?"

"It's Mike."

"Hello, Mike. It must be a beautiful day on Lake Waramaug."

"I'm in New York," Mike said.

"A pity; it's gorgeous up there."

"You know, don't you?"

Stone now had to decide between his two clients. "Lance called," he said, avoiding the decision.

"I'm embarrassed," Mike said. "I've already fired the two men who let it happen."

"I wouldn't be too hard on them," Stone said. "After all, we have to assume he's still safe, just not in custody, so to speak."

"We checked all the airports in the area," Mike said. "No sign of Pablo."

"I wouldn't try too hard to find him," Stone replied. "He doesn't seem to want protecting anymore."

"I can't argue with that," Mike said. "We'll stand down."

Stone hung up. Now, he thought, if I could just be sure that the Mossad and Al Qaeda have stood down.

59

Stone was at Elaine's with Dino when Lance Cabot walked in and, without a word, sat down, waving at a waiter. He did not speak until an icy martini sat before him.

Stone and Dino exchanged a glance.

"Good evening, Lance," Dino said.

"Is it?"

"It was until a moment ago," Stone said. "What do you want?"

"Peace on Earth," Lance replied, speaking into his martini, "or at least in this little corner of the earth."

Stone had never seen Lance so dejected, and he fought the tendency to feel sorry for him. "All right, what has disturbed the peace of your corner of the earth this evening?"

"I did it to myself," Lance said.

Dino spoke up. "This man is an impostor. The real Lance Cabot would never say a thing like that."

"I agree," Stone said. "Are you feeling bad about sending that nice young fellow Todd Bacon off to the Aleutians?"

Lance brightened visibly. "No, I didn't send him to the Aleutians after all," he said. "Instead, I sent him back to the Farm for torture-resistance training. That way, he will actually be tortured."

"Oh," Stone said, reluctantly admiring the way Lance's mind worked.

"I'm feeling better," Lance said, downing the remains of his martini and waving for another.

"I'm glad we could be of help," Stone said.

"Where is Pablo now?" Lance asked.

"Why do you want to know?"

"Frankly, I thought I had overreacted to the idea of a threat against him when I assigned those Strategic Services people to protect him, but it turns out there really is a threat."

"Uh-oh," Dino said.

"Funny, that's what I said when I heard," Lance said.

"Heard what?" Stone asked.

"The boys over at NSA have picked up more satphone chatter about him."

"And what was the source of the chatter?"

"Northwestern Pakistan," Lance replied. "Less than forty miles from the former cave facility at Tora Bora."

"Speaking of Tora Bora, any more news?"

"Estimates are that we killed about two hundred of the bastards in the bombing raid," Lance said, "and not a few mules."

"Does any of them have a name?"

"That will take time; we'll have to count noses—or rather, missing noses."

"Anything on the condition of bin Laden's nose?"

"Nothing, as yet."

"Let's get back to the chat about Pablo," Stone said.

"Oh, yes. It seems they have made the connection between Pablo and the bombing raid, and they're even more furious than usual."

"And how did they make that connection?"

"I don't know for sure, but I have my suspicions."

"And what do you suspect?"

"I suspect that Moishe Aarons—or one of his people—frustrated with their lack of success in laying hands on Pablo, may have leaked the connection to someone who knows someone in that part of the world. News travels fast, even over there."

"I suppose it does," Stone said, trying to figure out how to deal with this.

"Mind you," Lance said, "that is *very* Machiavellian, even for Moishe."

Stone was beginning to regret that he had spoken so harshly to Aarons. "Lance," he said, "do you think that this translates into an immediate threat against Pablo?"

"Oh, yes," Lance said, as if he had been misunderstood. "If what happened at my brother's Lake Waramaug house is any indication."

Stone waved for another bourbon. "All right, what happened at Lake Waramaug?"

"The house was set afire by unknown arsonists about an hour ago. It's still burning."

"Was anyone hurt?"

"No, but the house is going to be a total loss, and I'm going to have to find the money to pay for its rebuilding and the replacement of certain valuable antiques. God, it may take an act of Congress."

Stone was appalled. "No insurance?"

"Well, yes, but filing a claim would just provoke a lot of unwanted questions from a claims adjuster, and those might find their way to a congressional committee."

"I see," Stone said.

"Stone," Lance said, "if you know where Pablo is, you'd better get him out of the country, and pronto."

"Pronto," Stone repeated tonelessly.

"Yes," Lance said.

"Excuse me for a minute," Stone said. He went into the empty dining room next door, the one Elaine used for big parties, and called Pablo.

"Yes?"

"It's Stone."

"Good evening."

"What time can your airplane be at the place we discussed?"

"I'm told by the pilot ten a.m. tomorrow morning."

"Then I need to pick you up at eight a.m. sharp. Where can we meet?"

Pablo gave him an Upper East Side address. "We will be standing just inside the door of the building promptly at eight. What will you be driving?"

"A black Mercedes E55 sedan," Stone said.

"You sound very concerned," Pablo said.

"I am, but I can't tell you any more now. I'll explain everything on the way to the place."

"All right," Pablo said. "Should I be armed?"

"It couldn't hurt," Stone said. They said good-bye and hung up.

Stone returned to the table, where Lance and Dino were ordering dinner. "Spinach salad, chopped; rib eye, medium rare," Stone said to the waiter.

"Did you manage to make contact?"

"Yes," Stone replied.

"Did you impress upon him the danger he's in?"

"No," Stone said, "it would have just made him nervous, and I don't want him nervous."

"Anything I can do to help?" Lance asked.

"Please, Lance," Stone said, "don't help any more."

60

At a quarter to eight the following morning, Stone opened his garage door, walked out to the sidewalk and looked around. His street was uncharacteristically empty, and he was grateful for that. He backed out of the garage, closing the door with the remote, drove up to Park Avenue, and took a right.

He turned left in the East Sixties and saw the awning with Pablo's street address on it. He did not stop, but drove slowly around the block, checking both sides of the street for loitering men and his rearview mirror for a tail. Nothing.

He circled the block and pulled up in front of Pablo's building, pressing the button that unlocked the doors. Pablo and his wife hurried from the building, each carrying only a small duffel, and jumped into the rear seat.

"Put your luggage on the front passenger seat,"

Stone said, again watching both sides of the street, "and keep an eye out for trouble."

He turned up Madison Avenue, then left on East Sixty-sixth. A moment later they were crossing Central Park. Stone took the opportunity to check his rearview mirror again, and he did not like what he saw. "Black Range Rover behind us," he said. "Three men."

"That's my car," Pablo said, "with my two security men and my butler, who will return to the city with the car when we are gone."

Stone took a few deep breaths and tried to get his pulse to return to normal. "How are your men's driving skills?" he asked.

"Excellent," Pablo said, "particularly the one now driving."

"Good. I don't want to have to worry about them if we have to evade something." Leaving the park, he turned right on Central Park West, then left on West Seventy-second Street. A few blocks later he turned north on the West Side Highway and increased his speed to seventy miles an hour.

Soon they were on the Henry Hudson Parkway, with its well-engineered curves and its beautiful stone bridges, constructed by Roosevelt's Works Progress Administration in the 1930s. He drove north for another three-quarters of an hour, then joined I-684, heading north. Traffic was light, and they were making good time. Stone chose this time to tell Pablo about the events of the day before.

"I'm sorry to hear that," Pablo said. "It was a very beautiful house. I feel I should pay for it."

"Let Lance Cabot worry about that," Stone said. "He has deep enough pockets, and it was his fault anyway. He knows that."

"There's something else I feel I should do," Pablo said, "that I would like you to do for me."

Stone heard the sound of a check being ripped from a checkbook, and it was handed forward. It was made out in the amount of $100,000, to the doctor in Rye into whose swimming pool the Agency's Mercedes had landed.

"Would you send that to the gentleman with my apologies for the inconvenience?"

"Of course," Stone said, "but I'm sure he has already convinced his insurance company that he is covered for falling objects."

"Nevertheless," Pablo said.

Stone turned onto I-84 and drove east. Past the Southbury exit he got off the interstate and drove on surface roads toward Oxford-Waterbury Airport. The Range Rover kept pace. Stone made the final turn onto the airport road and looked up. "Look," he said, "Gulfstream landing; that's very good timing." The big airplane settled behind the trees.

Stone drove up the hill to the little terminal building. He didn't try to drive through the gate, figuring it would take too much time to get it opened, but pulled into a parking space. "Let's go," he said, getting out of the car. The Range Rover had pulled in beside them, and three men got out.

Stone grabbed the two duffels in the front seat. "Follow me," he said. He trotted through the little lobby and was buzzed out through the doors to the ramp, where the Gulfstream sat, its engines running, its door open. He shook Pablo's hand and hustled the party aboard, and as the door closed, Stone turned back toward the building and saw a gray van come to a halt at the locked gate to the ramp.

Stone grabbed the butler's arm and hustled him back through the building. "There's a van at the gate to the ramp," Stone called to the receptionist. "Don't open it or there will be trouble." He hustled the butler outside. "Get out of here," he said, getting into his own car. As he waited for the man to back the Range Rover out, he looked toward the van and saw a bearded man arguing with the intercom at the gate, and then he saw the Gulfstream turn onto a taxiway and head for the runway.

Stone got the car started, then got out his cell phone and called Lance.

"This is Cabot," Lance said.

"It's Stone. I'm at the Oxford-Waterbury Airport in Oxford, Connecticut, and I've just put our friend on an airplane, which is about to take off. There is a van with four men inside trying to get out onto the ramp." As he looked toward them he saw the Gulfstream race down the runway and lift off. "Pablo is gone, but I see a firearm on the belt of the van's driver. Can you get anybody up here?"

"I'll call the Connecticut State Police," Lance said. "That will be the fastest help I can get to you. Whatever you do, don't mix it up with those people, just get out of there."

"Believe me, that is my intention," Stone said. "Good-bye."

The Range Rover had backed into the drive very slowly and was now beginning to roll down the hill toward the highway.

Stone backed out slowly, too, so as not to attract attention to himself. It didn't work. Three more men got out of the van, and each had a light, automatic weapon. One of them shouted, turned toward Stone, and raised his weapon. From behind him came a mechanical thudding, which was the sound of automatic fire striking his rear window. A glance in the rearview mirror revealed a row of dents where the bullets had struck the armored glass.

Stone floored the car and burned rubber all the way to the first bend in the road. The Range Rover was dawdling its way toward the highway. Stone flashed his lights and leaned on the horn but got no reaction, so he swung around the car as he lowered his window, pointing to his left, signaling the butler to turn that way.

At the main road Stone whipped to his right and stomped on the accelerator. He had one advantage: his Mercedes E55, with its AMG engine, was faster than

anything on the road he was likely to encounter. It was half a mile to the interstate. He pressed a button on the steering wheel and instructed the phone to dial Lance.

"Cabot."

"I'm turning onto I-84 West," Stone said, "driving very fast. Please let the Connecticut cops know the bad guys are in a gray van—four of them, heavily armed."

"Will do."

Stone put the car into a four-wheel drift and connected with the on-ramp, then floored the accelerator again. "I don't know why these guys want me, but I've taken automatic fire," he said to Lance. "Bye-bye." He punched the OFF button and drove onto the interstate at 110 miles an hour, narrowly missing an enormous truck. He threw the car into the fast lane, and a moment later he was doing 140 and still accelerating. From somewhere far behind him he heard the whooping of a police car.

Stone was up to 160, weaving in and out among cars and trucks, but the traffic was light, and he didn't kill himself or anyone else. He figured the cops were probably just in time to see the van follow him onto the highway. In the rearview mirror he saw the lights of at least two police cars that had apparently blocked the interstate. He eased off the accelerator and began to slow down. He was decelerating through 120 in the center lane when he saw the motorcycle.

The Harley Hog and its driver had parted company for reasons he did not understand. The driver was doing flips and rolls in the grassy median, and the Hog was skidding along on its side, making sparks. There was a truck to his right and two cars to his left, so he was left with no alternative but to drive over the big machine, braking as hard as he could. His car struck the bike and became airborne.

Everything happened very fast after that; the car was turning end over end, and Stone was straining against his seat belt, his face full of airbags. Then the lights went out.

61

People were shouting at one another as Stone slowly came to, upside down, suspended from his seat belt, his arms below his head, deflated airbags everywhere.

The voices seemed to come from a great distance. "He's coming to!" a man shouted. "We can't move the car, and I can't break the window. Get that thing going!"

Stone saw the man kneeling outside his window, the thick glass muffling his voice. Some sort of engine started, something like a chain saw. Stone found the window switches and pressed one. To his surprise his window slid down—or, rather, up. The machine noise became deafening.

The man was shouting something at him, but he couldn't understand over the noise. Stone thought it better that he take a nap.

*　　*　　*

When he opened his eyes again they were filled with blue sky; then a man in a uniform leaned over him.

"Is your name Barrington?"

"Yes," Stone managed to say.

"We're getting you to a hospital right away," the cop said. "Is there anybody you want us to call?"

Stone thought. Not Lance. "Mike Freeman, Strategic Services, New York." He felt himself being lifted; then he went to sleep again.

Stone woke in a darkened room.

"Ah, there you are," Mike's voice said from somewhere.

Stone took a deep breath, and it didn't hurt much. "Turn on the lights," he said softly.

The blinds opened and sunlight flooded the room. Mike was silhouetted against the window. "There's nothing wrong with you, you know. You're woozy because some EMT gave you morphine; I'm not sure why."

"Well," Stone said, "it's pretty rosy in here where I am."

The electric bed moved Stone into a sitting position. "I could use a drink," Stone said.

"Later, my friend."

"Did I break anything?"

"Not even a rib. No head injury, either. I saw a picture of your car; it's a mess. You're a very lucky guy. They had to cut you out with that Jaws of Life thing."

"Can I have some water?" Stone asked.

Mike poured some from a bedside flask and handed it to him. There was ice in it; it tasted wonderful.

A man in a white coat came into the room. "I see the morphine is wearing off," he said. "The EMT said he gave you the morphine because he figured you must hurt all over."

Stone tried moving things. "Everything seems to work," he said.

The doctor gave him a neurological examination, then patted him on the shoulder. "I want you to stay here overnight for observation. If you don't die before morning, you can go home." He walked out.

"We're at Danbury Hospital," Mike said. "I'll stay at your place in Washington tonight and drive you home in the morning. Get some rest." He tucked something cold under the covers and held a finger to his lips; then he left.

Stone sat the bed up a bit farther and felt for the cold object. It was half a bottle of Knob Creek, with a straw taped to it. He smiled.

The following morning they wheeled Stone out of the hospital through a side door, where Mike was waiting with one of his big black SUVs. The two of them settled into the backseat, and the driver drove them away.

Mike handed him a plastic bag with a lot of stuff in it. "They cleaned out the glove compartment and found your cell phone on the ceiling," he said, "but your car is not coming home. By this time, it's probably a small cube in a junkyard."

"Well, that's what insurance is for," Stone said.

"Don't worry about it; I've found you something of ours to drive until you buy something new."

"Thanks, Mike. What happened to the guys in the gray van?"

"They rolled it half a mile behind where you hit the Harley. Cuts and bruises. The four of them are in a special part of the Danbury Federal Prison, where Lance's people are questioning them. Turns out they're four guys from Waterbury who are partners in a car-painting business, all radical Muslims from a storefront mosque. One of them has a history of raising money for some sort of charity that sounds like a front."

"How did the guy on the Harley do?"

"The rider is banged up a bit, but the Harley is history. It blew a front tire and threw him off; nothing to do with your being behind him. How are you feeling?"

"Sore and stiff, but okay. The bourbon hit the spot. I finished it last night."

Mike dropped him at his house and held out a car key. "There's something armored in the garage. Drive it for as long as you like."

Stone looked at the key. It said *Bentley*. He dug into the plastic bag and found the remote control, opened the garage door. There was a shiny green Bentley Flying Spur inside. A promotion!

Joan came into the garage and hugged him. "I'm so

glad you are all right. When I heard about it I thought I was out of a job."

"Gee, thanks," Stone said.

"Just to cheer you up, Herbie is waiting for you."

"Swell," Stone said. He walked into his office and found Herbie asleep on the sofa.

Herbie stirred and raised his head. "Hey, Stone."

"Hello, Herbie."

"I hear you spread your car around half of Connecticut."

"Close."

Herbie sat up. "I wanted to thank you."

"For what?"

"For getting my money out of Jack's business."

"You're welcome."

"It's a mess all over again."

"What's a mess?"

"The Gunn company. TV says they got away with nearly two billion."

"Herbie, start at the beginning."

"Stephanie and David. She came home from the office yesterday and told me to pack a bag and come with her. I did, and we drove out to Teterboro, where there was a Boeing Business Jet waiting. David and his girl were there, too."

"Go on."

"Stephanie said we were going to the South Pacific, to Attola. I asked her when we were coming back, and she said we weren't, unless I wanted to live in a federal prison."

"And why are you still here?"

"I told her she didn't tell me we were leaving the country, so I didn't bring my passport. And you know what she did?"

"No, Herbie."

"She kissed me and said, 'Well, fuck you, kid; you're out.' Then she got on the plane and they left. I didn't hear anything else until this morning, on TV."

Stone began to laugh.

"What's funny?" Herbie asked.

"I was just thinking that there are two very pissed-off ladies right about now in the DA's and the U.S. Attorney's offices."

"If you say so," Herbie replied. "Oh, there are some guys in your waiting room that want to talk to us."

"Us?"

"They're FBI agents. I told them I wouldn't have anything to say until my attorney arrived, and Joan said you were on the way, so they waited."

"Okay, Herbie," Stone said, hanging his tattered coat on the back of his chair and sitting down at his desk. "Trot 'em in here and let's see if we can get you out of this one."

And Herbie did.

ACKNOWLEDGMENTS

Once again I am grateful to my agents, Morton Janklow and Anne Sibbald, for their tireless efforts on my behalf over the past thirty years. They are peerless.

Again I am grateful to my editor at Putnam, Rachel Kahan; my publisher, Ivan Held; my publicist, Michael Barson; and all their colleagues for keeping my career on the boil.

AUTHOR'S NOTE

I am happy to hear from readers, but you should know that if you write to me in care of my publisher, three to six months will pass before I receive your letter, and when it finally arrives it will be one among many, and I will not be able to reply.

However, if you have access to the Internet, you may visit my Web site at www.stuartwoods.com, where there is a button for sending me e-mail. So far, I have been able to reply to all my e-mail, and I will continue to try to do so.

If you send me an e-mail and do not receive a reply, it is probably because you are among an alarming number of people who have entered their e-mail address incorrectly in their mail software. I have many of my replies returned as undeliverable.

Remember: e-mail, reply; snail mail, no reply.

When you e-mail, please do not send attachments, as I never open these. They can take twenty minutes to download, and they often contain viruses.

Please do not place me on your mailing lists for funny stories, prayers, political causes, charitable fund-raising, petitions, or sentimental claptrap. I get enough of that from people I already know. Generally speaking, when I get e-mail addressed to a large number of people, I immediately delete it without reading it.

Please do not send me your ideas for a book, as I have a policy of writing only what I myself invent. If you send me story ideas, I will immediately delete them without reading them. If you have a good idea for a book, write it yourself, but I will not be able to advise you on how to get it published. Buy a copy of *Writer's Market* at any bookstore; that will tell you how.

Anyone with a request concerning events or appearances may e-mail it to me or send it to: Publicity Department, Penguin Group (USA) Inc., 375 Hudson Street, New York, NY 10014.

Those ambitious folk who wish to buy film, dramatic, or television rights to my books should contact Matthew Snyder, Creative Artists Agency, 9830 Wilshire Boulevard, Beverly Hills, CA 98212-1825.

Those who wish to make offers for rights of a literary nature should contact Anne Sibbald, Janklow & Nesbit, 445 Park Avenue, New York, NY 10022. (Note: This is not an invitation for you to send her your manuscript or to solicit her to be your agent.)

If you want to know if I will be signing books in your city, please visit my Web site, www.stuartwoods.com, where the tour schedule will be published a month or so in advance. If you wish me to do a book signing in your locality, ask your favorite bookseller to contact his Penguin representative or the Penguin publicity department with the request.

If you find typographical or editorial errors in my book and feel an irresistible urge to tell someone, please write to Rachel Kahan at Penguin's address above. Do not e-mail your discoveries to me, as I will already have learned about them from others.

A list of my published works appears in the front of this book and on my Web site. All the novels are still in print in paperback and can be found at or ordered from any bookstore. If you wish to obtain hardcover copies of earlier novels or of the two nonfiction books, a good used-book store or one of the online bookstores can help you find them. Otherwise, you will have to go to a great many garage sales.

Read on for an excerpt from
Stuart Woods's next thrilling novel,

SON OF STONE

A Stone Barrington Novel

On Sale from Putnam October 2011

E laine's, late.
　　　Stone Barrington and Dino Bacchetti sat, sipping what each of them usually sipped, gazing desultorily at the menu. Elaine came and sat down.

"Having problems deciding?" she asked.

"Always," Dino said.

"Are you being a smart-ass?" she asked.

"I'm torn between the pasta special and the osso buco," Dino said.

"Yeah," Stone said, "Dino is always torn."

"Are you being a smart-ass?" Dino asked.

"I'm just backing you up, pal," Stone said.

"Oh."

"Have the pasta," Elaine said. "It's terrific."

"How can I pass that up?" Dino asked, closing his menu.

"Dino," Stone said, "you're veering toward the ironic again. Watch yourself."

Elaine looked at Dino. "You're lucky there isn't a steak knife on the table." She flagged down a passing waiter. "Two pasta specials," she said, her finger wagging between Stone and Dino.

"I'll have the osso buco," Stone said.

"I just sold the last one," the waiter replied.

"Tell you what," Stone said, "I'll have the pasta special, with a chopped spinach salad to start."

"Me, too, on the salad," Dino said.

"And a bottle of the Mondavi Napa Cabernet," Stone added.

"Good," Elaine said; then she got up and wandered a couple of tables away and sat down there.

"That was close," Stone said. "You could have gotten a fork in the chest."

"I didn't want the pasta," Dino replied.

"Then why didn't you order the osso buco to begin with?"

"They were out."

"You didn't know that."

"Does it matter? They wouldn't have had it anyway."

They sat in silence for a moment, Stone sipping his Knob Creek, Dino sipping his Johnnie Walker Black.

"When does Ben get home for the holidays?" Stone asked. Benito was Dino's teenaged son.

"Tomorrow," Dino replied. "I get him first. Mary Ann will have him for Christmas dinner at her father's."

"Could you bring him to dinner tomorrow night?"

Dino looked at him oddly. "Since when did you especially want to have dinner with Benito?"

"Since Arrington decided to come to New York for Christmas and bring Peter."

"You didn't tell me."

"I didn't know until tonight. I was just leaving the house when she called. They're due in early tomorrow afternoon." Stone showed Dino the photo of the boy that Arrington had given him. "This was over a year ago," he said. "I guess he's bigger now."

Dino gazed at the photograph. "Amazingly like your father," he said.

"How would you know? You never met my father."

"I've met the photograph of him in your study about a thousand times," Dino replied.

"Oh, yeah."

"Does he know?"

"Who?"

"Peter."

"Don't start that again," Stone said.

"I didn't start it—you did, some years back."

Stone's shoulders sagged. "All right, all right."

"When, exactly, was it? I know you know."

Stone cast his thoughts back. "Right before we were going to the islands for the holidays, to St. Marks. The night before, actually. I had bought her a ring."

"You never told me that. You were really going to ask her?"

"Yes, I was. That morning it started snowing. I got to the airport and got a call from her, saying that she was stuck in a meeting at *The New Yorker*. She had written a piece for them, and she was working with the editor. She said she'd get the same flight the next day. I was pissed off, but my bags were already on the airplane, and I didn't want to go through *that* a day later, so I left. As it turned out, while she was at *The New Yorker*, they assigned her to write a profile of Vance Calder."

"Uh-oh."

"Exactly. Turns out I got the last flight out of the airport before they closed it because of the snowstorm. She was stuck in the city for another day. Then Vance arrived in town and they had dinner. I met the flight the following day, and she wasn't on it, and I couldn't get her on the phone. Finally, a few days later, I got a fax at my hotel."

"A Dear Stone letter?"

"Right. She was marrying Vance."

"And when did she find out she was pregnant?"

"I'm not sure. I was out in L.A. four or five months later, and—"

"I was there, too, remember?"

"Yes, I remember. And when I saw her there, she was obviously pregnant."

"Did she say whose it was?"

"No, because she didn't know."

"The two . . . events were too close together, huh?"

"Right."

"When did she know?"

"Not until after Vance's death, I think."

They were quiet again. "Had she seen the photograph of your father?"

"Sure, she was in the house a lot when we first met."

"So she knew sooner than Vance's death?"

"I don't know; she may have been in denial."

"Did Vance know?"

Stone shook his head. "She told me the subject never came up."

"When did she finally admit it to you?"

"When we were in Maine a few years back, remember? Then, when you and I were staying at her house in Bel-Air last year, we had a frank talk about it. She said she had had a brush with ovarian cancer and had surgery, and that seemed to get her thinking about Peter's future. She wanted me to spend some time with Peter, but it hasn't happened until now. He's been in boarding school in Virginia for more than a year."

"So we're looking at a family reunion, huh?"

Stone grinned ruefully. "I never thought of it that way. Arrington and I have spent so little time together over the years."

"So how are you feeling about this?" Dino asked.

"Scared stiff," Stone said.

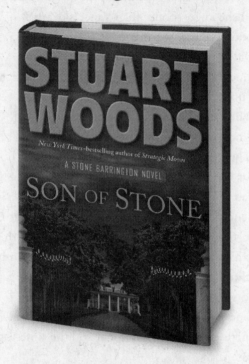

Also Available from
New York Times Bestselling Author

STUART WOODS

The Stone Barrington Novels

L.A. Dead

Cold Paradise

The Short Forever

Dirty Work

Reckless Abandon

Two Dollar Bill

Dark Harbor

Fresh Disasters

Shoot Him If He Runs

Hot Mahogany

Loitering with Intent

Kisser

Lucid Intervals

Strategic Moves

Bel-Air Dead

Son of Stone

Available wherever books are sold or at
penguin.com

New York Times bestselling author

STUART WOODS

The Will Lee Novels

Chiefs

A depraved killer claims his innocent victims even as three very
different generations of policemen seek to stop him.

Run Before the Wind

Restless and dissatisfied, Will Lee dreams of sailing on crystal-blue
waters—until an explosion of senseless violence drags the young
American drifter into a lethal game of terror and revenge.

Deep Lie

CIA analyst Kate Rule goes head-to-head with a brilliant KGB
operative who's the architect of a secret plot to invade Sweden.

Capital Crimes

From a quiet D.C. suburb to the corridors of power to a deserted
island hideaway in Maine, Will Lee, his CIA director wife, and
the FBI will track a killer, set a trap—and await the most
dangerous kind of quarry, a murderer with a cause to die for...

Mounting Fears

It's been a rough week for Will Lee. His vice president just died
during surgery. Meanwhile, rogue CIA agent Teddy Fay is
plotting revenge on the president's wife, CIA Director Kate Rule
Lee. And now some nuclear weapons are "loose" in Pakistan. The
prevention of WWIII falls in Will Lee's hands.

**Available wherever books are sold or at
penguin.com**